GW01271385

A FINE & PRIVATE PLACE

Also by John Simpson
MOSCOW REQUIEM

A FINE & PRIVATE PLACE

John Simpson

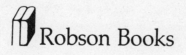

Robson Books

FIRST PUBLISHED IN GREAT BRITAIN IN 1983 BY
ROBSON BOOKS LTD., BOLSOVER HOUSE, 5–6
CLIPSTONE STREET, LONDON W1P 7EB. COPYRIGHT
© 1983 JOHN SIMPSON

British Library Cataloguing in Publication Data

Simpson, John
  A fine and private place.
  I. Title
  823'.914[F]

  ISBN 0-86051-189-8

All rights reserved. No part of this publication may be
reproduced, stored in a retrieval system, or transmitted in
any form or by any means, electronic, mechanical, photo-
copying, recording or otherwise, without prior permission
in writing of the publishers.

Printed in Great Britain by The Garden City Press, Letchworth

Phototypesetting by Georgia Origination, Liverpool.

'I will never imitate those who rub out their traces, disown the past, and are dead, although they pretend they are alive with the help of mental acrobatics. My roots are in the East; that is certain. Even if it is difficult or painful to explain who I am, nevertheless I must try.'

Czeslaw Milosz, *Native Realm*

'I begged my gods, whose names I do not know, to send something or someone into my days. They did. It is my country.'

Jorge Luis Borges, *1972*

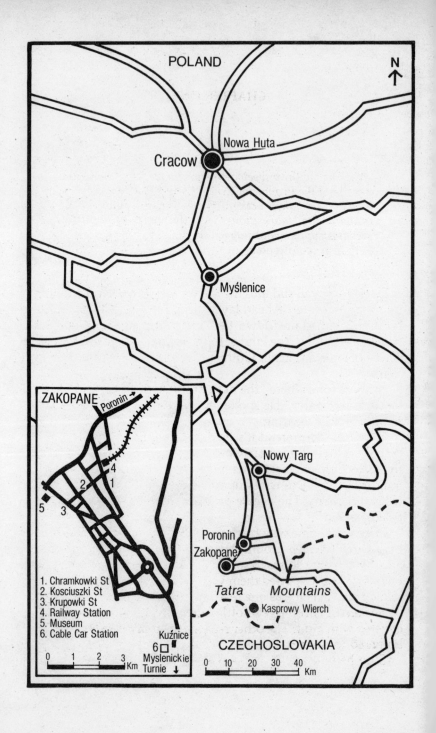

POLAND

N

Nowa Huta

Cracow

Myślenice

Nowy Targ

Poronin
Zakopane

Tatra Mountains

Kasprowy Wierch

CZECHOSLOVAKIA

0   10   20   30   40
Km

ZAKOPANE

Poronin

4

2   1

5

3

1. Chramkowki St
2. Kosciuszki St
3. Krupowki St
4. Railway Station
5. Museum
6. Cable Car Station

Kuźnice

6 □
Myslenickie
Turnie ↓

0   1   2   3
Km

CHAPTER ONE

'Working with praiseworthy vigilance, the Security Service of the Provincial Civic Military Headquarters in Cracow has taken action against persons involved in broadcasting fabrications and anti-socialist lies by means of equipment smuggled in from Western sources.'
— Polish radio report.

A black *Nysa* van slid into the back street like a shark moving into shallow water. Ahead lay a seedy block of flats standing by itself, with stains down the stucco and washing hanging from the windows; the kind of building that looked old the day it was completed. Lenin Gothic, they used to call the style in Warsaw.

'It's here somewhere,' the man sitting in the back said. 'I can feel it in my water.' He spoke too loudly, because of the earphones he was wearing.

They love to pretend it's instinct, the driver thought, and craned to look in his rear-view mirror. As he had predicted, the detection engineer was peering at the signal strength indicator which was wired up to what looked like an ordinary transistor radio. The needle peaked, dropped back, and then peaked again.

They were some way from the block of flats still, separated by a patch of open ground overgrown with the kind of rank grass which only seems to sprout in cities. The driver hoped no one would have spotted them yet. A *Nysa* wasn't exactly hard to pick out, which was one reason why they tried to disguise it by letting the chrome get mottled with rust, and the bodywork covered with mud. The other reason was that nobody could be bothered to clean it.

'Stop here.'

The driver stopped there, cursing quietly. He needn't have worried. The noise in the headphones drowned out everything else for the man in the back as he drew a second red line across his map with a flourish, jabbing at the place where it cut the first line at an acute angle and snapping his fingers impatiently for the RT microphone.

'Base, this is 21. Target confirmed at Topolowa 52. Over.'

'Thanks, 21. Repeat Topolowa 52. Out.'

'Let's go,' he said, unplugging his equipment. 'Fast.'

He never liked to see the next bit. The driver found somewhere wide enough to ease the *Nysa*'s bulk around, and they sped back down the street and out into one of the main arteries of Grzegorski.

A big picture of Lech Walesa from the old days hung slightly askew on the wall of the flat. Someone had pasted a Solidarity sticker on the bottom right-hand corner, just by the frame. *Aby Polska Byla Polska*, it said: Let Poland still be Poland. There wasn't much else in the room; even with the housing shortage as bad as it was in Cracow, no one wanted to live in a block like this unless they had to. A broken couch, its entrails hanging down on the floor, was at one end of the room near the window, facing a kitchen chair with a couple of dirty mugs on its seat. In the middle stood a table with a ham radio transmitter set out on it.

The engineer hovered in the background, occasionally darting forward like a mother bird to tend the bewildering array of transistors and winding coils. He had assembled them from parts brought in by well-wishers in the days before martial law, when things were relatively easy. The different underground Solidarity movements had good reason now to be grateful to the forethought of people like the engineer: nowadays the radio link was all that kept the underground movements together.

He reached out his hand again to make a slight adjustment on the power output and looked at the field strength meter. The radio operator kept his finger firmly pressed down on the mike key.

'We have signs of unrest at the Fourteenth Special Steel Plant in Nowa Huta. Strike committee being formed. Possibility of stoppage within a week. Otherwise all quiet. Over.'

He took his finger off the mike switch, and grinned at the engineer. The radio operator, tall and thin, had a face with an unfinished, crooked look to it. His nervousness, the engineer saw, glancing away from the winding coils for a moment, wasn't because of the danger so much as the business of speaking over the microphone to so many unseen listeners.

There was an urgent rap at the door, and for an instant the two men looked at each other, knowing what the signal meant. The engineer calmly started gathering up the equipment, while the radio operator pressed the mike key again.

'We have word of a raid. This is Cracow-Nowa Huta station closing down.' Then he remembered his radio procedure and added the necessary code letters 'QRT'.

The engineer was dismantling the equipment on the table now, working unhurriedly. The radio operator helped him, but fear made him clumsy. They could hear a door being smashed open downstairs, and heavy boots on the concrete stairs.

'Set it up again,' the operator said, realizing it was too late to escape. He was so nervous he could scarcely speak clearly. The engineer did as he asked, working as carefully and methodically to put it all back together as he had when taking it apart. He knew the radio operator was right: they would never have got away.

The radio operator pressed the mike key again. The noise of men running towards them was quite loud now.

'This is Cracow-Nowa Huta. To everyone listening in Poland and in other countries, this is our last message. Don't lose hope. Solidarity lives, even if it only lives in our hearts.'

He had thought of this moment so often and prepared so many things to say, and now he couldn't remember any of them. Outside the door the heavy boots halted and they could hear shouting. The door began to splinter inwards. The engineer gripped his shoulder.

The cracked, nervous voice began again, lips audibly smacking as the throat dried with fear. He said the only thing he could think of.

> *'Battle for freedom once begun,*
> *Bequeathed by father to his son . . .'*

3

The lines from Mickiewicz ended in a sharp staccato noise as a ZOMO riot trooper brought the butt of his gun down, smashing methodically through the equipment on the table. The signal disappeared, leaving only a faint hiss on the HF waveband. The radio operator, his face almost expressionless, stood up, and the engineer could do nothing but look at the destruction of his minor miracle of improvisation. They were bundled out together by four of the ZOMO, their feet raising little clouds of dust along the floor. The radio operator's shoulder hit the door frame heavily, his left foot trailed behind him.

'Stupid bastards,' the ZOMO trooper said as he swept the broken pieces of wire and glass and plastic on to the floor. Then he went over and jerked down the picture of Lech Walesa to add to the pile.

'Come on,' someone shouted from the stairway.

'Coming sir,' the trooper said, but he didn't move. He unbuttoned the fly of his black fatigue trousers and urinated long and loudly on to the little pile of debris he had made.

'Stupid bastards,' he said again, as he buttoned himself up.

It was raining steadily in Paris, but it didn't worry me. I walked quickly, head down, my arms across my chest to give the book I was carrying inside my jacket as much protection from the rain as I could. Cars flooded the Quai de Voltaire as thick as the rain and faster flowing: cyclists darted in and out between them like fish. Farther down the Quai the rain was leaking into the little *bouquinistes* fixed against the embankment wall, and the booksellers who hadn't given up and gone for a drink were standing glumly beside them, checking the plastic sheeting every now and then, and thinking of getting a job indoors.

Turning the corner I left the Seine and the traffic behind me. There were food shops here instead of the expensive places that sold antiques along the Quai, and the rain water which ran in torrents along the gutter carried with it the kind of rubbish food shops generate. In Paris there are fewer by-laws than in any other Northern European city except Brussels to stop shopkeepers from dumping waste into the gutter; so the gushing water carried not just the limp wreaths of clear plastic, and the ring-pulls from soft drink cans that you might get anywhere, but a uniquely Parisian admixture: leaves from plane trees and lime trees, a special type of wrapping paper, vegetable stalks, chicken feathers.

'*Homo sum; humani nil a me alienum puto*,' I thought as I looked down at it all, though I may not have got the Latin entirely right. Nothing human can be a matter of indifference to me: the greatest Frenchman of them all, Montaigne, had had that inscribed on a beam in the room where he wrote, and appropriately it was his *Essais* I was protecting from the rain. The torrent flowed on past me, until it came up against a dam positioned diagonally across the gutter — a solid wad of carpeting, the kind which the tough brigade of Paris streetcleaners call *chiffons*. The waters were diverted into the great open mouth of the drain, from where they would flow into the magnificent nineteenth-century sewerage system which was once the envy of the world; or the world of sanitary engineers, anyway.

I was walking with a purpose — stalking somebody, you might almost say. I knew the habitat, and my heart began to beat a little faster as I turned into the Rue de Lille, which marked its beginning — a long straight street on the Left Bank, on the fringe of academic Paris and likely to be colonized completely by it one day.

I opened the door of the book shop I'd been making for. A quantity of weather came in with me, and I stood on the mat gripping my Montaigne and letting the excess water drain off me. There were only three or four people in the shop, but the windows were misted with condensation which had begun to trickle downwards in dusty drops. I nodded politely to the gentle Russian-accented man who ran the shop, and looked round. No luck. I turned my attention to the books. The shelves went up to the ceiling, laden with volumes on Eastern Europe and the Soviet Union: serious studies, fiction, guide-books, collections of cartoons. I loved it, and had often come here in the past; but today I was using it like a hide near a water-hole.

Not having been here for a year or so, I found plenty that

was new and interesting, including a guide-book in Polish to the area around Cracow and Zakopane. I flicked through the pages, looking for some mention of the place where I'd been born, and where I had lived the first eighteen years of my life. 'Typical highland village with 18th and 19th century cottages in Tatra mountain style. Nothing of especial interest.' I put it back on the shelf.

After perhaps half an hour, when I was starting to suspect that I had misjudged the whole business, the door opened and the noise of rain and hissing tyres filled the quiet shop again. She didn't notice me, and I carried on pretending to read a book by some worthy Eastern European dissident. I wanted to make it seem like chance, even though she would know immediately that it wasn't. She spoke to the bookseller in her serious, quiet way and then moved across to look at the shelves opposite me. Something made her look up.

The green-gold eyes caught mine, and stayed there. How typical that the French should have a word to describe the glance of attraction that passes between a man and woman at such a moment, when there is no such word in English, German, nor even in my own Polish. For an instant, then, this *oeillade* locked Mary Pastorek and me together, and the critical moment was upon us.

'Hello Alex,' she said, and several of the customers looked round. 'How nice to see you.'

I was deeply nervous and in moving across to take her hand I let the Montaigne fall out of my jacket, and it lay on the floor like a shop-lifter's tin of rice pudding. The bookseller's eyes were quick, however, and he knew his own flock. I put it in my pocket without further embarrassment.

'Whatever are you doing here? You're looking very well, Alex.' The green-gold eyes still held mine and the message seemed friendly. I was careful not to break up the *oeillade* a second time.

'I have to spend a few days in Paris, and I couldn't come to Paris without looking in here.'

'Why didn't you tell me you were coming?'

If I gave you an honest answer, I thought, it might not help. Try though I might to forget it, our last conversation still rang in my mind.

6

'Oh well,' I said. It seemed to suffice.

She really was as attractive as I remembered her — tall and blonde and distinctively English, even if her father was a Pole. Though still embarrassed about her height, I saw; she was wearing dreary flat shoes — did they mean a short boyfriend, I wondered? I glanced at the baggy sweater under her raincoat, and she caught me at it. Whatever else happens, I resolved, this time I mustn't try to change the way she does things.

'I was just off to have a coffee with Jan Dolanski from the Institute. Did you ever meet him?' I shook my head forebodingly. 'He works in my office. Come and have coffee with us. He's very nice.' I doubted it, but I nodded anyway. The contact wasn't strong enough yet to bear an immediate break. Without much thought I paid for the gloomy dissident's work and waited while the bookseller packed it up and tied it for me in the approved Parisian fashion. I shook hands with him and told him truthfully it was good to see him again. It is an unpleasant feeling that one of the best corners of the best city in the world is off-limits to you because of a telephone conversation a year earlier.

It was raining too hard to be able to talk much. Still, she had an umbrella, and to get underneath it I had to hold her arm and keep close. She didn't seem to object to that either. But I was anxious about this Dolanski.

In the café, among the players of *baby-foot*, the bright-coloured bottles and the steam from reviving coats, I saw that I was right to be. Dolanski proved to be an elegantly turned-out man in his late forties, with perfect manners; just the kind of man you might turn to if you were a twenty-nine-year-old who had dismissed your boyfriend for alleged shortcomings of character. A sympathizer, a reassurer, a good friend who insidiously turns into a better one. Irresistible.

'Jan,' she said, 'I've found an old friend of mine in the bookshop — Alex Serafin, Jan Dolanski.'

He looked about as enthusiastic as I felt.

'Are you from Poland?' he asked, though it seemed to me that he knew already.

I nodded. 'Nineteen sixty-eight. And you?'

'Much further back,' he said in French, with the accent to prove it. Even after fifteen years in England, I reflected, no one

7

would listen to a sentence of mine and try to work out whether I had been born in Britain or not. It's something to do with the 'o's, but exactly what I have never been able to decide.

I tried to be wary but as always gave away more information than I wanted to. Jan Dolanski was perfectly pleasant, and said almost nothing about himself. Mary was determinedly jolly, as if she couldn't see that anything was wrong. I began to wish I hadn't come.

We progressed through coffee and on to *tarte aux pommes*. It was impossible to hold any kind of serious conversation with Mary while he was there and I decided that my strategy had been fatally flawed. All the same, I sensed that something of her old feeling still lingered, so I refused to give up hope entirely. If only Dolanski would realize that in this little gathering he was the one who was *de trop*, I thought, looking at him and catching a look so similar coming from him that I almost laughed.

'Alex is at Cambridge — the English one,' Mary said, looking more English than ever, though I noticed that she had gone back to her old habit of sitting sideways in her seat and twining her legs together to make herself look smaller.

'Oh yes,' Dolanski said, and showed me a few teeth.

'His subject is Slavonic history — perhaps you've read his book?'

He didn't seem to have read my book. Instead, he talked with some verve and determination about their office and what there was to be done that afternoon and other subjects in which my participation was less than total. He was, I gathered, on roughly the same level as Mary in the Institute where she worked, and there seemed to be some attempt going on at the moment by the nearby *Institut d'Etudes Politiques* to take them over. It was about as interesting to me as the *baby-foot* battle going on between two leaping youths in blue overalls. I was anxious not to stare too much at Mary; Dolanski looked like the kind of man who might not take to it.

He stood up, and started fussing around Mary in the way that older men sometimes have, shepherding her out with a good deal of gratuitous physical contact, and we all spilled on to the pavement together; except that since there was only room for two to walk abreast, I had to choose between wading through the gutter at a level six inches or so below the other two, or walking behind them and shouting to Mary to keep my end of the conversation going. It wasn't a great success.

But there was one to follow. As the two of them headed for the massive entrance to the Institute, Mary turned to me, and there was definitely something in her eyes that time.

'When am I going to see you again?' she said. Dolanski, not liking the turn the conversation was taking, moved into the inner recesses of the courtyard and flashed his identity card to some hidden figure. He hadn't said goodbye to me, I noticed.

'How about tonight?'

She paused. There was clearly something she had planned. Then she said, 'That will be very nice. Shall we have dinner?'

I cast around for somewhere where we hadn't had a row. 'That Hungarian place, off the Boulevard St Germain?'

She smiled again. 'I'll see you there around eight.'

For once, I arrived at an appointment ahead of her; my time-keeping had been a particular bone of contention between us in the past. I had spent the afternoon in a state of nervous excitement, practising conversation lines and trying to find ways of passing the time. I had even returned to the bookshop, and struck up another conversation with the bookseller. He told me about Sakharov and Bukovsky, but I paid too little attention, and soon found that the dissidents of the 1980s were mingling with stories of Chekhov's visit to Sakhalin Island in 1890, and I ended up not being certain who was in which prison camp when. I was so confused I said something to him in Polish, and that confused him in his turn. Afterwards I wandered down the Boulevard St Germain, looking in the shops and buying myself a shirt I didn't need at a price I didn't want to pay before going back to my hotel and passing an interminable couple of hours.

Later, there was embroidery round the restaurant wall for me to look at, as well as the menu and the beautiful woman who ran the place and called in Hungarian to the crone who did the cooking. A drink I ordered to give me a little courage nearly took my head off. The door opened a few times, and people who were not Mary came in and sat down. A

9

Hungarian-American couple sat uncomfortably close in the little place and talked in heavily-accented English, nodding and smiling at me from time to time as though I couldn't possibly understand them.

'Polish,' the woman said, pointing her eyebrows meaningfully at me. The husband turned and looked and agreed. 'Or Czech,' he said. After that they ignored me.

The door opened again, and it was Mary, just as I was deciding I must have imagined the whole business. She was wearing a vaguely familiar dress. What's more, she was smiling. She looked so good that I risked a reference to the old days.

'What's this, role reversal?' I asked. 'I thought I was the one who had to be late.'

The smile stayed, thank God. She even laughed. There had been a crisis, it seemed, Dolanski had had to leave early, she had had to finish some paper or other.

'Dolanski,' I ventured. She looked warningly at me but the moment passed.

The food was excellent. Not even the Polish shops in Ealing sell sausage as good as the ones we ate for hors d'oeuvres, and the goose tasted better than any I'd had since I'd left home. The Hungarian-American lady beside me masticated loudly with her mouth open, but it couldn't spoil my enjoyment.

It was like it had once been, before the bad times. We laughed, and talked about ourselves and each other, and there was no hint of the rows and the harrowing occasions when she had left me, or I had left her. I even risked a joke or two about Dolanski and she didn't mind.

'I like him, but that's all,' she said. 'He's very helpful in the office, you know, and sticks up for me when we have arguments with the other units.'

'Other what?' I asked.

'Other units.'

'Sounds like the Coldstream Guards.'

She laughed again, a plus point: she had never particularly liked it when I had laughed at her work before. It all seemed to put us back where we had been, three years or so ago.

'How's everything else?' I asked, trying to sound innocent.

'How do you mean?' She knew perfectly well, of course.

10

'You know — are you seeing anyone, or anything like that?'
The words sounded silly even in my own ears.

'No one very special. A few people, here and there, that's all.'

From this I deduced that there was someone, or had been.
The way she looked down at the table-cloth and made a little
pile of crumbs convinced me. 'How about you?'

'Like you, really, I suppose. No one that really stands out.
No one to match you.' Oh God, I thought, I hope Judith
Pringle never knows I said that.

I had been badly hurt by the way Mary had ended things,
but after the first few months my bitterness had faded away,
and I had simply felt an emptiness which I had not managed to
fill. It had taken me all this time to get my courage up to see her
again.

Outside, it was cold and the wind blew hard along the
Boulevard St Germain, which gave me the excuse to put my
arm around her.

'This Dolanski,' I said.

'What about him? He's nice.'

'Was he — ? Did he — ?'

'He didn't seem to like you either,' Mary said, looking, if
anything, down at me. I saw for the first time that she had high
heels on. She must have remembered that I liked her to wear
them.

'He's got a reason,' I said, choosing my words as carefully as
the drink I had taken on board would allow. 'But do I have a
reason to dislike him?'

'Only a very small one,' Mary said.

I stopped and laughed, and after a bit Mary laughed too.

'Poor bugger,' I said.

'Oh, I don't know, he's got his collection.' I looked at her,
wondering if she'd been finding a little fault with his character
as well. 'Antiques,' she said. 'He collects them.'

'Takes one to know one,' I said.

After that I kissed her.

Mary had a flat in a seventeenth-century house in the Rue des
Fossés St Bernard. Though it was a long way we walked all of
it, right along the Boulevard.

11

I remembered the flat clearly from before. It had two big rooms, one at the back and one at the front, joined by a passageway with bathroom, lavatory, cupboards and a kitchen off it. Although it wasn't the topmost flat in the building, by some architectural quirk the bedroom had a small roof of its own, on which the pigeons settled. Mary liked the pigeons, and I didn't. Sitting on her bed in the lovely room at the back, with its Louis XV panelling intact, Mary had answered the phone to me and put me out of her life — at least for a year.

There were new books, and new plants, and new records. There was, not surprisingly, no photograph of me, but then there wasn't a photograph of any other man, only the picture of her dyspeptic, disapproving mother. Mary was earning more money now, I could see that. I stood up and looked around the shelves, in the way that makes people dislike me, early in our relationship. My book was there, so she must have bought it herself; I had been in no mood, eight months before, to send her a copy. She too was a Polish specialist, and all the books were there — Davies and Halecki and Hensel, lives of Pilsudski and Lech Walesa, histories of Sobieski and the Jagiellonians, volumes of poems and plays by Mickiewicz, Slowacki, and more modern writers. For the most part I approved, but I didn't say so, remembering how she had once accused me of being patronizing.

'How is your father nowadays?' She had come out of the kitchen to ask me.

'Not too good. Liable to heart attacks, apparently.'

'H'm,' she said, and a look came into her eyes, as though she'd thought of something I could do for her. But it vanished quickly, and she said, 'I'm sorry.'

'And yours?' I picked up a frame in which a grey-haired, handsome old Pole in a Harris tweed sports jacket was energetically digging his garden and smiling at the camera. Her father was fine, it seemed. I liked him — a nice old boy who had flown in the RAF and who disapproved of Solidarity because it was a trade union. Her English mother I liked less, probably because she disliked me. Having married a Pole herself, she had decreed that her daughter shouldn't marry one in her turn.

12

Mary came in from the windowless kitchen with a tray of coffee. At this stage it was still unclear to me how what was left of the evening would develop. The coffee was a bad sign, I thought — a kind of farewell gesture. I remembered cups of coffee from before.

We sat for some time over the coffee. I made mine last as long as possible, to leave the options open. Why do you have to plot everything you do, she had asked me in one of our final rows. And then, why must you always be so demanding of attention, like a child?

'You're paying more attention to the record player than you are to me,' I complained, and wished I hadn't.

'Sorry.' She came and sat beside me — close beside me. The songs from the Auvergne came to an end, but she didn't bother with the other side. Her hair was loose on her shoulders.

After a bit she said, 'Why don't we go to bed?'

'I thought you'd never ask.'

An hour or so later, lying on the bed from which she had taken that last telephone call, I said to her, 'Would you come and spend a weekend in Cambridge some time?'

'Yes, I would.'

'Let's make the arrangements now — let's not do it over the phone.'

She seemed genuinely not to understand what I was talking about.

I extended my stay in Paris for a couple of days, almost — but not quite — moving in with Mary. On the third evening we went to the Hungarian place again, then walked home along the banks of the Seine. We'd eaten well, and drunk well, and I felt relaxed and happy.

The street-level door, between the restaurant on one side and the *charcuterie* on the other, was ajar. 'It's the people on the ground floor,' Mary said as I pushed it open to let us in. She didn't seem to care too much. 'I'm always asking them to lock it. But what can you do? A dog got in here once, and did no end of damage.'

I laughed at that, as I'd laughed at just about everything else that evening. All our quarrels seemed to have been forgotten; it was as if a tape had been wiped, and nothing was left except the pleasure of being with her again.

'Has anybody ever told you you're a great long streak of loveliness?' I had to look up to say that, and it gave me great pleasure.

'Has anybody ever told you that for one so small — '

I didn't let her finish. I'd had a hard day at some Solidarity demonstration with her, handing out leaflets and listening to speech after speech, and marching, and holding lighted candles and all the rest of it. I put my arms round her, drawing her towards me as we waited for the lift. It was a dreadful lift in almost every way: slow, resentful, disobedient, mildly dangerous, and it seemed to take for ever to reach the fourth floor.

The landing was lit, but dimly. If the French lack anything, it's a social sense; and when the light-bulbs gave out in Mary's building no one did anything about replacing them.

'It's too dark. I can't see,' she said, pushing me off and still giggling.

She passed me the key. It was amazingly complex, like a letter of the Mayan alphabet, and needed to be twisted and turned in the keyhole in a complex series of movements before the lock would spring open. I pushed and twisted and turned it now, which made Mary giggle all the more. It was a long and noisy process.

Both of us had expected a sudden flood of light to pour out into the narrow hallway when the door opened. But the flat was even darker inside.

'Didn't you leave your hall light on?' I asked and felt, rather than saw, Mary nod. Somehow, too, I could tell that she was frowning anxiously. The laughter, the slowly aroused sexual excitement, had all evaporated.

I didn't want to go inside. Instead I stayed on the threshold and reached my arm in to switch her hall light on. 'The switch is up,' I said with relief, remembering that up was the French way for on. 'It must be the bulb.' Even so, I didn't go in.

14

'Try the others.'

I did. No lights came on. I felt even more relieved. 'A fuse must have gone,' I said. 'Fortunately when it comes to fuses I'm something of an expert.' Mary was holding on to me now, and didn't laugh.

The fuse box was in her bedroom, and as we went in the pigeons stamped on the slates, making small eerie scratching noises. Apart from that, there was only the ticking of Mary's bedside alarm clock. She sat down on the bed, unwilling to go too far away from me in the darkness. No light came through the window, because of the high wall only a few feet away.

'I'll take the fuses out one by one, and look at them in the hall,' I said. A little light spilled in from the landing outside.

'Don't leave me here, Alex.'

'You sleep here in the dark every night.'

'But it feels funny.'

I breathed in, and noticed something. I sniffed again. 'Can you smell anything?'

'No. What is there?'

I knew what it was now: the smell of putty and cigarette smoke which seems to follow French workmen around. I didn't tell her; there was no point in alarming her unnecessarily. 'Let's look at the fuses out there.' The smell was making me nervous.

Mary clung on to me as we walked down the corridor to where we could at least see something, however faintly. In the front doorway I peered at the fuses.

'They seem all right to me,' I said, 'but I still can't see properly. I'll go into the sitting room and open the curtains.' The smell was even more pungent now, with an added tang of sweat. 'You stay here and hold the door open.'

But she didn't want to do that and, holding hands, we edged cautiously into the dark room, past the dining table. It was then I trod on something. She must have too, because she stumbled. The floor seemed to be strewn with things. I gripped her hand more tightly and moved towards the curtains. They were heavy curtains, of dark brown velour, thickly lined and blocking out the light completely. I gripped one to draw it back, and suddenly movement and light exploded beside me.

I must have yelled out something, and Mary screamed once,

15

very long and loud. But by the time I could move the man had already reached the doorway, the light from his torch showing where he was. I ran after him, crushing things underfoot as I went, banging into furniture, pulling a handful of books out of the bookcase as I tried to get a grip to make a sudden turn.

By the time I reached the front door of the flat he was out by the lift, heading for the spiral stairs that ran round the lift-shaft. I was determined to catch him.

The spiral was too tight to see ahead of me, but I could hear him as he thundered down. He sounded faster and fitter than I, but I was taking the stairs two and three at a time now, leaping down them as though possessed, remembering from a year before how I could get extra leverage from the rail that ran round the outer wall. Sometimes it was light and sometimes dark, and I still couldn't get a proper look at him: nothing more than the occasional sight of a dark head of hair and a dark jacket as he slipped round the perpetual turns of the spiral.

Then he wasn't running any more: the echoing noise of feet ahead of me had stopped, and I stopped uncertainly too. I knew where he was now, all right. The staircase opened out on the mezzanine floor, just before the last, slightly grander, flight to the front door. I would see him then, and he knew it. Anger, I suppose, made me brave. I went cautiously round the last curve, and saw a short darkish man raising his arm to throw something. I ducked instinctively and jerked to one side. There was an explosion and a shower of glass. I don't know how long it would have taken me to realize he was throwing light bulbs at me, because I heard Mary scream, three floors above me.

I turned, leaving the dark man to escape, and headed up the stairs again, my heart pounding and my breath coming painfully. It took a huge effort of will to carry on running; as I staggered to the top, I saw Mary standing in the open doorway, her hands over her mouth, staring into the sitting room.

I put my arms around her for a moment, to try and stop her shaking, then made my way into the sitting room, alone. Now that the curtains were open I could see what had happened: the desk had been rifled, the books pulled out from the shelves, the records flung on the floor. Filing cards lay like a trail for a paper chase, leading to whoever was still in the room.

I could smell him now that we were at close quarters: the sweat and the putty and the cigarette smoke had been his. He still held a handful of filing cards, and through the gloom I could see that he was stuffing them into a pocket while he moved his free hand about him, like a blind man, his eyes fixed on me. He was searching for something to use as a weapon.

I saw it before he touched it: a heavy alabaster lamp I had always told Mary was ugly. It looked even uglier now, as his fingers curled round its neck. His teeth gleamed in the faint glimmer from the street lamps outside. That meant he was smiling.

But lamps have cords, and he had to wrench this one from its socket. While he was doing that, I dived at him. He brought various things down in his fall, including me, and there was the sound of glass breaking. That's her mother's photograph, I thought; you shouldn't have done that. Mary was behind us now, but in the dim light and the general confusion I suppose it was too difficult for her to work out whose head was whose, and she didn't intervene. She stood there yelling instead.

Maybe that rattled him. It certainly gave him the strength to free one of his arms and start beating me over the head with the alabaster lamp. French slang calls the brain the Sorbonne, and I wanted to go on teaching. I let go of him and put my arms over my head to protect it from another go with the lamp. That was enough for him. The smell, which had reached a new peak of intensity while we were rolling around on Mary's mother's picture, suddenly lifted off me like a great weight, and breathing was a good idea again.

Mary threw something at him as he stood up, but he was a big man and the vase she had chosen crashed harmlessly against his chest and broke on the floor. He looked at me as I started struggling to my feet, and even in the faint light I could see the look of enthusiasm in his eyes as he drew his foot back and kicked me in the ear.

When I came round, Mary was bathing my face and policemen were swarming round the flat, crushing more glass underfoot. There were broken light bulbs everywhere; apparently

Parisian burglars remove them to give themselves a better getaway chance if their victims return early.

The police inspector was less than sympathetic and, despite the state of my head, wanted me to give him a notebook full of details. I told him what I could, but it was clearly not enough.

'It appears to be a political crime,' he said grandly. I looked at Mary, unable to take it all in.

'They stole the Solidarity files,' she said. 'I was looking after them.'

'The men smelled French to me,' I remarked. The inspector obviously disapproved.

'It is possible that French criminals were involved,' he said pompously. 'I must ask you to come down to the station when your condition has improved a little. We require further statements, and some identification of photographs.'

I nodded, and my Sorbonne almost closed down.

'Can't you see he's injured, Inspector?' Mary demanded.

The inspector was unperturbed. 'I shall have to make a full report about this. Other organizations may be involved.' It sounded bad. I looked up at Mary, and tried to wink, but that was bad too.

Cambridge felt safe and friendly after the excitements of Paris. I had looked at hundreds of photographs of faces at the headquarters of the Paris police, and further hundreds at the offices of the French internal security service, and failed to recognize a single one of them. I was left in no doubt that the fault was mine, rather than that of the files. The inspector who was dealing with the case quickly lost interest in it, when a better one, involving two women bank robbers, came along. Mary's Solidarity friends were certain it was agents of the Polish government who had carried out the break-in, and the job of replacing the lost filing-cards was begun. I left with the mystery completely unsolved, and Mary promising to change the locks on her doors and come and see me in Cambridge. Selected parts of it made a good story at High Table.

Outside my door, I heard the clatter of an impatient pair of feet on the stone staircase, followed by an annnoying triple knock. I bellowed something, and the gaunt figure of my star pupil Tim Dankley came in and flopped into my best armchair. Knowing the ways of my students, I had placed a cup of instant coffee for him beside the gas fire, rather as country people used to put out curds for the little people.

Dankley's black hair, which was already starting to recede fast, lay in a wad on his skull like a wet toupée. I didn't entirely like Dankley and Dankley didn't entirely like me.

'Well then,' I said, to break the silence. I pulled out his essay from the previous week and waved a hand at it. 'Not altogether bad, though I didn't feel you had much understanding of the basic question.'

Kick them down at the start, I thought, it's the kindest way in the end. The basic question was one I didn't have much interest in myself, and had set in a moment of absent-mindedness: ' "Poland Ever Faithful" and "Poland the Haven of Toleration" — can both descriptions be right simultaneously?' Dankley's essay was characteristically rather good, and he had found one source which I had never come across; unless, that is, he had made it up. I looked across at him as he tried to work out what I had written in the margin, and decided that I would probably have liked him better if he had made it up. But I knew he hadn't; he was just naturally clever.

We went through the subject for as long as I could stand, but since neither of us was much excited by Catholicism's triumph in seventeenth-century Poland, we soon drifted off on to other topics: seventeenth-century Germany, nineteenth-century Russia, twentieth-century Russia — the cue for Dankley's current worship of Trotsky. I rather liked Trotsky myself, but something obliged me to counter Dankley's enthusiasm. He had found some quotation with which to carry on an argument from the week before.

'In 1905, Trotsky says the Tsar's imposition of martial law on Poland was the constitution's tribute to the political temperament of the Polish people.'

Since that was impossible to deny, I tried counter-quoting. I enjoyed my arguments with Dankley, even looked forward to them.

'Trotsky also says, if I remember rightly, "What does

another month of emergency rule matter in the history of that long-suffering country?" '

That produced silence for a little, then Dankley came back for more. 'But he means — '

I knew perfectly well what Trotsky meant, but I wanted to wrong-foot the pair of them. 'He also says "What do a few lives matter in a revolution that devours tens of thousands?"' '

'It's rhetorical. Anyway, where does he say it?'

'In his account of martial law in Poland in October and November 1905. By rhetorical, do you mean he was making a joke?'

'A joke?' Dankley looked as though he didn't know what the word meant.

'You mean individual lives don't count in a revolution that costs tens of thousands of them?'

'It's not that, it's just — '

I knew I had him now. Not that I had scored some amazing ideological point; far from it. I had simply shut him up about Trotsky for the time being. By next week he'd be having another go at me. He was a decent enough character, and simply being intense didn't constitute a crime. Maybe it was his certainty that annoyed me; his feeling that the key to everything lay in the reasons behind what people did: judge the reasons and you could make your judgement on the effects. I knew the argument perfectly well; I'd used it myself enough times.

There wasn't much more of the supervision to go, but I spent the remaining time trying to be pleasant and we parted on friendly enough terms.

I tidied up when he had gone, reluctant to have his or any one else's imprint on my sitting-room, and sat back in the last of the evening light, looking at my books and at the view of the rooftops from my window. I remembered the look of contempt on Dankley's face when I had told him once that I wasn't prepared to do anything to support Solidarity activities in Cambridge.

How can you not get involved?, he'd asked. Very easily; just watch me, I'd said. And I couldn't resist pointing out that the University Conservative Association was just as strong a supporter of Solidarity as the different Marxist and Trotskyist groups were.

20

It can't just be that, he'd said; it must be something else. So what if it is? It's between me and myself, I'd said, mistranslating a Polish phrase in my agitation. It's nothing to do with anyone else. We aren't in the socialist paradise yet, you know: we can still keep our personal reasons to ourselves.

And there were more personal reasons; reasons I did my best not to think about more than I was obliged to. My gas fire roared and the room began to take on a pleasant evening haze, so that the rooftops outside became difficult to see. I paced around, with the thought of Cracow in my mind, and then went over to the bookshelves to get something to distract me. But it so happened that my hand fell on a book by Jerzy Andrzejewski, in which partisans battled against the SS, and no one had the luxury of being neutral. I read it for a little, in the circle of light from my reading lamp, but it brought Cracow so strongly back to me that I could see myself again in the dark of its streets, walking down to the square where I was to carry out the task that had been imposed on me. I had been angry and frightened in equal measures: angry because I had drawn the short straw, frightened because of the dangers.

I broke out of my thoughts determinedly, and made myself another cup of instant coffee: the taste, I thought, would be bad enough to take me out of myself. I leafed through a couple of student essays, but not even the effort of reining in their smart-aleckry could keep me from thinking about the square in Cracow and the monstrous Soviet war memorial in its centre. I could see it clearly now, though it had ceased to exist fifteen years before: a soldier, twelve feet high, who held his rifle in one hand and raised the other over his head, shaking his fist at me and everything I stood for.

I put a patronizing tick in the margin of the cleverer essay, and scribbled something the student would find hard to read. From my desk I could see into the little court at the rear of the college, where tubs of early geraniums were just being put out. But I knew I couldn't stave off the thought of that evening in Cracow any longer: and I felt it would have a value, even if only to understand precisely why I was unwilling to enter other people's comfortable arguments about what should happen in Poland.

I looked down at my hands: they were clean and pink and

soft from years of work in libraries and behind desks. They had seemed enormous to me that night, as I put the parcel I had been carrying with exaggerated care down on the steps of the war memorial. I got up and walked around the quiet room: the fit was on me now; there was no point in trying to shake it off any more. I threw myself down into my best armchair, remembering how my shadow had struck the buildings on the far side of the square, and how it shot off into the darkness at every move I made. I had felt as conspicuous as a floodlit building.

Could it really be the same person — the dissatisfied, flippant academic on the borderland of middle age, and the enthusiast who had believed in passion as the most important human quality? I could scarcely remember what my younger self had been like, though I remembered the fear of that night clearly enough, and the precise details of what happened. My hands had trembled around the parcel I was holding, and the light from the street lamp glinted on a disc-shaped object as large as a coin which had been taped to the top of the parcel. The object had belonged to me: it was a wristwatch my father had given me when I went to university. This was how I planned to repay the gift.

The gilt on the watch gleamed brightly in the light; the hands were touched with phosphorescence. The second hand, which turned on a small circuit of its own, had stopped. Just below it, at six o'clock on the main dial, a thin iron nail had been fixed into the glass of the watch. The minute hand was set at twenty past the hour; which hour, I can't now remember, and it doesn't matter. Minutes and seconds counted, nothing more.

I had squatted down in the shadow of the statue. The sounds of rioting had long died down, and the curfew was in force. I could hear little sounds: my own heart thumping away inside me, the scraping of a piece of gravel under my foot, the shuffle as the student appointed to keep a look-out shifted his position in the doorway of a building opposite. He had caught my look and turned his head away: that meant that no one was coming.

I touched the winder of the watch. The familiarity of the thing should have made it easier, but the feeling of it was somehow frightening, and shocked the expectant nerves of my

22

finger-ends. It had taken a great effort of will to grip the winder between my thumb and forefinger.

It turned almost freely, but as the spring tightened it became harder, and I thought I might break the spring and ruin everything; I half hoped that I would. But my fingers slipped on the milling of the winder and I knew I had wound it to its fullest extent. In the unnatural silence I could hear the loose insistent patter of the watch as it ticked the seconds away.

Then I was on my feet and running. I barged into a signpost, hitting it with my shoulder, and the shock deflected me. I ran in a wide arc across the scrubby patch of grass, heading for a side street thirty yards away. I had felt my legs weakening, but there was a sense of violent exhilaration, a delight in destruction, which kept me going.

The cars which had been wrecked in the rioting lay crushed and abandoned, like cans of food wantonly destroyed. The tanks had done that, when they put down the rioting the day before. As I reached them I forced myself to slow down. I had just under ten minutes: I had seen them on the face of the watch. There were riot police down here, the predecessors of the ZOMO, and I could hear them arguing and laughing at the end of the street. But they didn't hear me, and my steps were muffled by the rubber shoes I wore.

The second hand was still moving busily around its circuit, marking each half-second with a tick, and moving the minute hand imperceptibly up to the twenty-ninth minute mark. I was at the door of my cousin's flat by now, my chest heaving, my forehead covered with sweat that hadn't been generated by heat so much as fear. He let me in without looking at me. We were both waiting for the explosion.

When it came, it was as though it was in the street outside. The windows shook, and a wail of burglar alarms sounded almost before the pressure-waves had passed us by. Dust and plaster filtered gently down from the cracked ceiling. My cousin and I had shaken hands: the Red Army wouldn't be shaking its fist at us any more.

I got up and took my empty coffee cup into the bathroom. I was trying to be tidier nowadays, especially with Mary about to visit me. She wasn't the kind who found masculine squalor attractive. I felt the freezing water on my hand as it splashed into the cup and rinsed out the dregs. The bathroom itself was cold. The whole place was cold.

My cousin had brought me the news of the boy the next morning. What a thirteen-year-old had been doing, wandering through the streets after curfew, it was impossible to say. He must have seen the parcel on the steps of the memorial, and maybe gone to have a closer look at it.

When the bomb went off he was only twenty feet away, no doubt running for his life after seeing what it was. The explosive and the casing around it had been forced into the surrounding atmosphere at a speed of fourteen thousand feet per second. It had caught the boy squarely in the back, stripping the exposed flesh from his hands and the back of his neck, and flinging him forward so that his skull fractured on the cobblestones. A portion of the casing had lodged in his back, entering the kidneys.

I forced myself to go to the square after that. The statue had ceased to exist, the cheap composite material it was made of blasted all round the square. Most of the windows were out, and a couple of people had been slightly hurt by flying glass. You could see where the boy had died, even though they'd cleaned up the place as best they could. It was cleaner there, from the scrubbing they'd had to do, though there was still a darker substance in the cracks between the cobbles.

Only three British newspapers had carried any account of the bombing, and they were all completely inaccurate. I knew, because I was able to check them for myself, having left Poland for good a few weeks later. 'What do a few lives matter in a revolution that devours tens of thousands?'

I put the cup away, and the book back on its shelf. I wanted company, and thought of ringing Mary, but my phone was out of order. To my relief, the bell started ringing for dinner.

Seventeenth-century divines, eighteenth-century statesmen, nineteenth-century generals glimmered faintly from their frames around the walls, their faces hanging in the

24

surrounding gloom like eggs. Everything was red-gold from the light of a couple of hundred candles, and the flames guttered and swayed as the assembled college shifted its weight from foot to foot, waiting for the Master to get through the requisite number of Latin syllables.

He read out the grace like a fast and careless hurdler, ploughing his way through the barriers as he went: a corpulent mathematician who had lost whatever faith he might once have had long before most of the people in the Hall had been born. His voice droned on, taking the representative sharp edges off the Latin words and turning them out rounded and unspecific, like pebbles on a beach. The end came with great suddenness, just as it seemed he would never stop: 'Per Jesum Christum Dominum et Salvatorem nostrum, Amen.'

Honour was satisfied; chairs and benches scraped with the general relief, and the candles fluttered more furiously than ever.

'Grace seemed especially ample tonight.' Stilgow, the man on my left, was a disappointed sixty-year-old who had twice been defeated in college elections for the Mastership. He taught mediaeval French literature, and his long hairless white face made him look as though he had walked out of the pages of some Burgundian book of hours. He was utterly harmless, except for his down on the current Master; and the current Master was more than capable of looking after himself.

'Oh, I don't know, I enjoy the old traditions.' That was Patrick Binney, classicist, minor aristocrat, great capturer of the high ground: if Stilgow had praised the grace, Binney would have complained of the Latin pronunciation or disapproved of making people wait for their dinner. He was a natural predator in human relations, and Stilgow was easy meat.

'I thought it was too long,' I said, anxious to defend Stilgow. He had shrivelled at Binney's touch, like some exotic under-water plant, and I felt sorry for him.

'Maybe we take these things a little more seriously,' Binney said, smirking meaningfully. You had to admire it: in a few words he had isolated me completely, and I had been turned into the intruding Central European, godless, probably a Marxist, quite possibly a Kremlin plant. The kind of person

25

the college traditions should be defended from. Good material for a polytechnic somewhere. I was caught like a detachment of cavalry that had charged too far in its eagerness, and for once my English failed me. I bent my head to my soup in defeat.

'To our defender of the faith here, your suggestion was heresy.' A deep voice, rich and fruity, spoke from the other side of the table. George Grandison was a kind of Bjorn Borg of conversation, delivering lines of terrifying power which were almost impossible to return. Binney didn't even try, and covered his retreat gamely by talking to the man sitting on his right; which was unfortunate, since the man on his right was already talking to the man on *his* right at the time. It was my turn to smirk, even though I knew it wasn't the decent thing to do. Perhaps Binney was correct in his assessment of me.

Grandison was, I suppose, my patron, the man who had supported me in my early days at the college, and had over-seen my election as a fellow. Before that, indeed, he had plucked me from my hostel and helped me through my difficult early stages as a defector with some thoughtfulness and care. He reminded me of an oriental caliph, accustomed to obedience without question, but given to occasional acts of in-explicable generosity. His appearance was fearsome — his great head had a thin coating of iron-coloured hair and his face seemed on fire with the angry red patches of some skin disease — and yet he was famous for his conquests of women.

'It's patently clear to me that the whole episode will end in abject failure as far as the radicals are concerned.' It was Binney again, unwilling to surrender unconditionally and trying another sortie. He was talking loudly to his neighbour about the consuming topic of college politics at the time: Grandison's project to introduce more undergraduates from less privileged backgrounds into our notoriously élitist college. Binney leant back, planting the palms of his hands on the table, as though he had handed out a dialectical coup de grâce. A waiter hurried past on his way to the kitchens, and the candle flames down the length of the table followed him, changing the pattern of light on the faces of the men and women opposite me and breaking up their outlines, like the fragments of conversation that drifted across.

'. . . a decisive moment . . .'

'. . . just a question of cash . . .'

'. . . can you honestly say . . .'

The noise soared up into the belt of dark air that hung over the hall, above the range of the candle-light. Outside the atmosphere of warmth and conviviality, unemployment had reached three and a half million in Britain, Poland was in chains, the Americans were rejecting ideas for limiting nuclear weapons, intellectuals were languishing in the cellars of the secret police. And our college was arguing about whether or not it could go on being used to round off an expensive education.

'You feel there must be more important subjects for men to exercise their brains on.' Grandison rarely asked questions; he made statements, and his statements were surprisingly intuitive. He sometimes reminded me of Sherlock Holmes's clever brother Mycroft.

'There are more pressing problems in the world,' I said.

'Poland, for one.'

'I suppose so.' I always felt defensive about Poland as a subject raised by other people.

'Does Solidarity have a role now, a function to perform?' It sounded like an essay question he was setting one of his students.

'Oh, Solidarity,' I said. 'Too many people in this country support Solidarity in one breath and complain about union power in the next.'

'You don't seem on fire with patriotism.' Binney made a well-timed foray back into the argument with me, choosing a moment when I had plainly fallen out with my protector. 'What are your Russian friends doing with all this anti-nuclear nonsense, Serafin?'

'Here's a man who talks to a Pole about his Russian friends.' Since I felt unable to address myself to Grandison for the moment I had to say it to Stilgow.

'Ancient antagonisms,' he blathered in reply, as though it were the name of a fifteenth-century romance he was recommending to his students.

'About Solidarity,' Grandison said firmly. His voice was

compelling, and people further down the table stopped talking to listen.

Something inside me wouldn't let him make his point: a self-destructive urge, fostered by Binney but directed fatally at Grandison himself.

'Solidarity doesn't exist,' I said. 'It's over, gone, illegal, outlawed, and almost forgotten. Only people in the West even talk about it any more.'

There was an embarrassed silence, then everyone started to speak at once. Binney's handsome face took on a glow of gratified spite, and he turned sideways from me, looking in profile like a Roman emperor on a coin from some debased period: Elagabalus, say, or Gallienus. Grandison's red patches grew redder, and his lowering eyes switched away from me, his eyebrows sticking out like fingers.

The air was sweet and almost warm, and only an occasional line of brightness from a carelessly-drawn curtain cut through the darkness. Outside, beyond the college walls, a car was driving too fast and dogs were barking, but inside everything was quiet.

I could hear footsteps behind me, confident footsteps which neither went more quietly nor more noisily because of the feelings of others. I waited for George Grandison to catch me up.

'They'll take years to come round, you know.'

I realized with admiration that he was talking about his proposal to limit the entry from aristocratic fee-paying schools, as if our argument about Solidarity had never happpened. His tact was immense. He waved a large hand at the windows of the Senior Combination Room, from which we had emerged. 'Reactionaries,' he said, as though he had a bit part in a film about the French Revolution. 'They're enough to try the patience of a saint, especially if he's been at the Communion wine.'

That's it, I thought, my punishment. Justice demands that I pay my debt to society, but the payment is a small one. Grandison was offering me his interpretation: I'd been difficult with him because my patience had been tried by Binney — and because I had drunk too much at dinner. Maybe he was right at that. It was a mild enough rebuke.

Our feet echoed on the paving-stones and sounded hollowly as we walked through arches.

'But I don't quite understand why you don't support the people in Poland who want the same things for the country that you do.'

I didn't say anything at first, but there's something in all of us that makes us want to explain our position.

'It's just that everyone expects it of me — my wretched students, my colleagues, even you. I don't want to be switched on and wound up and paraded in front of everyone as the Pole who loves his country, that's all.'

'It's that business of the bomb, no doubt.' Grandison knew all about that. He knew about most things. He had been at Bletchley Park in the War, when they'd broken the Enigma code, and that was where his connections with Poland and with British Intelligence began. And because he never lost his links with anything, he had never lost his links with the Poles or with the Intelligence people. He was the one in our college who tapped bright undergraduates on the shoulder and suggested they should go to MI 6 for an interview. Spooks, I thought disdainfully; only the British find them fascinating, because they associate secrecy with sex. It must be their toilet-training.

'Maybe,' I said, and then, 'I've done my bit for political activism, and all that happens is that ordinary people get hurt. What doesn't happen is that anything changes.'

He was smoking a large and particularly foul-smelling cigar this time, and blew the smoke in my direction. He knew I hated it.

'You know what they say in American television dramas: "What are you trying to prove?"'

'When did you ever watch an American television drama, Grandison?' It was as if he'd shown himself knowledgeable about modelling men's mini-briefs; and for some reason I thought more rather than less of him for it. Perhaps he'd worked that out.

'We never lose our origins, you know. The call of the blood, the cry of the land.' It sounded like a quotation, but he had a way of making them up. Either way, it was a good ending speech.

He'd timed it to coincide with the ending of his cigar, too: the last half-inch spun away into the darkness, the end glowing like the jettisoned booster stage of a rocket. By now Grandison was bending down to unpadlock his bicycle, which stopped me capping what he'd said. When he straightened up his face was redder than ever.

'Don't give up Poland,' he said, hoisting his bulk into the saddle with surprising deftness. ' "Through fiery smoke, through brothers' blood and ashes." ' This time the quotation was genuine, part of something Ujejski wrote after the failure of the 1846 rising in Cracow. Grandison's gown billowed out, and he looked like a Viking long-ship setting sail as he pedalled for the narrow mediaeval door set in the main gate of the college.

He never does tricks without a reason, I reflected, as he negotiated the door with immense skill, leaving scarcely an inch of room to right and left of his great shape. His voice boomed its goodnights as he rode off to join his small birdlike wife. Perhaps it was all intended to impress me with his basic humanity, I thought; the trouble with people who speak in gestures is that they don't always provide you with a phrase-book.

I walked slowly up my staircase, feeling the smooth wood of the balustrade and the wear on the stone treads. I was a part of the wearing process now. I unlocked my door, glancing as I did at the lettering over the lintel. When I first came to England I had dropped the '-ski' from my real name, Serafinski, because I'd thought that 'Serafin' sounded more English. And by the time I realized that it didn't, it was too late. I didn't mind: '-ski' is only the ending many snobs added to their names in the eighteenth and nineteenth centuries to indicate a gentry background; and Serafin, my family's original name, is a good Polish name with a long history. Like Grandison, I was trying — and perhaps failing — to speak by gestures.

I slipped into the atmosphere of the sitting room: the odours of college polish and the elderly gasfire, and of a thousand or more of my books which filled two walls from floor to ceiling.

This room, these books, this Georgian panelling which hides God knows what in the way of mediaeval stone-work: these are my nationality, now, I thought. No one can make me a refugee here.

CHAPTER TWO

'Many Polish citizens have chosen to live abroad, and we have allowed them to go. But let us be frank: their motives are often selfish, and People's Poland is often better off without them. In most cases of this kind, we have no wish whatever to see them return.' — Polish radio broadcast.

There was a sudden disturbance in the usual night-noises of the house. The old man's throaty breathing changed its note, and he turned over slowly and clumsily, like a sea-lion out of water. Beside him, his wife whimpered a brief protest. Then the night-noises reasserted themselves — the ticking of the clock outside the door, the occasional creak of the house timbers, the old man's snoring.

The sound came again, louder and more insistent. Dr Galka sat up violently in bed, his heart clamouring with the shock of sudden waking.

'What is it, Jerzy? The door?'

'What do you think it is, woman? Don't fuss.'

The old man's tone was less irritable than his words; the two of them had suffered forty years of such disturbances together. But the years had not made him more orderly in his habits. By now he was sitting on the edge of the bed, one foot swinging speculatively in search of his slippers. His eyebrows, his moustache, his thin grey hair which normally lay in carefully-brushed wings over his ears — all were tangled out of shape by the heavy hours of sleep. How many hours? Dr Galka waved a thick hand towards the bedside table and connected with the alarm-clock: it was three fifty-two.

His wife lay back, now that he was fully awake, and she was

asleep before he had gone into the cold hallway.

The knocking began again, more urgent than ever. A woman stood outside in the cold, her face pale in the light that suddenly flooded out from the opened door. As she blinked and turned her head aside, her hand dropped guiltily away from her eyes, where it had been brushing away the tears of shock and anxiety.

She was a tall, angular woman in her middle forties. Though the night was close to freezing in the mountains she wore no coat, and her left hand gripped the curiously frivolous lace of her nightgown, her forearm shielding the thin outline of her breasts. Dr Galka had known her all her life: he had attended her birth in the year he came to the village.

'My dear Magda,' he said. He could guess why she was there. 'You must be freezing cold, standing out there. My poor girl, come inside and tell me what's wrong. Your father—?'

'There's no time, doctor, it's a matter of . . . We must . . . You . . .'

'Magda, my good Magda, I have to put my coat on, even if you don't think it's important to wear yours. And I must have my bag. While I'm fetching it, you can tell me what's wrong.'

He used words of reassurance as a salesman uses patter: to induce a receptive state of mind in the hearer.

She stepped into the hall, the light shining downwards on her sallow features, blanking out her eyes and stressing the habitual frown between her heavy brows, the pursed mouth, the wrinkles on the prematurely lined cheeks. Dr Galka glanced at her as he got ready. He knew everything about her, every mark on her body. The thought touched him, and he reached out and squeezed her arm. That triggered the flow of words.

'It's father. I heard him get up, and then while he was going back to bed he had an attack — it must be his heart, you always told him to look after himself but you know what he's like, he never listens to anything I tell him, and I can't move him and now he's just lying there with a dreadful colour and he can't speak or anything.'

She was suddenly silent.

'Why didn't you ring me?'

'I did. You didn't answer.'

'Old age,' Galka thought guiltily.

Galka lived a little way out of the village, and by the time they reached Magda's home he was glad to get out of the cold. She went to make some coffee, and Galka walked down the hallway. He turned the corner and saw the old man; his head was folded at an awkward angle as he lay on the linoleum, his body splayed out and his neck held upright by the skirting board. As Galka made his examination, Magda moved around pointlessly in the kitchen, listening in the dreary night-time silence to sounds she couldn't identify: the chink of something metallic, the rumble of a low voice.

'I'm sorry, Magda.'

She jumped as she saw his face, itself white and old in the light from the kitchen lamp. 'He's had a bad heart attack. He can't last long — a week, maybe two. I'm very sorry.'

She nodded. She'd been expecting it for a year or more. There was no fear of an outburst: she had controlled herself for a lifetime.

'We must get him into bed. Then I suppose we could have him taken to hospital.' He saw the alarm on her face. The old man hated hospitals, and had always made her promise never to send him to one.

'Well, I suppose the shock of that might be bad for him anyway.' Galka felt he needed an alibi, however spurious.

Later, when the doctor was sitting in the kitchen, Magda went into the bedroom to see her father. His colour was a little better now, and his breathing had lost some of its dreadful harshness. He was conscious and his bloodshot eyes searched helplessly for her, finally resting on her face with a look that seemed like an expression of sympathy. He mumbled something thick and incoherent, and Magda sank down on her knees by the bed.

The sound came again. Now the old man was looking at the framed print of the Sacred Heart, which hung on the wall opposite the bed. Magda caught what sounded like a word, and thought she guessed what he was trying to say.

'If only you'd taken some notice of me, father, I knew . . .'

But the old man, lying with the top of his sleeping-vest showing over the big double quilt, started speaking again. The preoccupied frown between Magda's black eyebrows cleared for a moment, as she realized what he was saying.

She went slowly to tell Dr Galka. 'He wants Alex to come and see him, all the way from England.'

I didn't dare move. Cambridge colleges were built on the monastic principle, and my bedroom was the monk's cell. There was enough space between the single bed and the far wall to stand in, undress and shiver, and that was all.

Her face was slightly towards me, her eyes were closed, her hair lay all over the single pillow we were sharing. She was so near to me that I could scarcely look at her, and if I had craned my head back I would have wakened her. I didn't want to wake her.

'Together, sleeping sideways'; where had I read that? I looked at the delicate mouth, the blue veins round the eyes, the smooth lines of the neck. Another quotation swam around in my memory, peering out at me like a fish in a tank before darting back into obscurity: 'A hundred years should go to praise/ Thine eyes, and on thy forehead gaze.' There was something else about adoring each breast, but that absurd bed made such a thing impossible.

The sun was moving, and I was getting uncomfortable. Also I had her hair in my mouth. I moved my arm.

'You're cramped,' she said. I had forgotten how quickly she awoke, how aware of everything around her. You could wake her up by asking her the date, and she would answer as she opened her eyes. She had opened her eyes now, and was watching me carefully. She was embarrassed, I could see, to be in someone else's bed.

'You're twenty-nine years old,' I said. 'You can do what you like.'

She scooped her hair away from me and laughed in a curious kind of way, without taking her eyes off mine. She's doing it now, I thought: making her judgements. I felt uncomfortably aware of the grey-brown fuzz that covered my chin, and wondered if I had sleep in my eyes. To distract attention from my physical shortcomings, I turned as best I could and stuck

35

my arms outside the blanket for the first time. I was very cold, and the rough grey wool with the college's initials stamped on it grated on my arms like sandpaper.

'They don't seem to heat these places.'

'Nothing we can do about it. It's the fens — the cold gets in everywhere.'

I thought about getting up and making some tea, but the gap between the thought and the action was so great I could do nothing.

'You can't have slept much.'

'On the contrary, I slept very well. I always do — remember?'

I remembered so many things, most of them unhappy. 'I remember so many things,' I said.

'Bad ones?'

'None of them bad.' Lying was a sin, a sin of necessity in this case. It had an effect on the fish swimming around in my memory.

'I remember one thing,' I said. 'A poem in a magazine here, which went, "Together sleeping sideways, / There's not much they demand, / A knee between his knees, / A place to put her hand." '

'The knees are right,' Mary said, looking over my shoulder at a poster on the wall, 'but not the bit about the hand.'

She put the bit about the hand right, still embarrassed.

Later, we lay quiet again, her head on my arm, her hair all round us, like one of those elaborate saint's haloes in a thirteenth-century Italian painting. It was warm, and smelled of shampoo and sleep, and it was fine enough to float when I blew at it.

'What type of tea do you drink in the mornings? Jasmine? Oolong?'

'Don't you just have ordinary tea?'

'Tea like mother makes?' I thought of her mother, spiky and upper middle-class and English, and no friend of mine.

'My mother was asking after you recently.'

'Ah.' I paused. 'She approved of your decision, I suppose.'

'She didn't know about it,' Mary said. 'I never told her we

weren't together any more.'

'Weren't or aren't?'

'This is scarcely aren't, is it?'

The verbs were starting to get away from me.

'I'll make you a cup of the first thing that comes to hand. It may be Oxo.'

It was freezing out of bed, and to make her laugh I dived headfirst into my dressing gown, arms straight ahead of me, shivering exaggeratedly. She was, as always, easy to amuse. I left her stretching out in the bed for the first time, while I went into my sitting room. It must have been fairly new when the king of Poland founded my first university, in 1364. I knelt down by the gas fire and struck the first of several matches.

'Did you know,' I called out, my voice thick with the effort, 'that King Casimir the Great had a granddaughter who could break horse-shoes in her hand and crush suits of armour in her embrace?'

'I forgot you liked strong women.'

'Not strong, just big.' I walked in carrying a tray, with a milk jug and sugar bowl on it as a concession to her neater ways. The tea was Keemun.

'You're as long as the bed,' I said, looking down at her. 'Don't blush — it's a compliment to you and an insult to the bed.'

In the time I'd been out, she'd appropriated a shirt from the drawer, and was wearing it. Women wearing my shirts have always acted out some transvestite fantasy of mine, but not in her case; she was so big it looked as though it were her own.

'Elizabeth of Slupsk, her name was.' I handed her a cup of tea. 'Crush that, Elizabeth of Slupsk.'

'I knew who she was. I didn't know about the suits of armour.'

I watched her, wondering if the wretched Dolanski ever made her laugh. I wasn't altogether anxious to be the court fool, someone to turn to when real life became a bore.

'Does Dolanski make you laugh?'

'Don't always be going on about him. He's intelligent, and he's sympathetic.'

'I'm sympathetic. I just keep it to myself.' I felt I was losing ground.

We sipped our tea, and I did my best not to drink mine too loudly, or indulge in any of the other habits one has when living alone, on the grounds that too much exposure to that kind of thing might cause unfavourable comparisons with Dolanski, who undoubtedly slept in silk pyjamas with a coloured handkerchief poking out of the breast pocket, and ate apples with a knife and fork.

We had finished with the tea, and were starting to work out the elaborate ritual necessary when two people, unused to each other's company, find themselves sharing a bathroom and lavatory. We were still doing it when there was a loud knock at the door.

For the moment we looked at each other, frozen in the embarrassment of having been caught out.

'It's not illegal, you know,' I said, after a second or two. 'People do this kind of thing quite often.' She nodded, seriously; it seemed to be an argument she was mulling over in her own mind. There were two doors to my rooms, an inner and an outer one, with a few inches between them. The previous night I had shut the outer one as well, for greater privacy. Maybe it was that that had brought a smirk to the college porter's face as he stood on the cold landing outside. His long nose, sloping chin and small bright brown eyes had made me dislike him even before I knew his habits of mind.

'Yes?' I put a certain amount of controlled irritability into my voice. It didn't stop him looking past me into the room. Men in his position know by instinct who has a girl in his college rooms, and this man must have caught dozens in his time.

'Didn't mean to disturb you, Dr Serafin, sir, but there's a call for you in the Lodge, sir. Your telephone not working yet, sir.'

'Couldn't you take a message?'

The ratlike eyes ran over me carefully, and darted back to the inner recesses of the room.

'Can't do that, sir, I'm afraid, it being a foreign lady and not speaking English like yourself, sir.'

I grunted ungraciously, as though the whole thing were his fault, even though it was now clear that it was a complex web of guilt, and his part in my discomfiture was relatively small. The voice of one woman on the line, the presence of another in my rooms — this was the stuff of which years of college gossip were made. I looked at Ratface, and his eyes unwillingly held mine for a second or two, then wandered back to the room again.

'I'll be down as quick as I can,' I called out as I went to get dressed. 'And shut the door after you.' I knew I was going to have difficulty convincing Mary that he hadn't guessed she was there.

I could tell at once from the look one of the other porters gave Ratface that the story had already started going the rounds. It was curious, I thought, that they should think I might not notice the half-concealed grins on their faces — as though being born and brought up in a foreign country made the clear actions of everyday life in England impossible to interpret, like another language. I looked at them poisonously and reached out a cold hand for the receiver, which lay on the broad wooden counter.

'Serafin,' I said, in the English way, the vowels flat and uncomplicated. There was a good deal of line noise, and for a moment nothing emerged through it. Then a woman's voice spoke.

'Alexander?'

Four syllables, and yet I knew precisely whose voice it was, though fifteen years had passed since I had last heard it say my name. There was even a kind of informality between us, as though there were no need for any preliminaries. I switched to Polish, saw the sly amusement on the porters' faces without really taking it in.

'I've been on the line for ten minutes, waiting for you. God alone knows how much it's going to cost us, and the operator keeps telling me that they need the line to give to somebody else.'

It was the same old Magda. Something very serious must have happened to make her phone, but though we were speaking for the first time since I left Poland, her first reaction was to complain about something. 'There's so much to be done here, Alex, and I'm all on my own.'

'It's father, then.' I had guessed it, and curiously I felt more sympathy for her than for him. There hadn't often been much between me and my father.

'He's had a bad heart attack — very bad. Dr Galka says he can stay at home, because you know what he's like about hospitals, so we've left him here and I'm having to do all the nursing for him as well as everything else.'

'At home': the words took me back instantly. I might have been standing in the passage-way of the house myself, twenty years younger, getting under Magda's feet and being scolded for it.

'Dr Galka': she had said the name as though I had never met any other doctors, could never mix him up with anyone in the much wider world I had lived in since leaving home. And of course I did remember him instantly. Like a lot of people in the village, Dr Galka came to my thoughts surprisingly often.

'He says he can't — can't die without seeing you, Alex. He wants to make it up between you. "I won't die easy," was what he said. I'm sorry. You always were his favourite, he said.'

I thought about my father. Karol Serafinski: his name somehow brought him back, and I could visualize him — broad-shouldered, with heavy overhanging brows and a strong, even brutal nose: the hawklike nose of the Polish highlander. In a way, I suppose, I had loved him, but love for me at that stage was mixed up with fear and uncertainty about his moods, and nowadays I would scarcely count it as love at all. My mother hadn't seemed to play a real part in his life and indeed, a year or so after I left Poland, she'd died. I often thought that my leaving must have hastened her death. My father hadn't been unkind to her; he was just so overpowering that he cut the light off from her.

And now he was lying in his big dark bedroom, which I could see as clearly in my mind's eye as I could see the grain on the wooden counter: a shrunken old body, with the tough, aggressive spirit flickering very low, and sustained, perhaps, by this single wish to see me once again.

Or was that really how it was?

'It isn't one of his tricks, Magda, to get affection and try to make me do what he wants? He really is seriously ill, is he?'

Magda was shocked, as she always had been when I had tried to show her how our father manipulated people's fears and love and emotions. 'How can you say such a thing, Alex?

It's almost indecent when your own father is lying there like that.' I could imagine her glancing down the passage to his room and lowering her voice, as though even now she might hear the bellowing voice demanding something from her. For some reason, it helped me to decide.

'Magda, I'm sorry, but I don't think I can come. There's too much for me to do here.'

'What can be more important than your own father's wishes?'

'Magda, it's no good, I'm not open to that kind of argument. I've had all that. Why do you think I've never been back? Because I don't want anyone putting moral pressure on me to do anything I don't want to do.'

I was starting to get annoyed. Everyone knows the lines are tapped — they even have announcements to tell you so — and I could just imagine all the secret policemen listening and nodding their heads in agreement with Magda. Let the bastard come home, they'd be saying, what right has he got to stay in the West when we need trained men in Poland? He is needed — the government needs him. Let him come home.

The line began to deteriorate in sympathy. Strange echoing sounds could be heard, coming in waves, as though the cable leaked and the sea had got into it. Someone started saying 'Allo?' in a French accent. Magda's voice grew more strident as she talked louder, and the emotion rose higher as well, as if to compensate.

'You don't care enough about any of us to come back, that's the trouble. Your own father, dying, and you refuse.'

'It isn't as easy as that.' I started to explain, but the tenuous connection, a thousand miles long, was broken almost before I had spoken the words. Maybe Magda had hung up in right-eous fury, maybe a secret policeman had lost patience, maybe the call had just decayed and died on us. Faintly, I could hear the Polish dialling tone, which had once been so familiar; just as the house was familiar, and my father, and Magda.

A decision of a sort had been taken, even if it was the cutting off of the telephone call that had done it. It was a kind of fate, and I had decided not to go almost without having had to decide. I pulled my dressing gown around me, and felt the cold wind on my neck and ankles as I went back to see Mary.

CHAPTER THREE

'Several members of an illegal, clandestine organization calling itself the InterFactory Workers' Committee of the NSZZ Solidarity have been detained by the Security Service of the Provincial Civic Military Headquarters in Cracow. At the time of the arrests, this so-called committee was engaged in planning various forms of disruption of the public peace.' — Polish radio broadcast.

For security work you need small, unobtrusive men who can walk down an empty street without being noticed; men whose heads don't show above the level of the crowd. Tadeusz Nowak was neither small nor unobtrusive, and you could see him from a long way off. Even huddled in a shop doorway in the dark he was noticeable: he was so big the small dark girl beside him was almost completely shielded from view. His bulk filled the space, the wind blew his shock of uncombed blond hair into his eyes and he was incapable of standing still. He moved all the time, banging his feet to keep them warm, and pounding one fist into the palm of the other hand to get the circulation going. He kept pushing his head out of the shelter of the doorway and looking in turn at the three roads that led to the point where he was standing.

Opposite him, people were shuffling slowly forward towards a small lighted window, and then heading off into the depths of the great arched brick building. The main feature was unremarkable in every way — a light comedy, filmed in the last days before martial law, which went further in the way of sexual explicitness than the authorities had previously allowed. Nowadays they seemed positively to encourage that kind of thing, in order to take people's minds off their problems.

The house was going to be packed, and through the glass doors Nowak could see the bulky figure of the cinema manager watching the audience come in. He could also see the figure of a gaunt, unkempt man in his late forties, who moved slowly along with the others until he reached the head of the queue. When the moment came, he took his ticket and passed from Nowak's sight into the worn plush of the cinema vestibule.

Inside, the thin figure walked up the main stairs with the rest of the crowd, but when they headed off towards the double doors and the darkness of the auditorium he broke away from the line and went up another flight of stairs to a little-used office on the third floor, passing a much younger man as he went. The younger man shook hands with him briefly, and pointed out the way to go before resuming his position on the stairs.

Five people sat round the table inside the office: a woman in her late thirties and four men. Several of them were wearing the badges of the Black Madonna of Czestochowa, the closest thing to a Solidarity badge that it was permissible to wear. The Nowa Huta leadership of the InterFactory Workers' Committee of Solidarity was already in session, and the untidy man who had just walked in was a prominent member of the national leadership in Warsaw.

They all knew each other from the days before martial law: Jan Bratowski had gone to Warsaw from Nowa Huta, and had often visited them in the past. There was no need for much preliminary talk.

'Our main object,' the woman at the head of the table said, looking down at the piece of paper in front of her, 'is to confirm the plan for the general nationwide meeting to set up a new controlling presidium.' She looked up at Bratkowski, her face handsome, her hair beginning to grey. 'We accept your date, and we have a place to propose to you, Jan.' He smiled back at her. He wasn't always certain about the determination or even the reliability of everyone in the Nowa Huta underground, but he liked her.

From their doorway opposite, Tadeusz Nowak and Anna Kapuszinska could see the glint of electric light in the small upstairs office, behind the drawn curtains.

'How long do you think they'll go nattering on?'

'Difficult to say, really. It depends on whether they can agree on everything. Then he'll want to see the plans of the place, and make his suggestions.' Nowak laughed suddenly, and banged his gloved hands together. 'All I can suggest is that if he doesn't like it, he can go trailing round Cracow and Nowa Huta like I've had to do, trying to find somewhere better.'

'He's nice, though, Bratkowski.'

'Fancy him, do you?'

'I always like the moth-eaten ones; they look as though they need a bit of looking after.'

'I see, I see.' Nowak laughed good-humouredly. He and Anna had been together for so long now that he knew her reactions to everything. 'I don't need looking after, I know that.'

'You're the most moth-eaten of the lot.' She dug a finger into Nowak's glove, and tickled his hand. 'I've got another idea.'

Nowak didn't answer. A jeep was coming down the westerly street, and they retreated immediately into the open doorway behind them.

'This could be trouble,' Nowak said urgently, and Anna shrank back into the passage-way. Now they could hear another jeep, and a rumbling noise that meant a truck was coming.

'It depends,' Nowak began to say, but he knew already that something very bad had gone wrong. Impatiently he pulled the glove off his hand and dug into his pocket for a whistle.

This was why he hadn't allowed anyone else to take the main look-out duty; nothing he could say inside the meeting was as important as the job of guarding it from the outside. In a few seconds he would have to decide either to blow his whistle or to see whether, after all, the riot police were heading somewhere else.

The jeep slowed down, the massive ZOMO truck a little way behind. In spite of Nowak's quick anticipation, the riot police were already starting to jump out. But not at the back of the cinema — they had chosen the building behind.

The whistle shattered the silence, but Nowak already knew that all was lost. If they knew the escape route, they knew everything.

44

Inside, look-outs heard the whistle and began the emergency procedure. One of them threw the door open and shouted out urgently at the people round the table. There was no panic; everyone filed out quietly, Bratkowski last. He had done this so often. They'd nearly broken the organization in Warsaw on two occasions, and it had been like this both times.

But the whistle went on blowing. That made the look-outs realize that even the emergency procedure would have to be changed. The ultimate fail-safe was for them all to scatter, making their own way out as best they could.

'Forget about the back way,' he called out. 'Head for the auditorium.' Nobody seemed to pay attention. Heavy boots clattered on the stairs, and shouting echoed from below. Bratkowski kept his head, and dodged down into the auditorium. He pushed a door open and ploughed into the audience, treading on feet and stumbling as he kept his head down and tried to find an empty place. He reached one and sat in it, pulling off his Black Madonna badge and throwing it under the seat. Over to his left he could see someone else coming and sitting down in an empty seat: to his disappointment it wasn't a woman. He apologized quietly to the people round about him, and leant back.

The lights flashed on, and there was a lot of shouting. The pictures on the screen grew pale, and the sound died.

'Everyone stay where they are,' someone shouted, and ZOMO men went running down the aisles and took up position at the bottom of the auditorium under the screen.

'There are some dangerous criminals who've escaped into the cinema here. If anyone knows where they are, they should stand up and raise their hands.'

Bratkowski tried not to turn his head, but he could see a couple of people at the end of the row raising their hands and looking down towards him.

'Solidarity,' he whispered urgently. 'Put your hands up.' He raised his own hand, and as a ZOMO officer came running up the others on either side of Bratkowski raised their arms too, uncertain what they were supposed to be doing.

'Someone came along this line a few minutes ago,' Bratkowski called out. 'Then he went somewhere down the front there.' He did his best to point out a part of the auditorium away from the other figure who had followed him in.

'That's right,' a girl said, with quicker wit than most of the others. The ZOMO officer ran down the aisle again, hoping to see where it was they meant.

'Thanks,' Bratkowski turned to the girl who'd agreed with him.

'Silence, over there,' a ZOMO man shouted out. Bratkowski sat back in his seat. He thought he might be safe now.

Outside, three people were being bundled into the back of the jeep. They'd already been handcuffed. The last of them was a woman, who looked round as she got in, and shouted 'Solidarity!' — knowing that she would only get the one word out.

The officer in charge of the jeep gave her a blow in the face with the top of his revolver. The sight on the end of the barrel cut into her cheek and tore it, leaving a welt that ran across half her face. Then he launched a kick at her as she got into the jeep, trying at the same time to staunch the bleeding with her shackled hands.

'Dirty bitch,' he said, and someone laughed.

From a window across the road, Nowak watched the prisoners being taken away. He could see the whole complex of buildings from up here, and although he waited for a long time, no more were brought out. Eventually the cinema audience were allowed to go. Nowak felt responsible for what had happened, but he knew that someone must have betrayed the whole plan to the security forces. Even as he and Anna turned to go away, he was working out who precisely had known about the meeting, and about the escape route at the back.

'There was nothing more you could have done,' Anna said, standing on tiptoe to give him a comforting kiss on the cheek.

'Someone knew,' he said.

The willows are the first trees in the Northern European spring to put on leaves, and those along the banks of the river were doing so to a considerable extent.

46

'Christ, it's cold,' I said, but I enjoyed it. The morning sun flashed in our faces, the wrecks of old boats lay in the water, and ducks stood on the bits above the surface and showed their offspring how to jump in.

'Tell me more about the call.'

'When I first came to the West I couldn't believe it: anyone could go anywhere, no passes needed, no little passports, no certificates of employment. It was up to you what you wanted to do or be. And what did I find? All these clothes for sale, and they still dressed badly, or they were too fat, or too thin, or they had spots. I couldn't believe the spots.'

Mary ignored the spots. 'Tell me about the phone-call.'

'My father's dying,' I said.

She held my arm more tightly, and said nothing for a while. Then, 'Are you going back?'

'No.'

She remained silent, and we walked on. I could feel her disapproval, but it seemed to me there was something else there as well.

'Does he want you to go back?'

'So it seems.'

'Please do, Alex. You'll never forgive yourself otherwise. I've done things like that, and sometimes I wake up in the night still and think about them.'

'Was I one of the things you used to think about?'

She didn't answer, and I blamed myself for my stupidity in saying it. But she was in a sympathetic mood, and gave my arm a squeeze.

'Is there any serious reason why you shouldn't go back?'

I had never told her about the bomb in Cracow, so I told her about it now. It took a little time, and I didn't leave out anything important. I didn't look at her while I told her.

'It wasn't your fault,' she said, as though I had broken someone's window with a football. 'You couldn't have known. And you were doing it for a good reason.'

She's another Dankley, another Trotsky, I thought: As long as the principle is right . . .

'And what about the boy's mother?'

'I'm not saying it doesn't matter, I'm saying that you can't blame yourself for what happened. But in the case of your father, you've got a choice.'

I admired her dexterity, but the confessional mood was still on me. 'He could be so unforgiving, you know. If I did something — I don't know, stealing apples or breaking a fence or something — it wouldn't matter how many times I said I was sorry. All he'd say was, "If you hadn't done it, you wouldn't need to be sorry." I'd be standing there with the tears running down my face, begging him to forgive me, and all he'd say was, "Don't do it, then you won't need to be sorry." '

To me, it sounded like a reason not to go back; but not a very good one.

We sat in a café, and looked out at the stylistic confusion of King's College. I wanted to be told what to do, and I wanted not to have to do anything unpleasant. Two women in their fifties were watching us, assuming that we were having a row; when I looked across at them fiercely they both started to talk at the same time. A girl brought in a stack of plates from the kitchen and there was the clash of china as she put them on the counter. A man asked for his bill as though the café had done him a favour.

'It can't have been easy to tell her you weren't coming.'

'You'd be surprised. With twenty spooks listening on the line and the prospect of five years in the slammer if I went back, it was the easiest thing in the world.' I was proud of my slang, and yet there were moments when I wondered if it wasn't the most foreign thing about the way I spoke English. Mary nodded, but not in agreement; she was acknowledging that she'd have to change tactics.

Even as he lay in bed dying, I thought, my father's will was as active as ever, influencing me across the entire face of Europe. The fact that I had been his favourite had enabled him to exercise more domination over me than he had over my sister; it was the parent, not the child, who was indulged.

We left the café, and gravitated to the market-place, where I always fancied I could detect something of rural Poland about the stalls. A silvery heart-shaped balloon bounced off my face as a child went past, trailing it from a string.

48

'Why don't you say something?' Her silence was wearing me down.

'I've got an idea, and I'm working out the details.'

There, I thought, you have the difference between us: I would start talking about the details the moment the outline of an idea came to me. I looked at the rubbish lying on the cobbles — the cabbage-leaves, the broken fruit boxes, the rotting over-ripe vegetables that the stallholders had abandoned all hope of selling.

'You see,' I said, as much to sabotage her train of thought as anything else, 'you ask me if I loved my father, and my answer is that love means something different for you and me. For you, it's a neat, clear-cut business, like your straightforward upbringing in Highgate. But out there, on the great Gothic plain—' I made a swooping movement with my arms, Dracula-like, and she decided to be amused. After that we talked about other things, but she still had the dangerous look in her eyes of someone mulling over a serious proposition.

' "Wedding customs of the Tatra mountains," ' she read. We were back in my rooms, with the gas fire roaring and burning up the atmosphere. 'It sounds rude.'

'Not really. They just eat a lot. There was a huge wedding in our village once, when I was about ten, and everyone came except the gipsies. The bride was dressed up in lace that was hundreds of years old, and all the younger men got drunk and danced in the fields. Some of the women did too. I watched from my father's best apple tree.'

She looked at me, noticing that I had ended the sentence too quickly.

'Tell me,' she said.

'I was up in the tree, that was all, and the branch broke, and all the apples came down with me. It was a long time before they could find the doctor. Maybe he was off in the fields as well.' I had lain there wondering how I could pacify my father, and then I was on the bed where my father now lay dying. Outside someone had called, 'Doctor Galka, Doctor Galka, there's been an accident,' and then my father stood over me saying, 'Do you think I care more about the apples than I do

49

about your arm?' and I knew I really had thought that. I told Mary about it, as I watched the blue flame of the gas fire. But even as I watched it, dredging up the memory from the past, I thought that perhaps, as always, my father had used the accident to his own advantage, binding me to him with new ties of guilt and indebtedness.

She listened gravely, like the foreman of a jury, and retired to consider her verdict.

'You know I work with the French branch of Solidarity,' she said. I nodded: we had obviously reached the moment.

'We've had word from the underground people in Poland that they need radio equipment in the Cracow area. There've been a lot of raids there recently, and they've lost some of their most important stuff. Your father lives not very far from Cracow, doesn't he?'

'I don't think—' But it was too late.

'It's the perfect way of getting the things to them.'

'Perfect for whom?'

'Oh, Alex,' she said, and a look came into her eyes. 'These people are the real Poland. Have you any idea of the courage it takes for them to go underground and fight for their ideals? Don't you think we owe it to them to help a little bit?'

I expect a look came into my eyes as well. 'It's just a form of blackmail,' I said. 'You're all at it — you, my sister, my father, everyone. Listen. I love Poland, I'm fascinated by it, I study it, I passionately want to know what's happening there and I just as passionately want it to be something better. What I won't do is get involved. I've had enough of all that. If I start climbing down from the terraces and running across the field, it's not going to help the game.'

We argued. It took us all afternoon, and it got us nowhere.

'It's pointless your sitting here telling me my duty is to go back to Poland, in order to save the nation with a couple of wireless valves.' I rather think I was speaking Polish by this time, to get an advantage over her. 'I notice you aren't falling over yourself to come with me.'

'I will come with you,' she said quietly. Her response came so quickly and so simply that I realized she had planned to say it all along, to offer it to me as the final argument, something thrown in to clinch the deal. I remembered that she'd once accused me of behaving as though she were someone to make treaties with.

'You planned all this, didn't you?'

'I've thought about it, yes.'

'And what would it represent between us, if you came?'

'What do you think it would represent?'

'Love?'

She inclined her head. 'It looks like it.'

'We may have trouble getting visas.' But I knew we wouldn't. She was laughing now, but somehow I couldn't do more than smile. I remembered the look she'd given me in her flat, when I had first told her that my father was ill. Even then, I thought, she'd seen the possibilities.

'I think it's an absolutely splendid idea. When do you go?'

'It's not a night-drop over France by SOE, you know.' I was annoyed that Grandison should have fallen into the spirit of the thing with such enthusiasm. 'I could get locked up for a long time.'

'Perhaps you're putting your value a little high.' He was irritated in his turn, I could see. He had lighted another of his foul cigars, and the room was starting to fill up with smoke; perhaps that too was part of his revenge on me.

'Well, there was that little incident with the bomb in Cracow.'

'My dear fellow, if they'd known about that they'd have tried you in your absence, and we'd have heard all about it. They didn't try you, *ergo* they don't know you did it.'

'But that's deduction. I want something more concrete if I'm going to take the risk.'

'More concrete?' The fumes poured out from him as though he were trying to put up a screen of smoke between us.

'Can't some of your friends find out more definitely for me? They're all spies, aren't they?'

He laughed. 'Even if that were true — which it isn't — I don't suppose anyone could say for certain what lurks in the minds of the police in Cracow.'

'But your friends could have a try?'

'I could arrange for you to meet someone who specializes in

51

Polish matters, certainly. But that would be a matter of private friendship between him and me. I have no links with the world of intelligence apart from that.' Another bland cloud of blue-grey smoke filled the air.

'If you don't have any links with them, what were you doing on the panel when they interviewed me about my time in the Polish army?'

'Merely there as an adviser, my dear fellow, merely there as an adviser.'

'When I offered them the inside leg measurements of the Polish High Command I thought you raised an eyebrow.'

'From what I can remember of the occasion, which is little, you found it hard to recall precisely what type of rifle you had been equipped with.'

We both laughed. The examination had been pretty uninformative for the intelligence people. It was only Grandison's interest in me, even then, which had prevented them from being downright unpleasant to me. He had read my doctoral thesis about the Cracovian Republic, or said he had; Grandison had been no mean bull-shitter for as long as I'd known him.

'So you're joining in the conspiracy of those who want me to go back, are you?'

'A conspiracy, eh? Who are my fellow-plotters?'

'My sister and my girlfriend.'

'Not the large redhead?'

'No, I rather dropped her. This is another one; you met her before. She works in Paris.'

'Ah, the large blonde.'

'Tall, rather than large.'

'And she feels you should go?'

'She's prepared to go with me. And she wants me to take a whole load of equipment to some Solidarity radio station.'

Grandison liked it all more and more, I could tell. It fed his schoolboy interest in secret things. 'For lust of knowing what should not be known . . .', I thought; all this will turn up in someone's in-tray tomorrow morning. Let's just hope it's in London rather than in Warsaw.

'If I had a son and the circumstances were similar, I should want him to come and see me,' he said, as though that settled the matter. He does see me as a surrogate son after all, I thought. 'Anything I can do . . .'

'You could put me in touch with your spying friend.'

'That goes without saying. When do you leave?'

I told him, and he blew a cloud of cigar smoke at the ceiling. 'I'll try and fix it for the day before you go. How long will you be in Poland?'

Three days, I told him; not a moment more. 'It's supposed to be easier to get visas now,' I said. 'If there's the slightest suspicion of a hold-up, I won't go.'

'I'm sure you'll find there won't be any hold-up,' Grandison said, purringly. I looked at him to see if he knew something I didn't, but the cloud of smoke was too thick to see through.

'I can't stand him', Mary said, with intensity and precision. 'He's old and lecherous, and he smells of cigars.'

'He thinks it's imperative that I go back and see my father.' I looked at her spitefully, watching her change tack. She would make a good Cabinet minister one day, I thought.

'Perhaps he's not as bad as . . .'

I laughed, and she became flustered and irritable. No one likes being caught out.

To some extent I had them all where I wanted them now: a group of people, all wanting me to do something dangerous because it satisfied their own ideas of how things should be. Stuff them, I thought, as I swung my legs over the arm of the easy chair and looked at my books. But even they betrayed me: *Fathers and Sons* by Turgenev; *The Return of the Native* by Hardy. I laughed again; it was like the I Ching or the *sortes Virgilianae*. Libromancy — if the booksellers catch on to that they'll make a fortune.

'Let's get this straight,' I said. Mary was sitting looking at the gas fire, her long body turned sideways in the best chair, her legs lying parallel to each other and stretching across towards me. She looked over at me in the serious way she had. 'If I go back to Poland to see my father, and take this stuff for Solidarity, you'll come with me?'

'Yes.'

'And will you carry on seeing me after we get back?'

53

That wasn't in the draft treaty; she stopped to consider it.
'We'll have to see how we get on.'

'But if we do, you will?' The auxiliary verbs were falling
over one another in my eagerness to get her to commit herself,
for once in her life, to an emotion rather than a principle. I
should have realized it was no good.

'We just can't say, Alex. It'd be silly of me to promise something I can't fulfil.'

She was right, of course. If I hadn't loved her so much, I
wouldn't have bothered to ask. I don't like the women's
magazine mysticism of it, but I felt the love like a kind of force,
carrying me into all sorts of things I would normally have
avoided at all costs.

That created a centre of resistance in me, and I looked round
for some way to prove to myself I wasn't totally dependent on
her and on everyone else.

'If I agree to go,' I started, and realized that I had now agreed
to go; 'then I'm not going to run extra risks by carting this
radio stuff around. If your friends in Solidarity want it, they'll
have to come and collect it.'

Mary was uneasy. 'Collect it from where?'

'That's their look-out.'

'No, but Alex, we'll have to send them a message in
advance. It's difficult enough to get that through; we can't just
say, "Come and fetch it". You'll have to decide on somewhere.'

'The only place I know I'll be is at my father's house. They'll
have to pick it up there.'

'Oh, Alex, that's mad. They'll have to come all the way out
to a little country village. . .'

'I've got to go all the way back to Poland.'

'We.'

I had diverted her for a moment, and now I started working
out an estimate of the day and the time I would be at the house,
if I got on the flight I wanted.

Once it had been decided, she became warm and friendly
again, and the seriousness evaporated. I couldn't leave it quite
so easily.

'One day you'll do this to me, won't you?'

'Do what?' She was getting sleepy.

'When you get a principle into your head, you'll sweep

anybody aside, won't you?'

'You and your theorizing.' She leant across slowly and kissed me.

'You will.'

Later that night, in the discomfort of the bed, I lay and thought about my father, as he was lying in another cold bedroom, stiff and drowsy and uncomfortable. From his point of view it was simple; I was his favourite child, we had fallen out, and he didn't want to die without being reconciled to me. Magda had been right: I couldn't ignore his feelings. But I couldn't work out whether I'd been swayed by that, or by the desire to bind Mary more closely to me, or by the pressure they were all exerting. I fell asleep before I had decided.

He seemed to know me immediately, and when I looked at him I suppose I could have known him too: a tall, untidy man in a rump-sprung suit. But in England, where everything is related to class, there are different ways of being badly dressed, and even to my foreign eye this man was badly dressed in an expensive, well-educated way. He wore a pink and nile-green striped tie, and was reading a copy of the *New York Review of Books*.

'What will you have?' he asked expansively. If we had been at the Ritz it might have been impressive, but we were in one of those appalling cafés that infest London, the kind with stained yellow formica tables and a big tea-urn. I told him what I would have.

'Strong tea, Luigi, and a piece of that apple cake for my friend.' I wondered if the man's name *was* Luigi; he stood there for a moment, looking at us, his exaggerated soup-strainer moustache moving slightly as he breathed. Then I watched him pour out the tea, lick his fingers, and reach over to pick up a piece of the cake.

'Dreadful place, I agree.' I hadn't said anything, but clearly I didn't need to. 'A thousand years of lack of interest in food have made a place like this possible.' We both looked across as Luigi went back to putting a scrape of margarine on white bread, and slapping a slice of wrinkled ham between a couple of slices. 'They have such a marvellous tradition of their own, and then they give us this. I suppose they despise us.'

The tea was dreadful: as strong as liquid varnish. It left a ring on the table, and I wondered whether it would eat into the formica.

'Grandison said you wanted reassurance. What can I reassure you about?'

'I thought he'd have told you.'

'He did.'

An old man was sitting in the far corner, trying to eat a doughnut without having the necessary number of teeth for the job. A middle-aged couple, probably Scandinavians, were looking at him with much the same expression as I must have had.

'Well, in that case—'

He moved his magazine out of range of a pool of the vicious tea.

'I can't give you any hundred per cent guarantees, Dr Serafin; my line of business isn't as cut-and-dried as that. But to the best of my knowledge and understanding, the Polish authorities aren't aware of what you did, and when they gave you a visa they weren't doing it to lure you back to the country. Is that the kind of reassurance you want from me?'

'How wide is your knowledge and understanding?'

'Pretty wide.'

'Wide enough so that you'd be likely to know if they *were* looking for me?'

'More than likely.'

'I see.'

'And all this business about radio equipment?'

'Take it. You'd be doing them a good turn.'

'You've been pretty well primed, haven't you?'

A girl started mopping the floor round the feet of the Scandinavians, giving them more cause for outrage.

'I know the background. Is there anything else?'

There were plenty of things, but the hard dryness of the man defeated me. 'No,' I said.

'I've done you a favour, Dr Serafin. Maybe you'd be kind enough to have lunch with me when you get back, and tell me

56

what's happened and what the state of things is there.'

'I thought you knew everything about Poland with certainty.'

It didn't faze him: nothing like that would. 'Every little helps, you know.' He gave me an insincere smile, and picked up his magazine meaningfully. 'Another cup of tea?'

'I think that would exceed the permitted adult dose.'

He laughed at that, and patted my arm. 'Look forward to seeing you when you get back.'

'If.'

'Don't worry. If you'd seen as much of this kind of thing as I have, you'd know it will all go perfectly smoothly.'

Luigi paused long enough to take the money, then got back to scraping the white bread again. He didn't wash his hands between the two transactions.

'You go on ahead,' Grandison's friend said. 'I want to get some more things.'

'Don't want to be seen with me, is that it?'

'You've been reading too many cheap thrillers.' He smiled again.

'I'll see you soon.' He turned back to the counter.

I was walking away when I remembered something else — something I'd meant to ask him all along. I swung round and almost cannoned into him as he came out of the shop clutching a greasy white paper bag. For some reason it annoyed him that I should see it, and he held it ineffectually behind his back.

'What about that break-in in Paris?' I asked him.

'You do worry, don't you, Dr Serafin? It was nothing: a standard small-time operation by small-time people.'

'Small-time Polish government people?'

'Nothing to worry you, anyway.'

'And it doesn't affect my trip?'

'Do we have to have the same conversation all over again?'

'I suppose not, if you say so.'

'I do say so.' He changed his grip on the bag and fiddled with his magazine, and then shook hands with me to show me the audience was over.

'All right, then.' I looked at him. He was the one who knew with certainty, after all.

CHAPTER FOUR

'Even abroad, our citizens cannot regard themselves as being exempt from their duties towards People's Poland.' - Polish radio broadcast.

In his double-breasted dark-blue overcoat, Jan Dolanski's tall figure slipped unobtrusively out of the main gate of the Institute and into the Rue de Lille. He stayed in the shadows, the occasional street light glinting on his silver hair as he walked fast, avoiding the puddles where he could see them in the near-darkness. The only time he showed himself in the light was at an antique shop soon after he had turned into the Rue du Bac. He bent and peered into the window, shading his eyes with one hand to see more clearly.

On a table which was itself a collector's item stood a fifteenth-century wooden group four feet high, with the original paint more or less intact: St Martin dividing his cloak with a beggar. The shopkeeper, knowing Dolanski's interests, had contacted him the moment it had come into his possession; it was, almost certainly, the work of a Bohemian sculptor whose work Dolanski always tried to buy if it came on the market.

Dolanski shifted his position greedily to see the flank of the horse more clearly; it was the treatment of the horse, in particular, that would confirm the identity of the sculptor. The group would look sensational in his small flat, alongside the some artist's St Roche and his dog which Dolanski already owned. The St Martin wasn't particularly expensive, by Paris standards: twenty-four thousand francs. But it represented almost a quarter of Dolanski's annual salary at the Institute.

He turned away from the window, bitter that he should

have to count every centime in this humiliating way, angry that works of art should be traded back and forth as investments, as hedges against inflation. Much of it was due to the Jews, he reflected. He walked on precisely down the Rue du Bac, crossing occasionally to look in the windows of shops on the other side. But the pleasure had gone out of it now.

The Métro station was almost empty. At the ticket office he said in his precise, scarcely accented French, 'Un ticket en première,' and then corrected himself when he remembered that the Socialists had done away with first-class carriages. Without needing to look at the direction-boards, he made straight for the Mairie d'Issy line. The train that glided in on rubber wheels was as empty as the platform, and before he jerked the handle to open the doors, he looked carefully around him. Sometimes, if he were suspicious in any way, he would abandon the whole business at this stage; or he would get out somewhere else and take a taxi. But tonight there was no one else on the platform, except for an elderly woman down at the other end.

Dolanski regretted the passing of the first-class carriages. To him they represented a badge of rank, just as his shoes or his well-cut, well-pressed ten-year-old suits did. It wasn't a luxury so much as a small tax that had to be paid if standards weren't to drop: a signal to himself that he hadn't given up the battle.

At the next station, he stood up and opened the doors. Again he looked around; again there was no one of interest on the platform. He changed to the Auteuil direction. This time the train was surprisingly full, and he was obliged to stand. He was starting now to work out what he was going to say, and paid little or no attention to the number of stops the train made; he knew them off by heart. At La Motte-Picquet he moved over and flicked the handle of the door, allowing the pneumatic pressure to open it for him.

The exit was almost opposite, but instead of going out he went and sat down on a bench, watching the other passengers who had got off with him, and waiting until the last of them had left the platform. Then, still precisely, he walked out, pushed through the swing dooors at the top of the stairs, and climbed a further flight to street level.

In the darkness of the evening he turned for a moment and looked at the floodlit bulk of the Eiffel Tower. No one was loitering there, and no one tailed him along the quiet road, or walked ahead of him either. More than once in the past he had turned for home at this point.

He could see the bar now: its red awning, bearing the dreadful English name 'Pub Victoria', signalled precisely the kind of place he found most distasteful. He still had his ticket in his hand, he noticed, and he dropped it carefully into a bin outside a butcher's shop. As he did so, he felt a slight lightening of the heart; he knew for the first time that he could see his way to raising the money for the St Martin, especially if the antique-dealer were prepared to be sympathetic. Dolanski thought of ways to make him sympathetic, and that took him up to the door of the Pub Victoria.

The noise inside was raucous, the air heavy with smoke. Dolanski disliked cigarettes as much as he disliked imitation English pubs. But he knew where he was going. At one of the dark-red plush cubicles, the man he had come to see was sitting holding a bottle of beer in his hand. The hand was so big, Dolanski noticed, that it completely hid the label. As Dolanski appeared through the cigarette smoke, the hand stayed on the bottle but the other gestured to the seat opposite. Utterly uncultured, Dolanski thought, as the gleaming spectacles with their thick black frames turned towards him, magnifying the eyes behind them. There were no polite preliminaries with a man like this. Dolanski reflected once more on the sacrifices that had to be made if one were to maintain a necessary level of existence.

I was committed now. I was even on Polish territory, since we were flying by LOT. And we were surrounded by men who worked for the Polish secret service. It's true the atmosphere was a good deal less tense on the flights from the West to Poland than those in the opposite direction. Not even the most devoted supporter of the Crow, the military government, would claim that a LOT airliner taking off from Paris and heading for Warsaw was likely to be hijacked by some

Westerner hungry for the free air of People's Poland. But the security men were armed, and they were on the lookout for trouble even when they were relaxing. And I was not only a returning terrorist, with a bombing in Cracow to answer for, but I was also carrying smuggled radio equipment for Solidarity.

From the moment I'd walked on with it, holding it in front of me the way a blind man holds the harness of his seeing-eye dog, I had been appallingly aware of my briefcase and its dangerous contents. Not that they looked dangerous, disguised as a couple of boxes of chocolates in one of those obsessively well-designed shopping bags Paris *chocolatiers* supply. This had been handed to me at a rendezvous in the Publicis complex on the Champs-Elysées; I had felt nervous as I made my careful way there, wondering if anyone was watching. And ever since I'd put the lilac paper-wrapped boxes into my briefcase I had felt even more nervous. Now, between my feet under the aircraft seat, the briefcase seemed to glow with an alluring kind of radiance. Other people felt it too. A stewardess asked me in a kind of French if I wanted to stow it in the compartment above my head. I had tried to keep my voice as natural as possible in saying no, but Mary nudged me warningly and I guessed that the words had sounded loud and strained. I was showing the hijacker's classic signs of disturbance, in a plane swarming with armed men whose job it was to spot potential hijackers.

Had they given us our visas too easily? They must have checked my background and believed the business about my father's dying; but had they come across anything to do with the bombing? And what about Mary's links with French Solidarity? A man settled beside me on the aisle seat, hemming me in. I'm trapped now, I thought, and grew querulous.

'Why do I have to carry it?' Mary and I had argued at great length about that, and I had been selected. It made sense in a way, I could see that. If we divided the consignment between us, that simply doubled the chances that it might be found. And since women do more smuggling than men — on the expectation that customs officials will pick on the men — we were going for the double bluff. I know it and you know it, I'd said to Mary, but will the Polish customs know it?

Somehow it hadn't seemed entirely real when we'd talked it

61

over in Cambridge and in Paris, but now it was real enough. I remembered how I had refused either to deliver the radio equipment myself or to allow Mary to deliver it. I had felt the need to assert myself somewhere. Now I wondered if I was here only because of the impulsions of others: Magda, my father, Mary, all the Solidarity people who had thanked me and congratulated me on my bravery in helping them, Grandison with his phoney father-figure business.

'Aren't you nervous?' I asked her, as she sat comfortably beside me.

She looked at me. 'I suppose so, a bit. More excited, really.' In spite of my nerves, however, I felt sure that I would get away with this, just as I had got away with almost everything. It's my gambler's nature, I suppose, the absolute certainty that the ball will land on red, the horse running third will overtake the other two, the right government will take power, things will get better. For me they always had; except in the case of Mary. Maybe that was why it had hurt me so deeply.

'What will you do when we get back?'

'Return to the Institute, of course.'

'You wouldn't think of coming back to England?'

'Not really, no. Not for the time being.'

I summoned her spiky mother, the energetic Harris tweed of her father, to my aid. 'Wouldn't your parents prefer it if you stayed in England?'

'They like visiting me in Paris.'

I thought of my own father. I wouldn't take one step out of the mountains to go and see him, he'd said when I left to go to England. As far as I'm concerned he no longer exists.

He'd relented, of course, over the years. There were our occasional letters, formal and not particularly informative on either side. But there was no love, no affection, not much interest, until he felt himself to be dying. Then, suddenly, he needed to see me.

I tried to talk to Mary, but her nervousness showed itself in a close attention to duty, and she was reading some improving book.

'Do you mind if I listen to my cassettes?'

She shook her head, without looking up from the book, though I knew she disliked gadgets. It was my latest toy, and I clamped the minute headphones on my head with anticipatory pleasure, ready to lose myself in Janacek's Glagolitic Mass and forget the flight and the arrival and the trials to come.

For the first time in my life, something powerful was happening: a dangerous return, a dying father. Without quite realizing what I was doing, I fiddled with the controls and turned the music louder, trying to drive the anxieties out of my head by pure sound. Mary reached her hand across suddenly and took mine, in a way that was rare with her.

'Thank you for coming', she said. It took me a bit of time to get the headphones off, and she laughed at me for that. I felt that we were back on our old terms, and the anxieties began to lift. But the moment wasn't allowed to last.

'You are going on holiday, or for work?' It was my neighbour, the man who had blocked me off from the aisle.

Even in my ears, his French had a rough edge to it, a nasal sound. I looked round at him: a thin-faced man with dark hair that seemed to be fading from his head, and two thin slanting lines of hair on his upper lip for a moustache.

'We are from Charleroi,' he said, as if that explained the moustache, and his large bleach-blonde wife leant forward from the seat across the aisle and smiled in confirmation. It was impossible not to smile back, but I didn't answer. The Belgian was examining me more closely now, observing my fair hair, my broad face.

'Maybe you're going home?'

My only defence against the Clark Gable of Charleroi seemed to be to refuse to speak French.

'I'm British,' I said, but softly, so my accent wouldn't show. The Belgian nodded, and said something to his wife, who leant forward and smiled again. I seized the chance to put my headphones on again. *Osanna vo vysnich*: Hosanna in the highest. The Czech words were sufficiently close to Polish for me to grasp them. But the Belgian had been right. I was returning home, in spite of myself, drawn there by a series of pulls which together were almost irresistible.

I knew then that it was the real place I was afraid of returning to, rather than the country of the mind which I had idealized over the years of exile. I would be forced to see not just the decency and beauty of the place, but also its smallness and decay. My father, dying in an inadequate little house that had once seemed so large; the lack of change in everything and everyone except myself. Would my mother be dead, or my father now be dying, if I had stayed? Would Magda be old and dried up and resentful?

Clark Gable nudged me, and I went through a weary parade of taking the headphones off all over again. He didn't seem to mind.

'We are going to the International Festival of Labour,' he said, his wife nodded cheerily like one of those dogs in the backs of cars. 'You too?'

'No, I'm going back to celebrate thirty-nine years of everything Marxism-Leninism has done for Poland.'

Mary looked at me warningly, but Clark Gable lapped it up. He explained what I had said to his wife, and one or two Poles looked round, then went on puffing away at their endless Sport cigarettes. They knew what was going on, even if he didn't.

'Food production up by minus twenty-four per cent, for a start,' I said, but maybe my French got in the way and muddled it up for him.

'Education and health too,' he said. I couldn't deny that; indeed, I'd argued the point over and over again with bores like Binney.

'Military activity up by several hundred per cent,' I said. 'Occupancy of prison cells increased to Soviet proportions.' He was starting to catch on. 'Foreign debts up four hundred per cent. Consumption of potatoes as opposed to meat up by three hundred per cent.'

'You are not a true Pole,' he said, with something approaching dignity. I felt sorry for baiting him now. Who was I, after all, to mock a man for his beliefs when I had none of my own? But I couldn't allow him to insult me or to have the last word.

'No, you're right. I get three good meals a day, and I didn't have to ask for permission to leave the country I live in.'

'For God's sake,' Mary hissed beside me. 'Did you realize how loudly you were talking?'

'It's true,' I said belligerently. 'Why shouldn't someone say it occasionally? It's all you ever talk about in Paris.'

'You're absolutely insane,' she said. It seemed to please her.

We slept for an hour or so then, and I was certain of peace and security on the Belgian front. I woke up to hear the chief stewardess telling us what temperature it was in Warsaw, and how much they hoped I would travel on LOT the next time I flew anywhere. Mary held my arm lovingly as the aircraft banked and we got our first look at the green woods and fields of my native country, set out for us at an angle as we cut through the lowest level of cloud.

I fiddled once again with my cassette player, knowing which passage I needed to hear, and turned the sound up savagely.

Agnece Bozij, v zeml'ej grchy mira, pomiluj nas: O Lamb of God, which taketh away the sins of the world, have mercy on us.

With a jolt that threw us against our seatbelts and made me afraid the plane would topple over, we landed in Warsaw.

There were so many unpleasant possibilities, it scarcely seemed worth while going into them all. The police might have found out about the Cracow bombing and be waiting for me. Or they might find the equipment I had in my briefcase. Everyone who had known about it in Paris Solidarity — and there had seemed to be an incredible number of people who did know — had insisted that they always sent things by courier, and that there had never been any problems. Well, only one problem. It transpired, after I had done a good deal of hard questioning, that a Belgian supporter of Solidarity had been given a long gaol sentence for carrying radio parts to Poland. We didn't want to tell you, someone said, in case it made you depressed. Since we're being frank with each other, I answered, tell me how many consignments of radio parts you have sent in to Poland this way. You'll be the second, the man had said. Then everyone laughed, and told me I was doing exactly the right thing.

But there was a kind of comfort in the thought that I could do nothing about it all now. The last chance to have got out of it was at Charles de Gaulle, and with Mary watching me carefully there hadn't been a hope.

She was watching me again now, the thoughtful green-gold

eyes on mine, the fine-shaped mouth a little pursed. She had some Solidarity literature, printed in Paris, with her and was running something of a risk herself, but as always she seemed more concerned about me. I envied her inner certainty.

'How does it feel to be back?' She gave my arm another friendly squeeze. I told her how it felt, and what I thought of airports in general, and Polish airports in particular. It made her laugh, and one or two of the other passengers turned round in the queue and looked at her with approval, her handsome long pale face creased up with amusement, her hair moving counter to the way she moved her head. I thought, I did the right thing in coming here, if it meant I came with her. For a moment I saw myself in another, altogether more flattering light: the adventurer, who had laid his freedom on the line for the love of a woman. But however much I tried it on, it didn't fit. Mary knew how reluctant I had been.

We shuffled forward in the queue; someone else had been judged fit to enter the country. Mary was excited now, I could see. She held my arm all the tighter, and kept trying to peer out of the airport windows to the drab green fields around us. She had only been to Poland once before in her life, in the summer of 1981. I had refused to accompany her.

We talked little; there seemed no point in drawing extra attention to ourselves now. Near me stood a soldier with his hand on his sub-machine gun, shepherding us into the control booths where our passports were to be checked. He looked stolid and obedient, but how could one tell what was going on in the mind within? Once again I started to tell myself that all of this was an adventure, of the kind I could bore my grand-children with. I glanced at Mary, and wondered if she would be their grandmother. The stolid soldier was looking at her too, in an appraising sort of way. I felt annoyed at first, and then thought that I should welcome any sign of humanity in the surrounding grimness of the Polish army. When his eyes flickered away from her to look at the man she was with, I tried to give an encouraging, friendly glance back to him. Immediately the stolid shutters came down again, and he was an automaton. The Polish army will never take action against the true representatives of the people, I had been told during Solidarity's heyday. I had once been in the Polish army, and I knew perfectly well that it did what it was told. Pointing that out hadn't made me particularly popular, either.

Another soldier joined the first. Their attitudes indicated that as far as they were concerned, we were all equally under suspicion until we had gone through each of the individual checkpoints between us and Poland proper. I disturbed the smoothly flowing pattern of the queue by changing a couple of hundred dollars at the bank counter and then going back to rejoin Mary in the queue for passport control. Several people took exception to that, but the soldiers looked as though they expected us to behave like animals anyway, so nothing surprised them. For the tenth time I read through the details in my British passport, noting the exotic place of birth and the familiar, uninteresting photograph that made me look older than I was. These next few minutes, I thought, will determine the course of much of the rest of my life. It seemed important enough to tell Mary about, but she had that dedicated look on her face, and I decided not to bother.

In front of me, Mary was handed back her passport across the wooden counter, said her thank-yous and moved on. I shuffled forward, pushing the dangerous briefcase ahead of me with my foot. Inside the wooden box was a boy in the drab uniform of the border guards. He was seventeen at most, and there were unpleasant clusters of hot pimples round his mouth. I pushed the familiar dark-blue passport across to him and wished him good day in Polish. There was no answer; his training hadn't covered such an eventuality.

I felt the familiar tightness in my chest. I had to concentrate all my attention on the pimples to keep my emotions under control. This was the moment when the men in suits would step forward and take me in for questioning, if they were going to. The soldier read each individual element in the English description of me carefully, word by word, then looked up to check it against the real thing. Height, five feet nine inches. Colour of eyes, grey. Colour of hair, fair. There was a mirror behind my head angled so that the soldier could see — what? That my hair was the same colour at the back? That no one was trying to crawl through while the guard's attention was distracted?

The cluster of pimples moved, and I tried to work out what

was being said. I smiled and said nothing, and it didn't seem to matter. The soldier looked back at my passport, and flicked through the visa pages until settling on a conveniently blank one and hammering it with an ancient multi-coloured stamp. Then the face, vacant as ever, turned back to me, and the hand pushed the passport towards me.

Mary and I grinned at each other, in our first entirely mutual display of emotion that day. I felt like kissing her, but that would have attracted too much attention.

We were only through the first barrier. A worse one still awaited us.

The long queue at the immigration desk meant that our luggage had already been delivered in the arrivals' hall. I could see my green webbing holdall from a distance, and Mary pointed out her suitcase. There were no trolleys, and the porters were deep in conversation by the side of the line of luggage. It was a good deal easier to carry our own things than to interrupt them. Mary, we had already decided, would go through customs separately, so that if one of us were caught, the other might just have a chance of getting away.

For the most part, the two customs officers seemed to be waving people through. The man ahead of me was carrying a couple of big cardboard cartons tied with string, as well as his suitcase, and they showed no interest. Something about me, though, seemed to strike them. There was a glance between them, and then one of them leant forward and made a weary gesture with his hand, as if to say, pile everything over here on the table.

My hands were shaking, and I was glad to be able to put the cases down. Mary, I had seen out of the corner of my eye, had already passed through, and was out in the concourse with the crowd waiting for the remaining passengers.

'Business?'

I shook my head. I knew now what they thought.

I had put on a suit and tie, knowing that Polish officials, like British ones, are impressed by the appearance of money. The trouble was, they thought I was a businessman. And business-men, unlike tourists, carried magazines like *Lui* and *Playboy*, which could be confiscated with a large fine, and then resold on the black market. I cursed my stupidity for not having worked that out in advance.

'Just tourist,' I said.

They had lost interest, but appearances made them obliged to continue with the examination.

'Open, please.'

I showed him my holdall first, hoping that its contents would bore him. He leafed quickly through the shirts and underwear, and sneered at the kind of things I shaved with; obviously I wasn't up to businessman's standards. He made a little chalk squiggle on the side of the case, and left it for me to close.

'And this one.'

It took me a long time to cope with the straps and locks on my briefcase, and the customs man grew irritated rather than bored. Other businessmen, who really were carrying copies of *Playboy*, might be getting through while he wasted his time on me.

I looked away, in a little movement of surrender. It was too difficult to watch him, and I felt my eyes might guide him to the two boxes if I did. Around me, a river of passengers was sweeping out into the arrivals' concourse. An old woman in a red headscarf was embracing a girl; a middle-aged man was looking on, smiling in an embarrassed way.

It all seemed a great deal more real than anything that was going on here.

'What is this?'

Five crystals and a power transistor: I confess, I'll tell you everything I know.

'A present,' was what I actually said.

'What kind of present?' The voice was without any excitement whatever. I pointed out the label from the Paris *chocolatier*, unwilling to trust myself to speak. My voice would croak too much.

He nodded. 'And what about this?'

I couldn't bring myself to look at what he had fished out. His voice had taken on a different tone. I couldn't even look him in the eyes now.

'I asked you about this.'

I forced myself to look at last.

'It's just that we don't often find people from the West

reading Lenin, that's all.' There was a suspicion of humour in his voice.

'Lenin,' I repeated idiotically. I had forgotten about him: *What is to be Done* was Lenin's essay on building opposition to a régime in factories and workshops; one of the less earnest Solidarity people had suggested there might be lessons to be drawn from it in Poland, and I had laughed and agreed.

Something seemed required of me: an explanation.

'I'm a university teacher,' I said. The customs man nodded, and waved me away. People who read Lenin wouldn't, by definition, carry copies of *Playboy* as well; certainly not university teachers. I walked towards the door, longing for the sight of Mary's handsome figure in her long tweed coat. The door opened. I was admitted. At last I heard the noise and smelled the smell of Poland once again.

CHAPTER FIVE

'The undeniably difficult situation we face demands that all honest and hardworking people in our country should be on their guard against signs of evil — in particular parasitism, an unhealthy introspection, and betrayal.' — Polish radio broadcast.

'Why does everyone always have to assume it's a woman when they're let down?' Anna drew a question-mark on his chest as he lay in the cheap, rough sheets.

'It's nothing to do with being a man or a woman. It's just a question of finding out who did it.'

'I would have thought it was more likely to be one of the ones who weren't arrested. What about Bratkowski? Or Smykowski, if it comes to that? They got away. Maybe someone helped them.'

'Or you, or me, for that matter,' Nowak said.

'You've got to trust someone,' Anna said, and he smiled as he ran his fingers through her strong curly hair.

'Turn over,' she said, and started to work on the muscles of his back. 'My God, you're enormous. A masseur should get double for doing you.' She dug her fingers painfully into his neck muscles, but he didn't say anything.

'Not Smykowski, anyway. I can't vouch for anyone else. If it's Smykowski, we really are screwed: he'll almost certainly be the next leader.'

'But why Ewa? Why pick on her?' Anna asked.

'No reason, really, just suspicion. She once worked for the newspapers, you know; her past isn't all that marvellous.'

'Oh, I see. She's from the intelligentsia, not like the rest of you. You've got to be all right, because you work on the shop floor. She's bound to be suspect.' This time she went out of her way to hurt him, and was rewarded by a yelp of pain.

'Nothing to do with it,' he said. 'What are you trying to do to me? I thought this was a massage.'

'It's a punishment session, to serve you right for your arrogance and your rotten male assumptions. Anyway, if Ewa told the police, why did they arrest her? If you remember, when they got the full presidium in Warsaw, the one who betrayed them wasn't picked up — whatever his name was.'

Nowak grunted his agreement into the sheets. 'Could be covering up,' he said, a little later. 'Why not? It means the rest of us are all circling round each other, trying to work out who did it. And if we think it's Smykowski who's betrayed us, then the whole thing breaks up of its own accord. That's the way these bastards want it to be.'

'We ought to move from here, you know,' Anna said, as though she hadn't taken in anything he had been saying.

He relaxed again, and laughed. But he asked, 'Do you really want to get out?'

'I don't want to end up in gaol with a load of dyke warders going the rounds at night-time.'

'You might find it suits you better.'

'It couldn't suit me worse than a great hairy lump like you.' She kissed him on the trapezius muscle.

'What can we do, though?' Nowak had already gone back to the real anxiety. 'We've got to assume that we're all okay. If we start doubting each other now, we'll be in trouble from the start, especially with a whole new presidium to set up.'

'Isn't there some way you can clamp down a bit on security? That's supposed to be your side of it, isn't it?'

'It was. Whether they'll want to keep me on after what's happened, I don't know.'

'If you hadn't stuck your neck out by blowing the whistle for so long, they'd all be in gaol.'

'If I'd done things better, I wouldn't have needed to blow the whistle in the first place.'

She punished him for that with another pinch. 'Don't always be blaming yourself. Someone else is the traitor. That's the one to blame, not you.'

'How do you know it isn't me?' He reared up his great

smiling face and looked round at her.

'I expect it is, then.'

'You're right, though. From now on, we don't talk to anyone. I won't even tell you anything. Do you mind?'

'Not as long as I can carry on working for you all. I don't want to have anything to tell the dykes when they put the thumbscrews on me.'

'It won't be your thumbs.'

She laughed, and then said, 'All I want to do is help, you know that.'

'You could help now. I've got to get up.'

'You've always got to get up when we get to the good part.'

They both laughed at an old joke, and from the room next door someone tapped irritably on the wall. Anna made a face at the wall, and started singing loudly.

The tapping got louder, too.

Nowak smiled again. He was glad to see Anna had recovered her spirits.

I was still exhilarated by the business of getting through undetected, by being in Poland. On the short plane flight from Warsaw to Cracow I'd felt something like panic at the thought that I was going to face it all again. To have to see my home and my father was one thing; to be brought face to face with the one part of my background that I had consistently idealized was altogether more disturbing.

The car we had hired from the Hotel Cracovia rattled along the pitted road surface, the wheels catching from time to time in the inevitable tramlines. Compared with the dreary blocks of flats, the untended road and the tinny cars, the great clean slogans — white words emblazoned on red banners hanging in front of the buildings — seemed fatuous. But things changed radically when we reached the Vistula.

In front of us were gardens, and beyond them the city, red and gold and brown, with spires and towers of dark slate, and gilded cupolas and weathervanes topping everything. It was a city that had outlasted wars and revolutions, a capital city in its day and then a small decaying provincial town in someone else's empire, then a republic of its own, and finally a major city once again. The most beautiful city in the world, perhaps; dormant now, but still the home of craftsmen and jewellers, waiting for new commissions.

Mary had been here more recently than I had, and was less astonished by its loveliness. 'We could probably find someone from the movement and hand over the things now,' she said. We had asked each other if the car might be bugged, and although it seemed unlikely we did most of our talking as we stood on a terrace and watched the flower-sellers.

'No,' I said. 'We've made the arrangements. Let's do it as we said we would.'

She disapproved, I could tell, but she believed in sticking to agreements. She stood looking at me, her hands bunched up in the pockets of her tweed coat. Her height meant she looked her best in slightly mannish clothes, and now, with the flower-sellers of Pijarska street behind her, she looked overwhelmingly attractive.

'If it hadn't been for you I'd be in Cambridge right now.'

'Doing what?'

'Arguing with someone, I expect.'

'So now you're in Cracow, arguing with me,' she said.

We walked on, but I was uneasy. I had already resolved not to walk anywhere near the square where the bomb had exploded, but how could I be sure I wouldn't meet the dead boy's mother? She could be any one of the drab old women I was passing in the street.

Even so, it was difficult to be depressed here for long. It was a poor city, but there was life in it, and it seemed far younger than I had remembered. There were older people, but they were fewer in number than before, quieter, humbler. Cracow now seemed to belong to the young. The sun was starting to go down, and a golden haze hung over everything. From the walls of the city, the red and brown tiles of the roofs stretched almost unbroken to the river like an irregular pavement; now and then great sculptured heads showed above the façades of buildings. It was unnaturally silent. Only the occasional hoot of a car horn and the hissing of the river broke the still-

74

ness. A few neon lights spelled out their gloomy slogans in the industrial suburbs. The smoke from tall factory chimneys formed a layer which stretched across the sky magnifying the last of the daylight. A shout echoed in the street nearby, and was answered from farther away.

I was twisting my hands around, trying to hurt them so that the pain would take away the anguish and the guilt. Do you think Poland is worth the death of one single thirteen-year-old boy, my father had asked, refusing to look at me. You don't think we planned it that way, I'd replied. Of course I don't. But it's too late now to say to that boy's mother that you're sorry, and that he died for the future of Poland. What future, anyway? How has anything changed because you blew up some foolish statue?

It's no good keeping on at me, father, I'd said. I've told myself everything you're telling me, ten times over. I wonder, he said, but I knew then that was his way of acknowledging that I had reached the necessary point of contrition. I suppose I shall have to help you to get out of the country before anyone finds out who did it, he'd said. And then, Don't go back to Cracow.

'I never wanted to come back here, of all places,' I said to Mary.

She moved in front of me and kissed me, first on the forehead and then on the lips.

'You mustn't ever feel any kind of guilt about it, any more than if you'd been driving and the boy had run out in front of you in the road.'

In some ways I prefered my father's outright anger, and his revulsion from me and from what I had done.

I could hear the bugle being blown from the tower of the church of the Virgin Mary, as it is at every hour to recall the Tartar invasion of 1241, and the complete destruction of the city. As the melancholy sound died away I could hear another sound I hadn't been able to identify properly earlier: the weird chirrup of some bird in the tower of a church we were passing. It seemed inexplicable to me, a symbol of something I couldn't describe, without any proper clarity of meaning, like a slogan in a foreign language painted on a wall. Mary seemed not to hear it, or if she did it didn't interest her. It came again, so it wasn't my imagination, but it was immediately drowned out by the laughter of a couple of teenaged girls, walking arm-in-arm along the cobbles behind us. They were joking about one of their boyfriends, then about me as I turned to look at them. Dark-haired, thin and attractive, they moved on down the slope whose cobbles were set in a pattern I immediately remembered with great vividness, though I probably hadn't thought about it since I left for England. A man nearby whistled a tune of which I could remember each bar, but only as the whistler reached it. There were vague words, too: 'Let us sing as we once sang, Round the —' Was it 'fireside'? With Mary walking silently beside me, holding my arm, I felt old and isolated and forgotten, and the golden city turned grey almost as I watched.

'You've no idea the risks these underground people have been taking here, to keep their radio station intact.'

There was an English enthusiasm about her, as though she were a schoolgirl again, describing a game of lacrosse.

'Oh yes,' I said. Other people's enthusiasms invariably brought a counter-response from me.

'You must surely feel something, Alex — you can't be completely unaware of what's going on around you.'

'Sure I feel something,' I said, and started pulling her towards me. It was a mistake, I thought at first, but then she responded gratifyingly enough.

The mood between us was changing constantly; perhaps it always had, but I couldn't remember clearly enough. Now we were close again, and together we went into a crowded, noisy café for a cup of coffee and sat opposite each other, acting like a couple of eighteen-year-olds on a date. I remembered the place vaguely from my student days, and when I looked round at the other people sitting at the marble-topped tables, it occurred to me that some of them must have been here then. It was that kind of place.

For some reason I pretended I was American and spoke no Polish, which both irritated and amused Mary, and I watched as the different emotions took hold of her. A man even came over to speak to us, on the grounds that he had a cousin in Milwaukee, but his English was so wretched I wasn't in any trouble. Mary, I knew, would have liked to get into conversation with him, but that frightened me. Someone might know someone else who might know me, and then I would become real again, instead of a disembodied observer, hanging around like Banquo's ghost, with only Mary able to see me and laugh with me. The others in the café gave me up as an impossibility, smiling and waving their hands to me if they felt obliged to, but otherwise turning away.

Outside in the street, we passed a bar with shutters that were almost closed over steamed-up windows. It was like the shutting of a camera lens: through the narrow gap I saw a man lift a glass with a deliberate, comically exaggerated movement, and lay his free arm on the shoulders of someone else. It was a gesture that made me feel more than ever alone, and even with Mary beside me, talking about her time with Solidarity and the need for more support, it was a long time before I could rid myself of the memory of the two sounds: the melancholy chirrup of the bird in the mediaeval church spire, and the formless roar of jollity from the warmth of the bar.

'Don't you feel isolated here, and alone?' Like I do, I nearly said.

'Not at all. Poland makes me feel more alive than anywhere else. When I'm in England, I feel well-behaved, but when I'm in Poland I feel completely Polish. My father may be a quiet sort of man now, you know, but in his young days before the War he was completely mad. Sometimes I think I take after him, but I need to be in Poland to bring it out.'

'All right,' I said, 'you're in Poland now: why not bring it out?'

She laughed, but once again a barrier came down between us. Even when I told her some of my experiences at the university, it didn't bring us together. We found the car and headed off through the dark city towards the south, into the area which had been my home. Mary fell asleep. The day had taken more out of her than I'd suspected, and I didn't disturb her, even though I would have liked her company. Darkness and warmth enveloped me. The tinny engine of the Fiat 126P sang and stuttered, the headlights picked out the shapes of trees and the sides of houses, and brought the white lines to life as they divided the road.

'And now, Frank, your phrase: "To dress up to the nines." ' It was hard to believe we were on a foray into potentially hostile territory, a thousand miles from safety. Frank Muir, his co-panellists and the others in the warm BBC studio in London seemed ten times more real than this journey did. Mary was still sleeping, but she held the portable radio on her lap, tuned to London, and it seemed that nothing untoward could happen while the chairman could still ask the meaning of stilted phrases, or which of four books was the odd man out. These sounds, I thought, were diffused throughout the whole world. In every hamlet, town and city on the face of the earth you could have heard Frank answering his comfortable questions, if only you had the necessary equipment. Everywhere, people were dying, or making love, or overeating, or committing crimes; and wherever they were, there was Frank, explaining the origin of his phrase.

'For Christ's sake turn that damned thing off.' For a moment, I had forgotten that Mary was asleep. She woke up, apologizing, and switched it off. Then there was nothing but the whirring of the cheap engine, and the occasional disturbance in the air as other cars passed us from the opposite direction.

'How do you feel?'

'A bit nervous, I suppose.'

'Nervous that someone will recognize you, or nervous about what you'll find?'

'Both, maybe.' I thought about it some more. 'No. Nervous about my father, most of all. It's hard to be away from someone so long, and then say the right things at a moment like that.' My God, I hate the lot of you, he had once said, as we were coming back from church. I wish I could get away from you all and start my life again. My mother had cried, silently, and I had thought about walking away from him, but I didn't. Now it seemed to me the most human thing about him.

'It'll be all right.' She touched my hand as it held the steering-wheel. Somehow her bland assumption annoyed me: how could she, with her uncomplicated middle-class upbringing, possibly know what would happen when I saw my father? I felt about as safe as I would walking up the slopes of a volcano that was thought to be extinct. Other people's platitudes offer little protection at such times.

What I said out loud was, 'Thank you,' and I took the opportunity to hold her hand for a bit. With my tongue I explored a small sore inside my mouth: an outward and visible sign of an inward and spiritual — what?

I slowed down by about ten or twelve miles an hour, careful not to drive too fast in case I ruined everything by getting stopped by the police. The car lights illuminated half a mile of the road ahead, and I began paying more attention to the way I was driving. No slip-ups of any sort.

'When do you think you'll see him?'

'It's too late tonight. It'll have to be tomorrow night, when we arranged for the Solidarity man to come over.' I looked at my watch, and felt a lurch inside me. 'Twenty-three hours from now.'

'Can you really wait that long?'

'If it hadn't been for you, I would have waited for ever.'

My frankness had a savagery which surprised both of us.

If you're irritable with someone, I thought, doesn't it mean that you must despise them? And if you despise them, how can you love them?

'I just thought you might want to see him sooner.' She sounded almost contrite. Now that we were so close, all her firmness and determination were starting to fade away. It made her all the more attractive, I thought; if only she could leave them off like winter clothes or those wretched flat-heeled shoes she prefers to wear.

'I've thought it out,' I said, talking and gesturing at the bare trees that formed a kind of tunnel over our speeding car, the branches and trunks grey in the hollow light. 'And that's the way I'm going to do it.'

Mary looked at me, and settled her head against the cold window, which shook with the vibration of the engine.

'Do you want me to come with you?'

I'd thought of that, too. Often, in the past, I had longed for the possibility that she might see what the house was like, understand the people I came from and get some glimpse of the things that had once been important to me. But not now, when we were so close to it. Petty things would make it difficult;

Magda would be seriously shocked by the idea, and there would be great problems in introducing someone else into the house at a time like this.

'I'd like you to see the house,' I said, and meant it. 'But maybe after I get back from seeing him we can drive round there, and you can see the village.' Her own father had belonged to a well-known banking family in Warsaw; even when he lived in Poland, he would have regarded a tiny village in a valley of the High Tatras as hardly better than savagery. Not much of a life down there, he'd said to me once, as we sat together in his drawing-room, and he was doing his best to approve of me. At the time I had been anxious to get the old boy on my side, and I'd laughed it off; later I would have resented it fiercely.

Mary nodded, and we grinned at one another. There's so much between us, I thought, and then realized how ambiguous the words were. We had so much in common, but there were things that made it hard even to speak to her properly.

The road was climbing now.

'This is the most beautiful countryside in the world.' I opened the window an inch or two, and sniffed at the cold, clear air. We were in the mountains; my mountains. The moon glinted on the still lake, and lit up a white chapel close to the water's edge. I looked across at Mary to show it to her, but she had gone to sleep again, which unreasonably brought back my irritability. In my saturnine mood I felt obscurely hurt that she wasn't looking, and I made the car go faster so that the view would pass that much more quickly, a punishment for an indefinable offence. When she opened her eyes again a moment or two later, the moon was hidden by a high mountain peak, and the lake was dark.

'Where are we?'

'This is the edge of the High Tatras.' I felt ashamed of my reaction, unable to tell her what had happened. 'We aren't far from the hotel now.'

'Was it built when you lived here?'

'If it was, I didn't know anything about it. But of course skiing holidays then were for well-to-do people from Warsaw; we peasants didn't get a look in.' I looked at her slyly, but she was determined not to be provoked.

'The signposts seem to be clear enough,' she said.

They were. We branched off the road and on to a smaller one which wound around the lower approaches of the mountains. The air seemed clearer than in the valleys lower down, and I sang to myself under my breath. The area is famous for its folksongs.

The hotel stood on one side of the narrow, poorly-maintained road, its name written slantwise across the side of the building. It was designed the way the State tourism board thought hotels in Switzerland looked. Not many lights showed, and there were only four cars in the car park. Our headlamps lit up the shapes of wooden swings and slides for the children of guests, and enlarged the shadows grotesquely, before shrinking them again as the car turned on the noisy gravel.

The empty hotel foyer looked like the set for a low-budget situation comedy on Austrian TV. Everything that could be made from cross-sections of tree-trunks was, from the board that announced the times of meals to the rows of hooks where the keys hung. Even the keys, I noticed, were attached to minuscule logs to stop you walking off with them. It did something to improve my mood when I noticed that.

I rang a bell on the counter, and tried to compete with the noise of a radio in some inner room.

'Give them time, Alex, they'll come.'

I rang the bell a bit harder in consequence, and a large blonde woman with an immense bust came unsmilingly out of the office.

I explained who we were, and when our reservation had been made. It took her a long time to search the almost empty register; while she was doing so she seemed to address a question to it in a low voice.

'Do you have any dollars to change?'

I took no notice. It would have been absurd to be arrested for trying to chisel a few more zlotys out of the system. She brought her head up out of the register and looked straight at me.

'Do you have any dollars to change?'

'Not really.'

She gave up the search and flicked a couple of forms in front of us, no longer interested in our reservations or anything to do with them. I dashed it off quickly, but Mary, more methodical, was still filling hers in when I saw the woman glance at her left hand to see if she were wearing a wedding ring. She didn't want to put us into the same room, you could tell.

'Passports.'

Even as she said the word, a slight feeling of anticipation went through me. Somehow, though I couldn't know the details, I felt that this was going to be a significant matter.

'When will we get them back?'

'You are in a hurry?' She hitched up the massive bosom, as though I had insulted her. I glanced at it involuntarily, wondering at the feat of engineering which kept it all in place, and said simply,

'We might want to go to another hotel.'

'You're booked here for three nights.'

I gave up, and handed the passport over. Mary did the same, though I felt her looking at me enquiringly. Perhaps she felt the same thing I had.

The incident annoyed me, but then everything annoyed me now. I picked up the suitcases and headed for the stairs, even though Mary was still completing her arrival form and fiddling in her handbag. As I went up, labouring under the burden of the cases, I looked back at the foyer. Mary was crossing the floor, passing the hatrack made from deer-antlers, and the blonde woman, her bust all the more disproportionate from that angle, was watching her with hostile eyes. Why do women always get the blame in Catholic countries, I wondered, and began to build a theory round it. It helped settle my mind.

The bed was surprisingly comfortable. I lay on it, looking up at the wooden ceiling, and trying to work out what I should

say to Mary. We had spent all afternoon here, and the room felt like a prison. We had made love once but it had been only an interlude.

I looked over to the window where she sat, reading a book about peasant movements of the Middle Ages. I knew all about it: I'd recommended it to her; see what Catholics are like when they're stirred up, I'd said, though in fact she was if anything even less of a Catholic than I was. Her expensive school had knocked it out of her. I brought my daughter up to go to church, her mother said sniffily to me, once. Have you seen her lately? I asked, and her father had choked with laughter, over in the corner. There were times when a look passed between her father and me; each recognized a fellow-sufferer.

I was anxious about going to see my father, of course, and not a little frightened about the business of handing over the radio equipment. Maybe Mary sensed my feelings, because she looked across at me and smiled, as an overture of peace. The mountains were behind her and her face was partly invisible to me because of the golden afternoon light flooding - in.

She looked wonderful and I told her so. She moved her head slightly, as though to discount the compliment, but it was true: the light, the mountains, the tall thin body, the long neck.

I looked at my watch: five-forty. 'I must get changed soon.'

'But you won't be leaving for another three hours — you said so yourself.'

' "Be Prepared" ', I said. 'Weren't you in the Girl Guides?' I knew she had been. Maybe it explained her toughness of character, her determination to see good prevail.

'Why don't you come back to England with me?' It was only the seventh time I'd asked her.

She shook her head seriously, and then laughed. 'You'll have to give up some time,' she said.

I turned to the presents I'd brought: a scarf and some perfume for Magda, a Dunhill pipe and some tins of their special blend of tobacco for my father; and of course the ludicrous boxes of chocolates, my present to the underground Solidarity movement.

I hoped they would enjoy them.

'There we are,' I said. 'Only three and three-quarter hours to go.' She thought I was making another joke.

We sat at dinner, an hour later, drinking the cucumber soup, *ogorkowa*, that I remembered strongly from my childhood. We were almost the only diners in the place, and Mary complimented the waiter on the good quality of the food. He hovered round us, beaming and rubbing his hands on the short white apron he wore round his waist. Her Polish, to my ears as well as his, had a charming old-fashioned quality to it, learned as it had been from an older father and from books. The waiter, elderly and bald, was glowing with the pleasure of being praised in such words. When he took away the dishes Mary looked across the table at me, and I knew then it was done for effect. But I didn't blame her; on the contrary, I rather admired her for her ability to recover so fast.

Around us, the restaurant started to fill up. A family party settled at a great circular table on the far side, and immediately began laughing and calling out jokes and mock insults to one another. The elderly couple at the centre of the party, whose wedding anniversary it seemed to be, sat embarrassed and smiling and pink, forced at intervals to kiss each other at the repeated demand of the younger relatives. The waiters who had earlier been standing around talking to each other were now swooping between the tables carrying big salvers of food. Above the diners clouds of cigarette smoke hung almost motionless under the bright lights that shone down on the tables. A little blonde waitress clicked her way across the wooden dance-floor, apparently unaware of the way her intricate movements between the tables were being followed by the male diners.

I looked across at Mary, and smiled at her in apology for my earlier anger. Slowly, she returned the smile, and reached across to touch and hold my hand. The influence of the smiling waiters and the noisy, self-absorbed diners was beginning to work on us both.

By now the band had assembled: four men, all in their middle to late forties, with midnight-blue suits and red bow ties. They worked their way through a selection from Abba and the Beatles and finished with *South Pacific*, without even working up a sweat. No one paid any attention, except for a handful of early dancers on the floor. A girl of around fifteen danced with a large woman fifty years her senior, and a man and woman the age of the musicians stood together in the middle, holding each other and scarcely moving, looking blankly over each other's shoulders. The musicians themselves moved as little as possible too, looking straight ahead of them as they played. When the electric guitar solo was over, and some people had clapped, the guitarist felt under his chair for his glass of beer and emptied it at a gulp.

I felt the excitement in me mount as the time to leave drew closer. We had finished our stuffed cabbage and dumplings, and were waiting for coffee. There was no one to overhear us, and the sound of 'If I Were a Rich Man' filled the smoky air like the noise of a thunderstorm. I leant across the table and went over the final details with her.

· 'I'll be back around midnight or one o'clock, so maybe you'd tell the lady with the cantilevered bust that I'll be late, and she'll tell you how I can get in. God knows what you'll tell her I've been doing.'

'She'll think we've had a row.'

'Tell her I'm a werewolf, and it's the full moon.'

'You don't want me to come, and sit in the car?' I didn't; it would mean I would have to be even quicker than I intended to be, and I didn't want to feel under that kind of pressure. But it was good of her to offer.

'You don't think you'll be delayed?' It was a strange question, and I stopped looking at the anniversary couple to examine her face for reasons.

'Not if your wretched friend arrives on time to collect the stuff. I shan't wait around for him, though — he'll have to come the next night. You don't have any way of contacting them?'

'He'll be there, I'm sure.' She herself didn't seem to know what she'd meant by her earlier question. For a moment I saw things from her angle: left alone in the hotel by a man smuggling strategic goods for Solidarity.

'I wonder how all these people have enough money to eat here,' I said, anxious to divert the conversation. 'And how the hotel gets the food.' I began to tell her about the black market vans that gathered up their goods from villages like my own, late at night or just before dawn, and converged at Cracow at five in the morning. Everybody knew everybody: suppliers, vendors, customers. There was no question of haggling, or cheating, or argument. Nobody said where the food came from, and no one was ever arrested for supplying it.

'Solidarity isn't the only underground movement,' I said, 'Poland is a country where underground movements are endemic.' The waiter came and hovered to hear a little more of Mary's genteel Polish, and went away satisfied. I saw him speaking to another waiter and looking over in our direction.

'We ought to work out what we'll do if something goes wrong.'

'You mean if I decide to ask for political asylum?'

She took no notice. 'You must always try to cover all the possible eventualities,' she said, looking down at the cloth.

'You think something's going to happen, don't you? You really think I'm going to get busted.' I was speaking in English, too loudly. She tried to quieten me, but that made me all the more angry.

'If something does happen, it'll be all through your bloody crazy idea of bringing the stuff. You'll be the one to blame.' The waiter looked at my gesturing from the other side of the room in surprise.

'I don't think anything's going to happen.' Her tone quietened me down. 'I just think that if we've got something sorted out in advance, that makes sure nothing bad will happpen.' It was difficult to disagree with her, so we talked about it for a while.

But neither of us wanted to think of the consequences if I were arrested. It seemed easier to leave it as it was and assume that I would be back at the hotel by midnight or thereabouts. The only thing worrying me was that Mary should have brought up the possibility in the first place; I knew the quality of her instincts by now.

'Money money money,' the singer was intoning, swaying slightly at the microphone, his maroon bow tie at an angle, 'It's a rich man's world.' It took me some time to realize he was singing in English.

'What about money?' I asked, reminded of the subject. We worked out how we would divide it up. I had accepted the possibility now that I might not come back. She had a hundred dollars, I had a hundred dollars, and we divided the zlotys in half as well. She had brought her own money, but less of it than I had.

For a moment I thought of asking her if she wanted to dance, but I was always slightly afraid of dancing with her because her height made my five-feet-nine look faintly absurd when we were close together. Instead we weaved our way through the dancers, who were spread more thickly on the dance-floor now. No one took the slightest bit of notice of us, and I realized that she could be a giantess and I a hunchbacked dwarf, and it still wouldn't make the singer look at us or catch the attention of the girls dancing with their grannies. As she went towards the door, I caught her hand and pulled her back. She seemed genuinely pleased, and we shuffled around with the others for a bit, banging haunches and treading on toes, and apologizing and being apologized to with friendly grins.

'All you need is love,' sang the man at the microphone, in an accent that cut through the cigarette smoke like Lithuanian.

'Maybe that's true of you,' she said to me, and I was so pleased that I didn't even look round when someone ground a heel into my shoe. After that we walked out, and the bald waiter smiled at us.

Untypically, the blonde lady was on duty at the desk as we returned. The absence of wedding-rings still seemed to be upsetting her, but I was able to tell her that I'd be back late, and we fixed up that she would be around to let me in. She looked about a year or two older than me, and I wondered if I'd seen her sometime in the past, thinner, less built-up, more attractive, at some dance like this. But I doubted it. We were a good fifteen miles from the village here, and anyway she looked like an import from a town: maybe Nowa Huta, I thought, with a highlander's snobbishness.

Upstairs, there wasn't very much to say. I was glad we seemed to be parting on a pleasant note; I had enough anxieties ahead without wanting to take any with me. All the same, the atmosphere of the room seemed to drop down over the two of us. I couldn't think how we were going to endure a couple more days here.

'So I'll expect you at around midnight.'

'Or later. Not much later.'

I hung around a little bit longer. I checked my briefcase to see that I had everything; the presents, the absurd chocolate boxes. The one thing I didn't have was my passport — it wouldn't be available until tomorrow, the blonde woman had said. But it was almost nine o'clock; I was anxious not to get to the house too late, and disturb everybody. I could see that Mary, too, was affected by the memory of all the arguments during the day.

'Don't be too long,' she said.

'I'll see you soon,' I promised.

'And be careful.'

It seemed to take an extraordinarily long time, even then: opening the door, looking back at her, closing it again. I felt I would remember everything about it for as long as I lived: the rumpled cover on the bed, the bleached wood on the walls, the balding grey carpet, the tall figure with her blonde hair tied back, standing in the middle of the room and watching me with a sad, resigned expression on her face; not sadness for me, I thought, but sadness for what we seemed to be in the process of losing. Then the door closed, and I realized I was on my own.

But going downstairs I felt exhilaration at that thought, and by the time I found myself in the cold night air the anxieties and unhappinesses of the day dropped away from me. Even so, I couldn't stop myself looking up at the hotel window in the hope that Mary might be watching for me, might even wave. The curtains stayed shut. I gripped my briefcase tightly, and walked on faster.

Ahead of me, the mountains loomed up against the clear night sky. Curiously, in spite of what lay ahead of me, I felt free of all restrictions; as though, like the prisoners in *Fidelio*, I was walking out of gaol with a song on my lips. The gravel of the hotel driveway crunched under my shoes, and as the hotel windows shone out yellow in the surrounding darkness I thought how impossible it was to live one's life cramped up with other people. In the clarity of the air, I felt I could almost speak to Mary, and tell her how petty I realized my anger had been; I felt that she would hear me and understand my meaning. I'm perfectly free, I thought, as free as I have ever been.

The tinny engine of the little Fiat started first go. This was likely to be the best time, I accepted that, before the reality of standing by my father's bedside came too close. The headlights cut their way into the clear air, and the tyres threw up the gravel as I turned out into the road. I was a free man, I told myself again. But the effect was wearing off. I started thinking again about Mary's face as she had watched me close the door behind me, and my elation faded. Memories of my father took over.

It was surprisingly unlike the way I had imagined it. For days now I had thought about the road that curved around the mountain, the woods, the lane up into the woods, and yet when I reached it I almost drove straight past. Partly it was the moonlight, of course, which changes the look of everything; but fifteen years' growth of trees and bushes also made a difference. The lane was scarcely visible now.

Yet when I stopped and got out to make certain, there could be no doubt about it. This was the main road from the village to the town of Zakopane, and every important journey I had made in my life had begun here — including the journey to England. I walked back a little way and found the lane.

I recalled looking out of the bus window at the lane when I left for England, never dreaming I would see it again under such circumstances. I climbed back into the Fiat and drove up it, until I judged that the car wouldn't be visible from the road, even in daylight. I had no intention of leaving it that long, but it seemed a sensible precaution to take.

Then I walked back down. I had deliberately abstained before from looking out across the valley, but when I headed towards it I saw for the first time how thick the trees on that side had now become: the valley was screened off entirely. I pushed through them, searching for the old continuation of the lane that had once acted as the village's short-cut to the Zakopane road, before the days of cars.

Below me the glacial valley lay like a great lake in the moonlight, stretching out from the mountainside where I was standing to the hills on the far side, five or six miles away. In the distance, like an island in the lake, lay the village, a mile from me: a cluster of houses around a spired church, each with a steeply sloping roof to ward off the heavy snows of winter. In the moonlight, the colours of the houses were distorted, and it was impossible to tell whether they had been painted since my time or not. It was almost entirely silent, as I looked across the lake of meadowland. I found myself grinning in the darkness, and whistling some inappropriate tune. I could smell the valley now, the smell of earth and pine needles and rotting leaves, and I felt a powerful sense of belonging which I'd never experienced anywhere else, not even in the small world of my rooms at Cambridge.

I knew what it was then, all right: it was the land, which people like me had farmed and owned for hundreds of years. For the moment the village was still in sight. It was a gentry village, like one out of every seven in Poland; no different in appearance or in general poverty from any other village, but the families living in it were descended from the small knights of the early Middle Ages, and their land had been cut and subdivided with each generation that passed. The only thing that hadn't been whittled away was the pride of the families who lived there. Some people wouldn't speak to others, and never had since 1509 or thereabouts, while others wouldn't demean themselves by marrying into lesser families in the vicinity. When I had announced one evening that I was seeing a girl from a village about ten miles away, there was a dreadful silence and no one spoke for a long time, until my father said, 'Do I understand that you are going to take a peasant-girl out?' as though I'd announced that I was going to a strip-show. In fact my father might have preferred that; at least I wouldn't have to marry the stripper. I did take the girl out in the end, but it was scarcely worth it, and since sex was an activity which didn't officially exist in our area, not even among peasants, the evening wasn't a success, and I had to wait until I went to Cracow for one that was.

90

We had a coat of arms which hung over the mantlepiece in the kitchen, my mother wore gloves when she worked in the fields, and we called peasants by their surnames and each other 'sir' and 'madam'. Now, of course, I find it all rather quaint and gentle, but then I hated the extra shackles that it represented.

The slope was so steep now I could hardly keep myself from running. I slewed my way down through the dwarf pines, clutching my briefcase, clasping the narrow tree-trunks as if I were taking part in some ludicrous peasant dance. I was glad that there was no one to witness my home-coming, for all sorts of reasons.

The smell of the sap in the tree-trunks and the roughness of the bark on my hands brought back a distant recollection which I could half sense without being able to grasp properly. I stumbled faster down the slope, more clumsy and absurd than ever, and feeling closer now to the source of the elusive memory. I stopped to get my breath back, and to ensure I was heading in the right direction; the village was completely hidden now that I was lower down on the mountainside. All round me the noises of the night cut through the silence: the distant barking of a dog, the sound of the wind blowing through the branches of the dwarf pines, the occasional low call of a bird higher up the mountain. Then came a pause — followed by a sharp, high scream from thirty or forty yards away.

Even in the instant of paralysis I recognized the noise, and what I had been trying to remember. When it ceased I was left in the shocked silence, my heart beating fast and my ears ringing with the sudden quiet.

My father was leaning over me. 'Stop it making that noise,' I said plaintively, but my father simply frowned and shook his head and told me to be quiet. He was looking at the threshing object on the ground, unaffected by its screaming. Then he seized his moment and lifted the wriggling animal into the air, holding it by the wire noose which had trapped its leg and was biting into the flesh and muscle.

'It's a good one,' my father said, in a way that made me sick and ashamed. The animal hung rigid, head downwards, unmoving. Its eyes glittered in the faint moonlight. I was curious, in spite of my fear and distaste. I was, I suppose, about nine.

'What is it?'

'You don't know anything that's round you, do you? When I was your age I knew every animal in these mountains, and every bird too. Don't you honestly know what it is?'

He pushed it towards me, and I backed sharply away, keeping my balance only by throwing my arm round the bark of a dwarf pine, smelling the pungent odour of the sap.

'Is it a squirrel?'

'In a way.' He liked explaining things. He held the animal out, so that it turned and wriggled awkwardly, but made no sound, and pointed with his free hand to its tail and dark pelt.

'It's a marmot,' he said. 'There used to be a lot of them in these mountains once, but after the First War there were too many trappers round here, and they've mostly gone. They make good coats, if you can get enough of them. They used to want a lot of marmot coats in Warsaw and Cracow.'

'Let it go, Dad, please. It's frightened almost to death, and its leg must be hurt bad.'

'Don't be soft, boy. Animals don't feel pain like you and me, it's a known fact.' He jerked it towards me, and it screamed.

I moved backwards, sharply, and started to cry.

'If you don't like seeing it like this, you'd better put it out of its misery. Go on.' He seemed drawn along, somehow, by my revulsion, going further than he had originally intended.

I backed away down the slope. 'I'm not doing anything like that,' I said, licking my lips and searching for some way out.

My father looked big in the moonlight, and I couldn't see his eyes, deep in the shadow of their sockets.

'Don't be disobedient.' He didn't seem to know what to do, and the animal hung beside him without struggling. 'I thought it would be interesting to you — part of your education.' He was being defensive now, not wanting to say who had set the trap or how he had known it was there. 'You're lucky to be brought up in the mountains, so it's time you made the most of your luck.'

The animal started struggling once more; I shifted away,

horrified. It swung towards me, and touched me, wet and quivering.

'Let it go. I'm not staying with you.' I started for the trees, even though I was afraid of the dark and my father knew it.

'Come back here — don't you dare walk away like that when your father's talking to you.' His shouting made the dogs bark in the village below us. Somewhere in the woods the strong wings of a bird beat against the branches in alarm. The marmot screamed again, and I started to run now, tears streaming down my face, desperate to get out of range of the sound. Behind me my father stooped down to finish the task I had been too frightened and soft to perform.

The blood of the animal seemed to be on me, trickling down my face and inside my shirt, and its screams were in my ears. I threw my arms round the tree-trunks, smelling the sap, kicking stones and small boulders from beneath my feet, crying out in pain and horror, trying to wipe out the memory by the sheer intensity of running. And as I went, a new determination came over me: I would never talk about this night, that had begun so well, and to the best of my ability I would never even think of it again. It was past, and dead, and perhaps it had never happened, except in some unpleasant corner of my imagination. My hands were cleansed by the cuts and bruises from the rough tree trunks, and my mind was cleansed by the refusal to accept that any of it had actually taken place. I burst through the last screen of trees, and found my feet on the hard road at the bottom. I began to walk towards the village.

The moon was down now, and I could smell root vegetables in the dark earth. The cold was exhilarating. Across the road I clambered up a grassy bank, and walked along it a little way. I knew exactly where I was. A motorcycle buzzed its way along the main road towards the village, and a small animal of some kind slipped into the water of the ditch below me with a faint splash. Above me, reaching up to the Belt of Orion, stood a wayside cross. My nose and fingers told me it was flaking with rust and lack of care. I could see nothing of the figure of Christ which had once been painted on it, and would perhaps still have been visible: Christ in agony, the work of some nineteenth-century itinerant artist, which had been fixed in my mind all my life as an image of pain and misery. I moved away, brushing the brittle flakes of rust from the palms of my hands, and slithered back down the grassy bank to the road.

I was home. I felt exultant and intensely nervous. A farm dog started barking as I came up to a gate, but no lights went on there: that farm, I remembered, had always had the most aggressive dogs. A horse frightened me, looming up out of the darkness and then clattering sideways and back down the field, as I frightened it in its turn. There was no avoiding walking down the main street which led through the village, but it was past ten o'clock now and most people would be asleep. A few houses had lights in the bedroom windows, and I walked on the grass verge whenever possible, in order not to attract any attention.

By now the houses were close together, the gardens smaller and given over to flowers rather than to vegetables or grazing. Soon the road would turn into a proper street. But just before it did, on a little hill overlooking the centre of the village, I came across the high wall which surrounded the cemetery. My ancestors lay there, or in the church, reaching back to the time of the battle of Legnica against the Tartars. When I was a boy I had pictured my own grave, in a corner near the other Serafinskis but a little way away from them. Now, perhaps, my father would lie here soon; I felt a brief pang of guilt. The whitewashed wall glimmered in the starlight, and I ran my hand along the surface of it, remembering the sensation. Opposite, from the houses of the gipsies, I heard the barking of a dog, but it mattered less; gipsy dogs always barked, I recalled with the prejudice of childhood, but the gipsies never bothered to get up and find out why.

The road dipped into the valley where the village proper lay. There was an imposing house here, set back from the road and with a front garden that would not have been out of place in any dreary English suburb. I went past extra quietly: the family here had wanted me to marry their bucktoothed daughter Izabela, and my father had been half inclined to make me, since their family was better than ours. The thought that Izabela's father might walk across his front lawn and spot me slinking past was a real and frightening possibility. As it was, a figure was outlined against the curtains of a bedroom window, raising its arms as though getting undressed. Izabela, I thought, and walked on even faster and even more quietly.

Now I could remember the names of most of the people who lived in these houses. In the light from a street lamp I saw a round pebble, and picked it up, turning it over and over again in my fingers as I walked. The stone had been here for a million years, had seen every night since my family had settled here at the dawn of the Middle Ages. The wind got up and played roughly around me, and then I saw the long, low shape of the house where I had been born and brought up.

It was just as I remembered: the gentle downward slope of the field, the wooden fence, the bent fruit-trees, and the house itself — squat and rectangular, with a steeply-shingled roof and tall chimney. I saw from the extraordinary haphazard bundle of sticks piled on it, looking just like an Edward Lear drawing, that the storks still nested there.

A light was burning at the far end of the house: Magda's bedroom. I broke into a run. My memory took over, and told me where to vault the fence, and how to make my way through the apple trees and across the vegetable patch. Much of it would be overgrown, I knew, and these trees and bushes too were higher and thicker by fifteen years' growth.

Now I was side-on to the house, and could see six points of light shining out of its blind bulk: the thick light, dull and yellow, of a candle, leaking into the night from the holes cut into the wooden shutters of one of the rooms; there was no question which room. I moved towards it, but reluctantly. This was the moment I had resisted thinking about for days — maybe for years. I had to force myself to carry on, sometimes feeling damp grass and sometimes the heavy clinging earth of a vegetable bed under my feet. I blundered into things, cursing my clumsiness. Once I dropped my briefcase, with its precious contents. The whole business seemed to me juvenile, blameworthy, ludicrous.

The points of light resolved themselves into twin triangles; light shone from the holes in the shutters, and beamed out towards me like a lighthouse. It seemed to me that I could feel the warmth of it on my face. I reached the house, and knocked on the familiar panel, an intricate knock with a pattern to it, which came naturally to me from my distant childhood. Nothing happened. I knocked again, a little louder, but in the same intricate way, and whispered, hoarsely: 'Magda, Magda.'

Then I stood back and waited.

CHAPTER SIX

'The trade union law of 5th October 1982 ensured that we have trade unions which effectively safeguard the interests of working people. No unofficial organizations are therefore required.' — Polish radio broadcast.

In the empty factory yard newspapers and the wrappings from sandwiches blew about. It was starting to rain. The wind picked up speed around the corners of the yellow brick buildings and howled over the wet cobbles. There were no signs of life anywhere, from the delivery trucks which were stopped where their drivers had been told about the factory meeting, to the workshops which stank of dried oil, and of metal that had been heated and then allowed to cool. Tools lay where the assembly staff had thrown them. But if it was empty, it wasn't silent. No one had bothered to turn off the loudspeakers and they went on playing the cheerful music which supposedly aided production. A yellow cat walked uncertainly down the aisle between the lathes.

The life and warmth of the factory were all gathered in the works canteen, in the three-storey block down at the far end.

'Where's the butter? Where's the sausage?'

'Gone to Russia!' It wasn't particularly funny and it wasn't even true but it always got a laugh.

The atmosphere grew thicker with heat and tobacco smoke, and the stewards were forced to bustle round opening the windows. It was very badly organized: arguments were continually breaking out on the floor, and the men and women on the platform couldn't keep order.

'It's not the management, particularly,' said one man, pulling the microphone towards him like a Fifties crooner. 'They're not too bad, as managements go.'

'Go on, arse-licker,' someone called out. 'Lick a bit more'. The man on the platform got upset, and loosened the collar of his shirt with a quick movement. A red mark on his cheek flared up.

'Now you've embarrassed him.' There was more laughter.

'This is hopeless, friends, quite hopeless.' The chairman of the ad hoc committee was standing up in appeal, both arms in the air. 'We've got to have a bit of discipline, otherwise we'll never get anywhere.'

'Sounds like the bosses,' someone shouted from the back. The chairman could see that the moment of protest was slipping away from them, and that they would soon be left with no coherent strategy for negotiation, and no strength. He was a poor leader, he knew; he had only taken on the job because everyone else was scared. The last of the scheduled speakers was on the platform now, and still nothing was decided. He began the same old catalogue of what was wrong, with no positive suggestions for taking action. The chairman looked out at the hot faces through the blue mist of cigarette smoke, running his eyes over the valleys in between the tables, and the mountain ranges where people stood on benches and table-tops.

Some were starting to get restless. One man standing quite close to the platform nudged his friend and cupped his hand round an imaginary drink, tilting it and raising his eyes questioningly at him as he did so. The other man nodded, and they turned to push their way to the door.

The chairman watched the movement helplessly, knowing that it would grow until the meeting trickled away with nothing achieved. Then his eyes caught the face of a familiar shambling figure, a big blond man with an unruly crop of hair falling over his forehead who looked back at him, turning the corners of his mouth down as if to say 'What can you do, if they're in this sort of mood?' But the sight of him cheered up the chairman immensely: it was like the old days, just to see him. The chairman beckoned to him pleadingly but Tadeusz Nowak shook his head and smiled, warningly. It would be the worst thing possible for him to start making public statements now, with so many informers in the audience.

The chairman got his chance when the speaker came to an

abrupt stop and sat down. 'Friends, I'm going to call someone most of you will know, even if you won't agree with everything he's done and said in the past. But it's important for us to have as wide a range of views as possible. That's why I'm calling Tadeusz Nowak, ladies and gentlemen.'

Nowak was annoyed, but he knew he would be more conspicuous if he refused to speak than if he did. Nowadays many people at the plant were wary of him, knowing his old connections with Solidarity, but something in his stooping posture, his broad shoulders and his careless, rumpled clothes made him a friendly, attractive sort of character. He clambered up on to the platform and looked down at them all affectionately. They weren't, most of them, the stuff of which martyrs were made; they would back him to the end, then leave him to take the punishment. And yet, he knew well, they were capable of heroism too, and of great self-sacrifice, if they were appealed to correctly.

'This time,' he said, and the crowd hushed expectantly, 'this time it's different. We aren't the bosses any more. We're back here, and they're back in their offices. And this time we aren't talking about political demands or civil rights. This time we're talking about our working conditions, and what's wrong with them. You know it was Lenin — no, you may not like him, but this is a democratic meeting, give the poor old bugger a chance — it was Lenin who said you should judge a society by the way it treats the people who created its wealth. That's us. What does it mean about our society, eh?' The groaning and the laughter went on for some seconds, and the cigarette smoke billowed towards the platform in obedience to the flow.

'Exactly. I couldn't hear a word you said, and I agreed with every bit of it. But there's no point in getting together to complain about the way we're treated, and then not doing anything about it. That's like going whingeing and crawling to the union rep and asking him why someone hasn't turned on the generator this morning — where is the union rep, by the way, I don't seem to see him here? If something's wrong with the machinery it's up to you and me to put it right. Switch the generator on ourselves, that's what we've got to do. It's not difficult. And in the case of this factory, we've got to make sure that all those wonderful national agreements are actually followed, right here. And since five hundred of us can't do it all together, the best thing is to elect a team of five, or ten, or whatever you want, who'll do it properly. Does that—' his voice took on the braying sound of the convenor appointed by the management to the new, supposedly self-governing union — 'meet with general approval?'

There was a shout of laughter, and a forest of raised hands. 'Thank you. Now what about a few nominations?'

The nominations started coming in, his own name among them. Nowak looked at his watch, and estimated the driving time. Another half-hour at the most, he thought, and then he'd have to leave.

I stood there in the dark for a little longer, my shoes letting in a certain amount of the ancestral damp, and the briefcase which I had struggled so hard to bring from Paris weighing down my arm. The whole thing began to feel thoroughly absurd. Suppose Jan Dolanski were to see me now, I thought, or Patrick Binney. Especially Patrick Binney. I was tempted to make my way back through the vegetables and tell Mary I hadn't found anyone at home.

But of course it was too late. A shadow fell between the candle and the shutters, and the six points of light went out. A voice as familiar to me as some old, sour country dish I hadn't eaten since childhood came floating out to me. The intervening years faded; I was a spotty, cumbersome, pretentious teenager once again.

'Who is it? What's the matter? What do you want?'

I wished then, very hard indeed, that I had called Magda back to tell her that I would be coming after all.

I made a funnel with my hands, and spoke through the shutters' coarse, weathered wood. 'It's Alex,' I said. A sudden onrush of warmth made me add, 'I've come home.' Even as I said it, though, I started to doubt it. A different person had lived here, a long time before.

Inside something dropped; and I sensed surprise rather than delight in the noise my sister made. For once in your life be pleasant, Magda, I thought, but when she swung the shutters open and I saw her face in the candlelight, it was shocked and frightened. The skin was pallid and tight-drawn over the bones, the eyebrows were as strong as I remembered them. Having checked that it really was me, she disappeared again, only to reappear a few seconds later, a few yards away at the side door of the house.

'What in the name of God are you doing here?' she hissed at me. 'You always were a troublesome, difficult boy.'

I listened to her Podhale dialect, which I had allowed myself to drop over the years, and only used nowadays to amuse my sophisticated friends from Warsaw.

'I've come back to see father,' I said, trying to sound filial. God knows, it was true enough.

'To kill him, more like,' she said, her bony frame filling out the doorway. 'You said you weren't going to come. You refused to.' I started to put my side of the argument, but she came back at me with a line she must have used thousands of times when we were younger. 'Don't you ever think of anyone except yourself, Alex?'

But I was older now, and had gone ten rounds with professionals.

'Not when I'm standing out in the cold after coming all the way from England, no.'

Sarcasm wasn't something they had a great deal of experience of in the village, and my words had an immediate effect. Her face softened. The tradition of hospitality was unbreakable, even to errant brothers.

'I'm sorry, you must be freezing. Come in and have something to eat. I'll get it for you.'

I passed close by her in the doorway, but I didn't touch her; she wouldn't have liked that.

Inside, it was an anti-climax, of course. It was partly shabbier and partly better than I had expected. Objects I hadn't seen for fifteen years came back to me with a sudden vividness. The kitchen was unchanged in the way kitchens tend to be: a little dingier, a little less cared for, but arranged in recognizably the same way as before. I looked round. It was a room where people had worked very hard, for a very long time. There was a smell I remembered, and I tried to work out the strands in it: cabbage, certainly, and onions, and spiced meat, and something that could have been soap.

I turned and looked at Magda in the light. Her face seemed to have settled into its creases, and she looked smaller and more defeated, though she still had the long proud face of the highland people and the high-bridged nose. Her life had been a battle, her face the battleground. The victim of our gentry snobbishness, I thought. For the first time in my own life I saw her not as my elder sister, but as a woman; and I could tell that she had regretted every day she had spent in this house since she'd left her childhood behind.

'You look well,' she said quietly, and smiled her old tight smile. She couldn't bring herself to say she was glad to see me, but she did ask me what I wanted to eat. For Magda, actions counted for everything, and words were suspect.

'You were very silly, Alex,' she said, but the perfume brought her a sniff of the outside world, which she only read about in magazines, and it seemed to do her good. The scarf looked somehow rather sad, tied firmly round her neck, as incongruous as the bright red and white banners I'd seen in Cracow, neither scarf nor banners bearing the slightest relation to the state of affairs around them. I looked across at her, and saw there were tears in her eyes; tears of shock, perhaps, but signs of some kind of emotion, at least. I had always thought she would have chosen to stay in the village if the choice had ever been put to her; now I realized that she, too, detested her imprisonment, and all I had done by bringing her presents from Paris was to give her the faintest touch of a world she had never been allowed to see. She pulled the top off the perfume bottle again and put it to her nose.

'What's Paris really like?'

'It rains a lot, and there's garbage in the streets. But the buildings are as nice as in Cracow.'

She didn't say anything at all after that, but got up and looked at the soup she had been heating for me. There was coffee too.

'You make *barszcz* as well as ever,' I said, looking into the red bowl. It was true, but she didn't answer. She wasn't used to compliments.

I worked my way slowly through it, turning my attention

occasionally to the bread. I couldn't remember eating anything to compete with either the bread or the beetroot soup since I'd left the village. It wasn't only hunger and enjoyment that kept me silent; it was a way of putting off the questions I knew I had to ask. She cleared away the crockery and I had no excuse left.

'How's father, then?' I tried to make my voice as light as possible.

'Dr Galka says he won't last more than a few days now. That's why we didn't take him to hospital. You know what he thinks about hospitals.'

I did, and I rather agreed myself. Like so many people with dominating fathers, I found myself taking on his attitudes in later years, even though I'd spent most of my early life combatting them with all my power.

'Can I see him?' I didn't look at her when I said that, preferring instead to take in the different remembered objects around the room. There were scarcely any things there whose provenance I couldn't recall: a piece of flint that looked like a dog's head, and had been found during a picnic in the mountains when I was about seven; a crucifix of plaited straw that my mother had made one Easter and had put on the mantelpiece over the stove, where it had probably never been moved since except to blow off the dust; the faded wooden shield the size of a paperback book which carried our family's coat of arms, and which was so dingy now its details were invisible; a few pictures, cut out of magazines: Cracow, the Pope, Rome, the Pope, Cardinal Wyszynski, the Pope. The State's campaign for scientific atheism still had some way to go as far as our family was concerned.

'I suppose so.'

I didn't know whether to be glad or sorry. In some ways it had been enough of a shock seeing the house again; I wasn't altogether prepared for the much greater shock of seeing my father on his death-bed.

'These last days and weeks must have been difficult.'

'A bit.'

I noticed the mechanical way she was cleaning up a table that was already perfectly clean, and I reached across to put my hand on her thin, nervous arm. For a moment she responded, holding my hand in place, but the moment passed and

103

she broke away.

'I must get his gruel ready,' she said, with an urgency which was intended only to cover her trembling voice. Even a tyrant is missed when he dies, and although my father had been a tyrant to Magda, she was not altogether an unwilling slave to him. Don't behave like that, she'd said to me once; don't you know your father loves you? What, him? I replied, with the scepticism of thirteen. Of course; he loves us both. At about that stage, the final identification was made between my testy, difficult, domineering father, and the God who allowed Vietnam and nuclear missiles and the likes of Nixon and Brezhnev to infest and afflict the world. At times during my teens I wasn't certain which of them I blamed more for my life, my father or God the Father.

I got up and walked around the kitchen, looking at things more closely but not really noticing them. My legs were quivering slightly. Death is never an easy thing to look at, nor is impending death: one's own or any one else's.

My father had always been intuitive about his children, sometimes infuriatingly so; it was the quality which he had in place of the more openly expressed affection which other fathers showed. Even as I turned the well-remembered china doorknob and slipped into the room the grey-blue eyes had focused on me, and were identifying me. He knew exactly who I was and why I had come, and it didn't surprise him at all. Whatever you did, he would always counter it; he was never shocked, never upset except with anger, never taken unawares. There was a slight movement of his hand as it lay on the counterpane.

When I was younger, the great mahogany bed my parents had slept in had seemed to me like a massive castle. I had been conceived in it, and born in it, and I think my mother must have died in it. Now that my father was also dying in it, I saw that it was really nothing more than a rather tasteless piece of turn-of-the-century pomposity, with none of the magical qualities it had once seemed to possess. I couldn't think of anything to say, so I touched his hand, and felt some slight pressure in the dry and craggy fingers.

Fifteen years before, my father had been a powerful man, with the short legs and barrel chest of a wrestler. There was

104

nothing of me in that, I thought, glancing down at my own thin frame; but looking at his face, I could see myself there, even though it was grey and fallen with age: the narrow, lined face, the Roman nose, the prognathous jaw, the blue-grey eyes.

They looked at me now, without much in the way of expression; expression, after all, is something given by the muscles of the face, and the muscles of his were almost paralyzed. But the eyes were just as I had remembered them from my earliest childhood: strong and frightening if you had committed some misdemeanour, unforgiving eyes. Now there was another look in them, a softening that had nothing to do with his condition. In his old age, my father had become a little gentler. Sentimentally, I thought that the forgiveness which had never been there for me as a child was now there for the man. I felt the familiar prickle in my eyes and throat, and blinked, taking advantage of the excuse of looking round for somewhere to sit to hide my emotion.

He wasn't any longer the natural force he had once seemed, the powerful physique who could lift up his little son in one hand and humiliate him, making him slap his own face painfully, or cry out for mercy. Mercy. I watched the old eyes move away from me, as though they knew what I was thinking, and wander over to the picture of Christ on the opposite wall, and then back again, as if he were at last taken by surprise, by the disaster which had laid him low.

He murmured something, and I leant forward, embarrassed by the thick, incoherent sound. The lips moved again, scarcely disturbing the white crust that outlined them.

'What kept you?' he said.

I almost laughed aloud; how foolish to think that people change completely, just because their bodies are starting to give out on them.

'I had to come all the way from England,' I said, in the clear, patronizing tones of the healthy to the sick. 'You didn't think I wouldn't come, did you?'

'Couldn't see any reason why you should.'

I sat there for a little, watching him as he watched me, holding his hard old hand as he held mine. Whatever would he have said when I was a boy, if he had known I would leave the village, leave Poland, and start a life in another country? I wondered now, looking down at him, whether he might have approved; it was people who did what he wanted whom he used to scorn.

But his mind seemed cloudy, and that made it difficult for him always to know where he was or what was happening. How he would have hated that in the old days, I thought.

'It's not my back.'

I said something reassuring, but the words stayed in my mind, and it was only later that I remembered what he meant. Once, when I was fifteen or so, he had been doing some work on the roof, and had slipped off and fallen on his back. We crowded round him, looking idiotically down at him, and he had cried out petulantly, 'It's not my back.'

'Was it hard, coming back?' he whispered.

'No, not really; not when it was important enough.' For a moment I thought of mentioning the bomb in Cracow, and asking his forgiveness, but I decided against it.

I looked down at his hand. It was heavy and square and knotted, the veins showing dark purple in the shadow, the great fingers with their untended nails, the curved, adept thumb. I could see a scar on it that I remembered from my earliest childhood, when he had seemed as massive as a mountain, and I had clambered on to his shoulders and stood there, shrieking with delight and fear, while he had threatened to let go of my ankles.

Then he had told me that the scar had come from killing a bear, and that it had snapped at him with its teeth. But afterwards, anxious never to tell lies to his children, he had confessed that he had made it all up, and that it had been done while he was working with a knife.

I watched the scar carefully; strange how the accident of a moment should last so indelibly for sixty years, while the fall of empires and the death of millions left less of a mark. He seemed almost asleep now, and I looked at the white stubble round his chin, the irregular, yellow teeth, the grey skin-colour. It seemed impossible, I thought, that it should all have come to this. Yet life still churned on in the old man: the stubble itself, the growth of the fingernails, the blood flowing sluggishly round the purple veins all proved it. The contrast of

106

it all, the pointlessness, struck me powerfully. For the first time since I had heard of his illness I felt the tears rolling down my cheeks.

The blue-grey eyes were open now, and his mind seemed clear. He said something, moving his lips only slightly. I couldn't hear and asked him to repeat it, a touch of the old irritability came over him for a moment before his voice croaked quietly again.

'Once I took you to hospital when you fell out of the apple tree and broke your arm.' I nodded, thinking how odd it was that I should have told Mary about it so recently.

'You said if I stayed with you, you'd stay with me when I was an old, old man.'

I didn't remember.

'I broke the promise,' I said.

'No. Here you are, at the end.'

I didn't contradict him; it would have been pointless.

'The doctor said you were good.' Perhaps I had been. 'And now you're a doctor too.'

'But not a medical doctor, like Galka. I study history.'

'The history of your own country.' There was a pause, and the hand seemed to have taken on a little more strength. It seemed to me that he was lying suspended between the years, uncertain whether the history of Poland was frowned on or not, and probably not much caring.

'I study the old times,' I said.

'I saw the end of the old times. You could go where you wanted and say what you wanted.'

Some demon of contradiction got into me, even then — just as it always had in my late teens, when I was beginning to learn independence. 'At least you get a pension now, and proper medical care. That's something.'

His eyes looked past me, and the utter unimportance of it all shone through them. 'Perhaps you're right,' he said. I could hardly believe what he was saying. 'Not everything then was good.'

I dropped my head, 'I'm sorry, father, I'm sorry.' The reasons why I was sorry overlapped so much, I couldn't tell them apart.

'It's not my back,' he said, with a touch of the old

107

irritability, as I looked down at him. His eyes closed again, and I slipped my hand from his faint hold and dried the wetness on my cheeks. I stayed there, looking at him, for some time.

It was comfortable sitting in front of the fire, listening to the stove's wheezing, and settling into the cocoon-like state of family life in the country for a couple of hours. My face and left side were hot, my right side chilly as I faced Magda across the kitchen, and the cat marched between us before settling on the carpet in front of the stove. I dropped into the harsh dialect which was once so familiar to me, and which Magda had always spoken.

I was reluctant to let in the cold of the outside world, but eventually it had to be done; the man would soon be here.

'Magda, I ought to warn you about something.'

She looked up at me immediately, on the defensive once again. The intimate atmosphere had already vanished, even before I had told her what was going to happen.

'I brought something with me, a few things in fact, which I have to hand over to someone. He's coming here.'

I glanced down at my briefcase to check that the wretched thing was still there.

'Coming here? Someone from the village, is it?' I could tell that she was already trying to work out what it could be that I had brought with me. Magda's years of bitterness had given her intelligence an extra edge.

'Someone from town,' I said. It wasn't too explicit, since we used the word to mean both Zakopane and Cracow. She drew the inevitable conclusion immediately.

'Something you've smuggled. Something political.' It wasn't a question. She wouldn't look at me now, and her profile was towards me, sharp and disappointed.

'Something I've brought. I brought you the perfume and the scarf, and the pipe for father. I had other things to bring as well.' It was no good; she wouldn't be mollified.

'You've put us in danger, Alex. Me, and even father, lying in there dying.' Magda in full moral flight was alarming; she made awkward, jerking movements of her thin arms, and her eyes looked past me at some higher court of appeal. I had no

108

idea what her real feelings were about Solidarity; we had never mentioned the subject in our brief, uninformative letters. My father, who was a strong nationalist, was probably in favour, but he had never written anything to me about it either.

'It'll all be over in a moment. The man is coming here in a few minutes' time — half an hour at the most. He'll pick the things up and go, and that's the last we'll hear about it.'

'The last you'll hear about it, I'm sure. But what about us? You don't have to live here, Alex. You can do stupid things and get away with them.'

I let the storm work itself out, scarcely replying.

She wanted to give vent to her feelings; the act of talking seemed to make her feel better.

The visitor was late — almost an hour late. The quiet knock at the kitchen door came as a surprise, just when we had begun to get back on better terms again. Immediately the kitchen seemed to go cold as Magda went cautiously to the door and unbolted it.

For a moment all I could see of him was his breath, which billowed out in front of his face, like a ship making smoke. He sounded embarrassed, not knowing who it was he was supposed to meet, and not being willing to give his own name. Magda let him stand there for a little, to demonstrate her disapproval, but her sense of hospitality soon intervened and she invited him in. He was a good deal bigger than I; he came to warm himself by the fire, and his great hand enveloped mine and crushed it painfully.

'Tadeusz,' he said, in a pleasant deep voice, and I tried to coax the life back into my fingers. His face was pleasant too: big and open and untroubled, with a crown of absurdly curly fair hair which hung all round his head and made him look like a Polish Harpo Marx.

Magda had, in spite of her forebodings, decided he was someone to look after and feed, and the *barszcz* came out again. As he sat at the table eating, he began to talk a little about himself. He was careful not to tell us his surname, and he didn't tell us he came from Nowa Huta, though I knew that anyway. What he did start to tell us was the reality of life on the run: the cold, the lack of food, and the constant feeling that

109

you needed more sleep. Magda immediately became sympathetic, even though she had been telling me earlier that Solidarity was nothing but a bunch of idle factory-workers who had got the country into trouble. I felt mildly irritated, as though I was expected to be impressed by the difficulties and dangers of his life.

'It's good of you to have brought these things,' Tadeusz said, holding the two ludicrous pink-wrapped chocolate boxes almost hidden in his enormous hands. 'You ran quite a risk, you know.' Maybe he sensed a little of my irritability, and interpreted it as a sign that I wanted some praise and attention as well. Magda looked sharply at me, as though her earlier point had been established. That goaded me, I suppose, into a long account of why I had not been interested in bringing the boxes, and why I thought historians should beware of trying to play walk-on parts in the history they themselves are studying.

'Someone has to stay on the outside, making the judgements,' I said. It sounded unbearably pompous, even in my own ears. Tadeusz listened to it all, and then nodded his head, in the manner of one who has been convinced by a weighty argument.

'It's hard for people like me to be too objective,' he said, 'but maybe you're right; maybe some people have to stay out of it, in order to tell the story properly. That makes it all the braver of you to have brought all this.'

There wasn't much more I could say, so I handed him the copy of Lenin's *'What's to Be Done'*. He seemed to realize that it had a value. I felt myself drawn to him, as he bent over his bowl of *barszcz* making the kind of noises that would have made Patrick Binney get up from high table in college and eat in his own rooms. The kitchen positively rang with the sound. I didn't mind it: he was that kind of man.

Once he looked up at me, his mouth ringed with red from the soup, and his eyes were sharp amid the surrounding geniality. 'Everything must seem very provincial in Poland to you now.'

He wasn't a man you particularly wanted to flannel.

'Yes, in some ways. But it's still my home, you know.'

Sitting in the warm kitchen, hearing Tadeusz eat his beetroot soup, had brought something out in me which I couldn't yet define. Maybe, I thought, it's just one of those passing enthusiasms. It seemed rather more likely than that I was undergoing some major change of heart.

'That'd mean getting involved, though, wouldn't it?' He didn't look at me as he said it, concentrating on pulling a massive lump of bread off the loaf. I laughed, and didn't answer.

After he'd eaten he started making signs that he wanted to go, and it occurred to me that without him Magda and the kitchen would settle back into the kind of sameness I didn't particularly want to face.

'Are you going towards Zakopane? Because if so, maybe you would give me a lift to where I left my car.' It seemed a natural enough thing to ask, but immediately I'd said it I realized how cut off I was from the realities of his life. Even to tell me he was driving to Zakopane was a breach of security for him, and since he stayed free only by keeping one step ahead of the police I was a fool to ask. I suppose I must have showed my feelings, because he grinned and patted me on the shoulder.

'I can give you a lift to your car, anyway.' He didn't seem to have taken it too badly.

'Where did you park yours?'

'I wanted to be careful, so I left it on some waste ground a bit further along, down to the right.'

I looked at Magda; I couldn't remember any waste ground. She worked it out, and seemed nervous. 'Next to Rybka's house: he got the old wooden one — where the Tokarskis used to live — pulled down.'

'The bastard,' I said, and then it sank in and I started to laugh. 'It seems you've parked right in front of the village's only Party member.' I went over to the window to check; you could see Rybka's house, and the site of the Tokarskis' cottage, from the kitchen window, though it was some way away. My father would have appreciated the joke, even if Magda didn't.

I pulled aside the faded red curtains, which I thought I remembered, and peered out, holding my hand over my eyes to see better. The shutters were open still, but they cut off the view and I couldn't see properly where he'd left his car. I was just letting the curtain drop when a movement outside caught my eye.

The light from a lamp further down the street shone faintly

on a man in a lightish coat making his way through the small orchard that lay on one side of our house. What I had seen was the movement of his arm — he had caught himself on a twig and was trying to disentangle himself. He was so concerned with his sleeve, and with his irritable townsman's attempt to snap off the twig that had caught it, that he didn't notice me.

'Stupid idiot,' I said, though even as I was forming the words I started to realize what was going on, 'there's a man out there trying to walk through the orchard and getting stuck.'

'At this time of night?' Magda was saying, as though it was a personal affront to decent people. But Tadeusz had caught the implication in my voice and was looking at me, smiling. I must have looked at him questioningly. The police, I thought.

'Looks like it,' he said, confirming what I was thinking. 'Sorry.'

He picked up the chocolate boxes and shoved his coat on with the surprising speed of a heavy man. It was very quiet in the house now, and I thought I could hear the sounds of shoes on the gravel; not just one pair, either.

'I'll get out the back way,' he said, and as Magda was starting to protest about something said, 'Thanks for the *barszcz*. Better clear up the dishes.'

'UBEKs,' I thought; they must have followed him. The UB is the KGB of Poland: only nastier and more intelligent, as you'd expect. A blind panic seized me, and I couldn't bear to face them. Tadeusz was already out in the hall, and I pulled my coat off the chair where I'd left it, picked up my briefcase and hurried after him. I didn't even look at Magda, and gave no thought to my father.

'I'll show you a better way,' I said, breathlessly.

We headed for the door of my old bedroom, at the far end of the corridor. Behind us came an ominous knocking from the kitchen. Whoever it was didn't bother to use the ordinary knocker, but was hammering away with something heavy and metallic. I thought I could guess what. By the time we reached the bedroom I was in the lead, and I jumped on to the bed and started wrestling with the old-fasioned lock on the window. It took a moment or two, and Tadeusz lost enough of his composure to whisper at me to hurry.

'I am,' I hissed back irritably, and the lock came away in my hand, cutting into my fingers. But the window swung open, and I quietly pushed the shutters open too. Behind us voices were raised: Magda's, sounding admirably plaintive and annoyed, and a couple of deeper ones from the secret policemen. I clambered out of the window, which was small even for someone of my size — and a great deal smaller for Tadeusz — and dropped down quietly into the soft earth of a vegetable bed, crushing some early beans. I was in a small dead area between our house and the next one, which was about ten yards away. Only by standing in the main road and looking directly down between the houses could anyone see us, and as far as I could tell no-one was doing that. Of course, they could have stationed someone round the back, but that idea presented too many problems for me to cope with.

Tadeusz was still struggling through the narrow casement, and I seriously thought of leaving him to it. Perhaps my thoughts communicated themselves to him; certainly, as he stuck there, half in and half out, looking like a comic burglar in a silent two-reeler, there was a quizzical light in his eye that seemed to be summing up my motives. I stayed. He was, after all, an experienced outlaw and I was a law-abiding lecturer in history.

At last he prised himself out, and we heard a violent hammering from inside the house.

'Good job I locked the door,' he whispered and gave me a playful punch. Inside, a UB man was putting his shoulder, at least, to the door: I pushed the window shut and closed the shutters silently, my mouth opening and my tongue curling with the concentrated effort. I hoped no one would notice my bed had been trodden on.

There was the sound of boots ringing on the surface of the road now, and that meant the land at the back of the house was our only chance of escape. Even if they had it staked out, I thought, they might not see us in the dark. We headed that way as silently as we could and I tried to force my mind to work out the position. Policemen always went in their biggest numbers to the main door; say there were three of them there. They would have left one or two out in the street, another one or two, I assumed, by Tadeusz's car, and maybe one or two by the back of the house.

There were in fact four of them: big men in raincoats, looking like every detective movie I'd ever seen, and all concentrating their attention on the lighted window where I'd knocked to attract Magda's notice. All I could see of them was their shapes and the lighter sheen of their raincoats, but I could recognize them. They were about twelve yards away from us, and saying nothing.

Tadeusz had already seen them before I nudged him. It should be possible, I thought, to edge down into the garden, past the detectives, if we kept to the damp earth of the vegetable beds. I pulled at him to follow me.

Gardens change in fifteen years. We were only another ten or twelve yards past the waiting detectives when we came on the raspberry canes. The four heavies swivelled round together and a couple of them fidgeted with something then turned their torches on. For an instant we had both stopped, but the sudden stab of white light impelled us into a run; bumping into each other we fought our way through the raspberry canes until we got free of them. The torches twisted and turned in the darkness, the beams shooting off into the night, but it was enough to give them a sight of where we were. A shot crashed out, appallingly loud in the silence of the night, and I heard it crack in the air not far from me.

By now the UBEKs were shouting and flashing their torches this way and that, but before they could work out exactly which way we were going we hit the orchard. Twigs lashed us in the face and caught at our clothes, but the trees gave us the illusion of defence from flying bullets, and rendered the beams of the torches almost useless.

I was running with the speed of panic, taking no notice of the sudden troughs in the earth between the trees. Beside me, perhaps a little ahead, Tadeusz was thundering along, making an appalling racket as presumably I was too, but jinking and dipping his head to avoid the trees as they loomed up at us out of the darkness.

And then we were out in the open, and the UBEKs were caught in the orchard, breaking off the twigs and boughs with their heavy passage. Occasionally their torches flashed in our direction, but there were no shots now; they were too busy avoiding being whipped in the face by apple trees.

114

These were fields I knew well, and I moved fast and easily towards the only fordable part of the stream which divided our field from the next one. I risked a shout to Tadeusz, who was starting to head off at a tangent; it was safe — the bucketing flashlights showed the detectives were a good way behind us now, and still among the trees. There seemed no point in trying to disguise our path towards the crossing point; I doubted if the UBEKs would be following us that carefully anyway. I shouted another warning, using up my failing reserves of breath, and then we were over the stony banks and running down the beach by the willow trees, our heads almost on a level with the surface of the fields behind. Our shoes filled with icy water as we splashed across, but it helped to cool us.

On the other side of the stream I let Tadeusz clamber up the bank first, and got a little of my breath back while I turned and looked for our pursuers. They were there all right, perhaps fifty yards away at the moment, having broken out of the orchard at last. While we were down here the torches flashed aimlessly around and I could hear shouts of anger, then a lucky flick of somebody's wrist caught Tadeusz's head in the torch beam, like a bomber in a searchlight, and they were yelling and coming on again. One of them fired two shots before moving off, but the range was impossible. All the same, it was frightening, and somehow the fear of a bullet striking my spine or the base of my skull, made me forget some of my tiredness and the violent heaving of my chest, and my breath started to come a little more naturally.

We were heading for the woods now, and I knew that if we could make it we would get away altogether. There were two hundred yards to go, but the UBEKs still had to cross the stream.

An encouraging yell of pain erupted from one of them as he discovered the hidden drop and fell on to the beach of stones. More shots were fired, perhaps by mistake. I tried to shout something triumphant to Tadeusz, but I couldn't get the words out now, and he was looking almost all in. I pointed to the woods instead, and he nodded. It was no race for a man as heavy as that.

The flashlights were jerking about as violently as ever, only this time they weren't able to find us. I looked back to see what had happened: they had stopped in the middle of the field and were concentrating their attention on completely the wrong direction. And because they couldn't see us, they started loosing off their handguns in a blind rage at what we had done to them. Some wildlife may have suffered, but none of the bullets came within a quarter of a mile of us. While they vented their frustrations we headed into the woods off to their left, and stood there in the dark shelter of the trees, chests heaving, and shook hands as though we two had set some amazing new record.

All we had done in fact was to get a step ahead of the UBEKs. It wasn't long before the realization dawned. The muscles of my thighs were quivering, my calves were strained, and my shoulders were beginning to ache. And I was a hunted man.

'It's all right for you, you're used to this kind of thing,' I whispered. 'But what am I going to do? I've still got to get out of the country.'

We hadn't moved, and through the trees we could still see the probing flashlights of the frustrated UBEKs.

'Anything I can do for you, I will, and so will any of my friends in the movement. Tell them Tadeusz Nowak said so.' There was something about him which inspired confidence.

'We ought to head off,' he said. I agreed. There was no point in making for his car; that would be surrounded. And mine was some way off still. If only I could get back to the hotel, I thought; maybe they won't have discovered the connection between me and Tadeusz, and I'll be able to get away with Mary in the morning. It didn't seem entirely likely to me, even then, but there was nothing much else to look forward to. At least I was free: it was a proud thought, in its way. It was very dark in the woods, and I felt this was just as well; I must have looked a complete idiot, wearing a raincoat and carrying my absurd briefcase.

'You've still got the things I brought, I hope.'

We were walking along side by side now, trying to find our way through the forest by feel; sight and direction were quite impossible.

'If we lose those, I might as well give myself up to the police right now. Without them, we're nothing.'

'What exactly are they for?'

'If I told you, Dr Serafinski, it would make your life a lot harder —'

'If we got caught, you mean. Listen, if we're on the run together I think you could call me by my first name; it's a kind of introduction.' I tried unsuccessfully to make it sound like something different from the dialogue in a John Buchan novel.

'OK, Alex. But I mean it about the other things. Don't worry about them. If we are caught, I'll take the blame for everything; I've got less to lose.' He was almost a caricature of decency, lumbering along beside me and grinning when he saw me looking at him.

'That's the kind of thing they say in English thrillers. I didn't know real people said them.'

'You'd be surprised what people say when they're under pressure.'

I had the uncomfortable feeling I might well find out before I saw Cambridge again.

'Maybe we'll be lucky,' I said. 'Maybe they'll shoot us down in cold blood.'

Nowak liked that. His gigantic, bone-crushing hand came down on my shoulder and pushed me forward a few paces I hadn't intended to run.

The wood, roughly the shape of a lozenge, wasn't a large one and we were in the middle of it now, though I dare say we'd wandered a little from our path. But even in the darkness it was starting to be apparent where the wood ended — it was a little lighter ahead of us and to our left, and we headed in that direction. When we got to the edge of the wood I felt a stab of fear: in our confusion we might have turned round, and would now find ourselves walking straight into the UB men, refreshed by their wait. But we didn't.

In the starlight I could see the mountainside ahead of us, and I knew that if we scrambled up it we would eventually come across the road which ran along the edge, and that my car would be somewhere there. Between us and the start of the mountain slope was a field which we had to cross: black ploughed earth which clung heavily to our shoes as we walked. It was tiring work, and our speed soon slowed down to a measured plod. I hunched my back like a farm labourer and trudged on, the earth grabbing at my feet. A car raced invisibly from one point along the main road behind us to another, sounding its horn. It sounded official.

The walk across the ploughed field was the worst thing we'd had to do so far, and there was no longer any immediate fear to drive us on. My legs burned with the mechanical effort of lifting my feet and putting one clogged shoe in front of another. My breath began to gasp and whistle.

But eventually it ended, and I pointed out to Nowak a patch of mountainside relatively bare of trees where we could climb up.

'You know the way, I'll follow you.'

'Where do you come from?'

'Nowa Huta,' he said, in a way that showed me he was proud of it.

Some perversity in me made me want to puncture his pride a little.

'We don't hear much about what Solidarity's doing in Nowa Huta,' I said. 'In Wroclaw and Gdansk, yes, but not in Nowa Huta.'

'We get along,' he said, and I felt reprimanded.

'I went to university in Cracow,' I said in answer to his question. So, it turned out, had he. We even had a few mutual friends, though he was a good five years younger than me. I climbed up the steep mountain slope, holding my briefcase in one hand and pulling myself up with the other, while exchanging names and stories with him about our university days. We talked so loud and laughed so much I forgot the need for caution, until we started to find the going easier and I realized we were getting close to the road.

My Fiat was there, exactly as I had left it, and there were no signs of any policemen. It gave me a savage excitement to hear the car churning and grinding in reverse gear as the wheels tried to bite into the carpet of dead leaves. We shot out into the dark road, our lights still off, and turned in the direction of Zakopane. It was only then it occurred to me I would never see my father again; maybe never see Magda, either.

Another thing to feel guilty about, I thought, as we drove along — though for the time being I didn't feel anything except relief at being free.

'Are you comfortable, Tadeusz?' He was crammed into the front seat of the tiny car, almost squeezing me out of the driver's seat.

He turned round and gave me one of his grins, as bright as the lights of an oncoming car. 'I'm free, that's what counts.'

It was my own feeling of a moment before, but now I was less certain about it. For a start, who was to say how long we were going to carry on being free; and secondly, surely the UB would have the sense to block off the roads?

'Not necessarily.' Nowak knew the ways of the UBEKs a great deal better than I did. 'I doubt if they'll have expected us to get this far; they'll think we're out in the woods somewhere, and in a few hours they'll bring in dogs and try and hunt us down. They won't like the thought that we'll have got clean away.'

But we hadn't got clean away. Our road took us down into the glacial valley, about a mile and a half from the village; it was the point of maximum danger, even according to Nowak's optimistic assessment.

'If they aren't putting up roadblocks,' I asked, 'what's that?' It was at the crossroads where rumour had it that suicides were always buried.

The arm of the crossroads leading to the village was blocked off by three men, each carrying a sub-machine gun, and each in civilian clothes. They had rigged up a line of red lamps, but there was no other barrier.

They weren't particularly interested in us; that was clear from the start. When we first saw them, they were facing down towards the village, apparently not interested in anyone coming — as we were — from the mountains and heading for Zakopane along the main road. Strictly speaking, our way wasn't blocked at all.

'Don't take any notice of them,' Nowak said, his voice harsh and loud with tension.

I meant to do what he said. But one of the three UBEKs turned and looked at us, and half-heartedly waved his arm at us.

'He wants us to stop,' I said, panic rising.

'Pretend you haven't noticed.'

I couldn't do it. Another of them turned and waved his arm

119

as well, and I felt obliged to stop. Maybe it was all those years of living in England. Nowak said nothing — it might have been better if he'd shouted at me. The three policemen were close now, and one of them waved at us with his sub-machine gun. I stopped, a little short of the crossroads itself, and the man with the gun was forced to walk the three or four yards towards us. Nowak still said nothing.

'Where are you going?'

I started to say 'Zakopane,' but Nowak spoke across me. 'Poronin,' he answered. The policeman had a torch, and he shone it into the car. Then he started to say something, turned away, and opened his mouth to shout to the others.

'For Christ's sake get going,' Nowak hissed so loud the policeman must have heard him. For a moment I was too scared to do anything, then I saw one of the other policemen unshipping his gun, and I crashed the car into first gear and screamed away from them at a rate which threw us back in our seats.

'Head down,' Nowak yelled, but he was too big to protect himself properly in such a tiny car. Behind us, as we raced away, one of the policemen recovered himself quickly enough to fire off a burst. We were about thirty yards away when it happened, and for a moment the force of the sub-machine gun was such that he fired high and wide. But towards the end of the burst he got the weapon under control: a bullet shattered the rear window and buried itself somewhere in the instrument panel. Another, a fraction of a second later, cut through the bodywork of the car slighly lower and to the right, and smashed into Tadeusz Nowak's arm.

He gasped, and immediately there was blood everywhere — on him, on me, even on the windscreen. 'I'm sorry, I'm sorry,' was all I could say. It sounded stupid and panic-stricken, but I couldn't think of anything else. The crash of the bullets and the horror of the blood and the wound filled the car. There was a smell of fresh blood. Nowak, by contrast, seemed to have shrunk. He lay half against me, and half against the small in-adequate door of the car. He was conscious still.

'What shall I do?' I asked stupidly, willing him to tell me. Without him I could scarcely even think.

He was gritting his teeth with the pain of his arm, and his

face, when he half-turned it to me, was white with shock and loss of blood.

'We've got time to get to Zakopane,' he said, speaking determinedly but so softly I could scarcely hear him over the tinny racket of the engine.

'And when we get there? I don't know anybody there.' Nobody trustworthy, I meant; nobody who would know what to do with a seriously injured man.

'There's a sanatorium there, for rheumatic trouble.' His voice was very faint. 'I can't remember the street.'

'You'll have to make yourself stay awake, then,' I said, showing the first sign of determined, logical thought since it happened. 'Can't you give me any clear idea?'

He seemed to be fading already. 'On the road to Olcza,' he said. 'A big place. On the right.' I knew Olcza, though I didn't know of any sanatorium there. Still, it was a small place, a little way out of Zakopane, and finding a big building like a sanatorium wouldn't be too difficult, I thought. 'OK, I'll get you there as fast as I can. Don't worry.'

All I could think of was how much better it would have been if I'd done what he'd said right from the start.

He half-turned his heavy, drawn face towards me again, knowing what I was thinking. 'It's all right,' he said, as though I were the patient and he was the man who was going to look after me. 'It wasn't your fault. I'll be okay. Don't blame yourself.'

He was holding his arm tightly now, trying to ease the pain, or perhaps to stop the bleeding. I thought that probably the bullet hadn't severed an artery: after the initial outpouring, the flow was slowing down.

'All that matters is the radio parts,' he said.

A sudden wave of panic struck me. 'Have you got them safe, for God's sake?'

He nodded, without even having to check. They were the most important things in the world now, he seemed to be saying; though how he was going to get them to Nowa Huta from Zakopane I didn't know.

'Could you take them?' he asked.

'I've got to get out of the country,' I said, but I knew that it was a weak argument.

121

'They'll help you. Can't do without parts.'

I couldn't see what decent alternative I had. But in many ways it was the most dreadful moment of my life so far, when I realized how deep I had got myself into everything.

There was no going back, I could see that clearly. I was already in very serious trouble, and Mary probably was as well. We had passed the turn-off to our hotel while I was still trying to work it all out; then I made the decision. The only chance either of us had of getting out was to throw our lot in with the underground, as Nowak had suggested. To be arrested by the security police meant certain imprisonment for smuggling — and there was my past to reckon with as well. There was just a possibility that the Solidarity people might somehow or other get us out of all this. But I had to offer Mary the choice; I couldn't just disappear, leaving her to the police.

I put my foot hard down on the brake, and all but stalled the engine. Poor Nowak must have taken quite a jolt, but he was a brave man and didn't complain. Perhaps he wasn't altogether conscious.

'Tadeusz, you're going to have to be patient with me a bit more,' I said, as I wrestled the little car round and headed back for the hotel turn-off.

He said something, but I didn't catch it.

The hotel was mostly in darkness, since it was now almost midnight. Mary's light was on still, I noticed. I drove the car into the car park, and left it in the shadows, some way away from the building, just in case someone wondered if Nowak was a courting couple; he was certainly big enough for two.

The large blonde lady opened the door to me, and it was only when she did so that I realized I probably had some of Nowak's blood on my coat. So I started taking it off almost immediately. My actions probably looked a bit strange, but I improvized by acting as though I'd had too much vodka that evening. When I get excited I behave much as I do when I've been drinking, so acting the part wasn't altogether difficult. I fought my raincoat and swayed in the doorway and addressed the amazing upholstered bosom which she presented to me.

'Everyone tucked up and asleep?'

'Everyone but you, Dr Serafinski.'

'And you, dear lady.' I edged my way round her, and walked unsteadily through the hall. She hung back, worried that I might make a sudden lunge at her.

Passports, I thought. No matter what happens, we've got to get our passports out of here.

'Have you got our passports all ready and stamped?' I had to lean heavily on the counter of the reception desk to ask that. When she had taken them from us the evening before, she had put our passports somewhere behind the desk, close to the door into her inner sanctum.

'Not ready yet, Dr Serafinski. But you surely won't be needing them till the morning.' I looked at her carefully: an element of humour seemed to be creeping into the conversation on her side. But she wasn't smiling.

'Any messages for me?' I wanted her to turn round, so I could get a look at the table and see if our passports were still there.

'If there had been, Dr Serafinski, I would have notified your — Mrs — the lady you're with.'

'Well, how about the key, then?'

'The lady has that with her.'

'Ah.' I couldn't think of anything else for the moment.

'If that's all for the evening, Dr Serafinski . .?'

'Laundry list,' I said, fixing on something at last. 'We need one.'

'Tonight?'

'I always make my laundry list up at night.'

To humour me, she bent down and tried to find a laundry list under the counter; and as luck would have it, there wasn't one.

'Perhaps in the morning?'

'Out of the question,' I said, with a drunk's quick change to irritability. 'You must have one somewhere.'

Grumbling, she turned away and looked in a cupboard at the far end of the desk. Her back was only turned for a few seconds, but it was enough. I put all my weight on my hands, leant as far forward over the counter as I could, and spotted the table. The passports were lying on it, one on top of the other.

'Don't worry about the laundry list, dear lady,' I said, with a touch of drunken majesty, as she turned, her face dark red with the exertion. 'I never do my laundry till morning anyway. Many thanks.'

I moved off unsteadily towards the stairs — and it wasn't all acting! I gave an affectionate wave as I reached the chamois head which hung over the staircase, looking concerned about things, but by that time she had stormed off into her lair to listen to the radio and complain about the guests.

Mary was awake and worried. I had no time for the affectionate kiss she tried to give me. It took me a couple of minutes to tell her what had happened, and she found it hard to get all the facts together.

'They'll know it was my father's house, they'll know I was there, they'll know I'm staying here, or they'll quickly find out, and they'll know you're with me. The question is, do you want to take your chances alone or with me?'

Mary was a rational person, even though her enthusiasms carried her away at times. She thought about it for perhaps fifteen or twenty seconds before speaking.

'I'll come with you.'

I could see she wasn't particularly keen. 'You've got to be certain.'

She paused a bit longer, and I sensed the various options racing through her mind again. I knew she must be aware that she'd got me into all this by persuading me to bring the radio equipment in the first place.

'Yes, I will come.' This time she sounded a little more convinced.

'Right. We'll leave most of our stuff here — it may just confuse them for a bit about what's happening. All you need is a coat.'

'And my passport. I'm not leaving my passport behind.'

'No,' I said. 'I've been working on that.'

We left some money to cover the bill, and hung the 'Do Not Disturb' sign on the handle of the door. It was unpleasantly quiet in the corridor, but the stairs provided the real problem. Each one seemed to have its own independent creak, of a kind you never notice during the day but which sounds like a twenty-one gun salute in the dead of night. It took us a

124

dreadfully long time to reach the chamois head, and even longer to reach the hallway.

It sounded as though the blonde lady lived in the room behind the reception desk; perhaps there was a whole apartment there. We could hear her moving about, now that the radio was off the air, and some down-trodden male figure seemed to be in there with her; his voice punctuated hers in a quiet way occasionally, only to be over-ridden and no doubt contradicted. Perhaps he felt I had had a point about the laundry list.

To reach the table where our passports were I had to lift the flap of the reception desk and get underneath it. Like the stairs, it creaked, and for an appalling moment the punctuated monologue behind the closed door stopped. By that time the passports were in my hand. I decided to leave the flap resting on the counter; she'd find out soon enough what had happened when she glanced at the passport table.

Mary hadn't been adequately prepared for the sight of Nowak. He was slumped down in his seat now, his head resting on the minuscule dashboard and his face an awful grey colour. She climbed into the back seat on my side, seeing his injured arm clearly as she did so. I could tell it was as much as she could do not to cry out.

'Maybe you could try to do something to help him as we go along,' I said. For the moment, I was more worried about getting the car out of the car park without letting everybody know we were leaving. The start wasn't too bad: the car park was on a slight slope, and I'd left the car in a position where I could take advantage of the downward camber. I eased the hand-brake off, and with a quiet reflective sound the little Fiat passed over the gravel of the drive. We got a good way down before I had to start the engine, but it took me a couple of goes before it caught and in my nervousness I gunned it up too much, so that it roared. The noise was devastating, but we were round the other side of the building from the blonde lady's bunker, and nobody appeared.

Mary was already doing what she could to tie up the wound in Nowak's arm. It seemed that the bullet had exited, though where it had gone to we never found out, and it had made a far nastier hole in leaving than in entering. That must be why the blood had spattered on the windscreen. As far as she could tell, the bones of the arm weren't broken; but she knew enough first aid to be certain that he would need expert care very quickly, and when I told her about the sanatorium in Zakopane she appeared relieved.

The drive to Zakopane was short and without incident, so that my mind was free to wander. I kept seeing my father's sunken face, hearing Magda accuse me again of irresponsibility. What had happened to them after I'd left? After *we*'d left . . . Nowak seemed to have slipped into unconsciousness again.

I found the sanatorium without much difficulty: a big modern low-slung building that could have been a school, a block of flats, or a discreet drying-out clinic for alcoholics. The problem was getting to the director. I rang and rang at the main door, but it was a good ten minutes before anyone answered. At last a sleepy porter appeared, refusing point-blank to wake anyone else up.

'I must speak to the director. It's an emergency,' I said, but I knew that sounded unlikely at a sanatorium for arthritics. 'A personal one,' I added.

'The director didn't leave any instructions about that,' the porter said, looking idiotic. We talked for a little about the likelihood that he would have given instructions for something he wasn't expecting.

'Leave it to me,' I told him eventually, the fear and shock and tiredness beginning to take over. And when he still hung around I pulled a ten-dollar bill out of my wallet and folded his hand over it.

'Well, if you're sure.' He at last let me inside. While he was working out how to spend it, I got hold of the internal phone and dialled the number the porter gave me. It still wasn't easy. But it appeared that the director was a friend of various Solidarity people, and he eventually agreed to come down and look at Nowak. I didn't tell him Nowak had been shot in case the ten dollars had worn off and the porter was listening.

A little later the director and I sat at a melamine table in his kitchen while Nowak lay in a private room somewhere in the sanatorium and Mary hovered around acting as his nurse.

126

'This is all very dangerous, Dr Serafinski. Not to say irresponsible.' He nodded his head at me magisterially, but the effect was spoiled by his pyjamas, which were striped with a dramatic shade of pink, and made him look like a cross-section down a stick of English seaside rock. Now the pyjamas had blood on them — Nowak's blood — but the director didn't seem to realize that. What he did realize was that his massive pink pyjamas trousers were in danger of gaping open in the front, where the cord hung, and he had to keep a tight grip on them most of the time, especially when Mary was around.

I nodded, taking his lecture seriously.

'This man should be in hospital, where there are proper facilities for treating him.'

I nodded again, knowing that doctors always like to get a little disclaimer of some sort into this kind of conversation; it makes them feel they've done the right thing by their Hippocratic oath.

'However, in the circumstances I suppose there's nothing much we can do about it. If we take him to hospital he'll be arrested, and so will you and the young lady. How does she speak such charming Polish, by the way?'

'We're all in your hands,' I said, unwilling to get down to socializing for the moment. 'If we can rest up here for a while, then I'll make contact with Mr Nowak's friends in Nowa Huta, and maybe they can smuggle him into a hospital somewhere.'

The director seemed entirely trustworthy, but I wasn't certain about the night porter, and said so.

'There's no real need to worry about him. He's slightly simple — you may have discovered that for yourself — and he only works the night shift. I shall do my best to ensure that he doesn't talk to anyone about this evening.'

'And there's my car. It's got bullet-holes in.'

'Ah.' He got up to think that one over. 'We have a lock-up garage here, where you may leave it. I don't think it would be very safe to drive it around. And I'm afraid I wouldn't be able to lend you another car to replace it. This is Poland, after all.' I smiled; it was brave enough of him to offer to hide the Fiat for us, and if he had offered to lend us another car I would certainly have refused. He was courting ruin anyway.

'Perhaps the best thing would be if you and the young lady

were to get a little sleep. We have a guest bedroom in our section of the sanatorium here, but I'm afraid you would both have to sleep in the same room. I don't know if . . .' His voice dropped away courteously, but I could tell he was interested.

'Very good of you,' I said; and of course it was. The penalty for harbouring us would have been at least three years in prison. For that, I felt, he deserved a modicum of information.

'Miss Pastorek and I have lived together for some time.' If it wasn't true, I thought, it wasn't for the want of trying on my part.

'Ah yes,' he said, in a slightly melancholy tone. He had, I later discovered, recently lost his wife. 'Such charming Polish.'

'Her father left Poland in 1939.'

'I see.' He wandered around, trying to make us each a cup of powdered coffee with his free hand. 'You are both more than welcome to use our facilities here, but obviously the more discreet you are, the better it will be for me.'

I thanked him, and drank my coffee. I was so tired I could have slept in the sink, even though I noticed it was crammed with the dirty dishes of bachelorhood.

'I'll go and fetch Miss . . . Pastorek?'

'Pastorek,' I said.

'A Polish name?'

'Possibly Slovak in origin.'

'Ah.' He faded out of the room, keeping a tighter grip on himself than ever.

It was as close to swimming in urine as I hope I ever get. The bright sunlight streamed in through the immense windows and cut through the foul fumes, showing me a fierce old man with a stark, blue-veined white chest who shot up beside me from the stinking depths and gasped for breath, the steam wreathing round him. I tried restricting myself to breathing out, and the sulphurous fumes kept away from me for a little, but it was a battle I was bound to lose.

Around me, other arthritis sufferers ploughed their way up and down the small pool, their faith and determination at least as strong as the mineral contents of the hot water. A physiotherapist bustled by and called one of them out for a massage, and I watched her go, her thick, powerful legs on a level with my streaming face. Then I turned to do a bit more swimming, keeping my head exaggeratedly high out of the water. Nobody took any notice of me, or cared who I was; there were always masochists who dropped in from the world outside and took advantage of a day's swimming to ease the pain in their joints. I was aching and stiff after the unaccustomed exercise of the night before, and it had seemed a good way of passing the morning; by the time I had smelled the water it was too late. Mary had been more sensible.

I grasped the porcelain rail that ran round the edge of the pool and looked around. Some of the more depressing cases were being pulled through the water in slings; bent and twisted people of all kinds sought relief here. I felt guilty for being so healthy, and guilty too for having bent my head and raised my shoulder as I walked down here, as though I were a fellow-sufferer.

'Good morning, Dr Chalubinski.'

It gave me such a shock that I let my head go in the water; there was the director kneeling down a foot away from me, wearing his white coat.

'What did you call me?'

'Dr Chalubinski. I thought if you came from round here you might enjoy the alias.'

I couldn't think what he meant.

'Our friend is awake, and would like to see you when you're ready.'

The director was waiting for me when I emerged from the shower where I'd washed away the disgusting waters.

'I hope our hot bath did you good.'

I was about to make some suitable comment, when it occurred to me that it probably had done me a certain amount of good. The aches seemed to have faded away, and now that I no longer smelled as though I had rubbed myself down with a couple of dozen rotten eggs I felt a good deal chirpier.

'Is Miss Pastorek around?'

'She's already up there with our friend.'

I let him lead the way, and after a bit he turned to me.

'I don't think you need to hold yourself like that, unless you really want to.'

I dropped the shoulder I'd hunched up and walked on normally, more embarrassed than ever.

Mary made an admirable nurse, though there was a bit too much enthusiasm for my taste about the way she smoothed down the pillow and brushed the hair out of Nowak's eyes. She glanced up at me as we came in, and smiled, but I felt that Nowak was upstaging me for the time being. He was looking a little better now, and his arm was neatly tied up. Over his head a calendar suggested that this was a good month to go into the mountains and pick flowers.

We grinned at each other, the grin of people who have been through an ordeal together.

'I'm sorry about stopping,' I said. Mary pricked her ears up at that, but Nowak brushed it aside.

'They would have fired anyway.'

'The bastards.'

'Yes.'

'I thought I'd head off to Nowa Huta and see if we can get you some help. Maybe you'd give me some names.'

Nowak nodded. 'I've thought about that,' he said. 'I don't like staying here too long. The director's been very good to us in the past.'

A Solidarity bolt-hole, I thought; where better than a place where people are constantly coming and going for treatment, and where no one in their right mind would want the kind of treatment that was offered?

'But there's something else anyway.' I looked at him; his face had taken on an altogether different expression, and its usual slightly apologetic good humour had vanished. 'It's urgent, and you're the only person who can do anything about it.'

My heart sank; Mary had used words like that when she persuaded me to come to Poland.

'If I can,' I said.

He turned to Mary. 'Do you think you could prop me up? I can't really talk like this.'

She obliged, but there was something else he clearly wanted to say to her, and didn't. For a moment or two there was silence, and then he brought himself to do it.

'Please don't think it rude if I ask to speak to Dr Serafinski alone.'

130

Mary and the director moved into the next room. I stayed sitting on the end of the bed.

'This is very difficult, Alex,' he said at last. 'We haven't known each other very long, but I feel I can trust you. I hope I can.'

'I sometimes stop when told not to,' I said.

He didn't smile. 'There's no one else.' He played around with the edge of the blanket for a moment, and I looked back at the calendar for hints about picking flowers.

'I have a close friend: a girl. Like you and Mary. Her name is Anna Kapuszinska, and I have known her for many years. Naturally, I don't tell her too much about my Solidarity work, because that would put her in danger as well. She's already in enough danger: she's an artist, and she does the printing for a lot of Solidarity leaflets, as well as handing them around. It's not easy, you know.'

I nodded, trying to work out what was behind all this.

'I've been thinking very hard, Alex. We've had some trouble recently in our underground cell. We lost a radio transmitter; not just for broadcasting to everybody, like a radio station — we've done a bit of that, but it's only for morale, you know, it's frankly not that important. But we had a ham radio set-up too, so that we would contact groups all over Poland. It wasn't just for our area.' He went quiet, trying to work out if he'd said too much or ought to give me a few more hints. I didn't need them: he meant that there was an underground radio system covering the whole of Poland, to co-ordinate Solidarity policies. It wasn't any great revelation to me: there'd been stories about it in the papers. All along I had guessed that this was why I had been asked to bring in some spares.

'We were raided a few weeks ago. It was probably bad luck — usually the operators move around so much that they aren't caught. We were lucky that we still had most of another set, and another operator as well, so the loss wasn't crippling.

'We think the radio was monitored by detectors, not given away to the UBEKs by a traitor. But other things have happened since. There was a meeting in Cracow, for all the underground leaders of the area. A man even came from Warsaw to arrange a conference for the whole of Poland. Almost as soon as it started there was a raid, and several of them were arrested. I was on duty outside and I saw the whole thing.'

I nodded. He was getting worked up now and his cheeks were flushed, but I didn't like to interrupt the flow. It was obviously something he'd been worrying about for a long time.

'And then there was last night. I told myself that you could have been followed, that there could be a traitor in Paris, that they'd allowed you to get through with the equipment in order to trap me. But maybe it wasn't like that. Maybe they knew where I was going.'

'Did you tell anyone?'

'Various people have to know anyway; there's no possibility of keeping everything entirely secret. I had to know where to come, for instance, and someone had to tell me. But I can't believe any of the people who've been working with me on this are traitors.'

He looked away, and started playing with the bandage round his arm, as though it hurt him, or perhaps as though he wanted to make it hurt him.

'I've had a bit of time to think it over this morning — nothing else to do. I've worked out who it is that's been betraying us.'

'Can you tell me?'

'There's not much point — you wouldn't know the person anyway. But I've written it down in a letter to the head of the underground presidium. I want you to take the letter, Alex.'

I'd been expecting something like this. I couldn't think of any way the radio parts would get to Nowa Huta now, unless I took them. So much for all my hopes of staying on the sidelines, I thought: I'm in among the players now. Maybe my lingering reluctance showed on my face, because he said, 'There's a certain amount of urgency about it, I'm afraid.'

I looked at him: a big man, the mane of yellow hair frothing on to the pillow propping him up. He was the only one, I thought, who had been apologetic about involving me, and he's the one person who's got the right to complain.

'They've moved to a new hide-out, and it's too difficult to describe where to find it. The best thing is to go to the Number Fourteen Special Steel Plant in Nowa Huta, where there's a strike on at present. Anyone in Nowa Huta will tell you where it is. Ask to see the head of the strike committee, he'll send someone to guide you to the new headquarters. They're in touch every day.'

'And you said it was urgent?'

'There's going to be a nation-wide meeting of the underground groups in Cracow, and our traitor knows all about it.'

I thought about the implications of that for a moment or two.

'When is it?' I asked, faintly.

'Three days' time.'

'Friday?'

'Yes.'

'Christ.'

There was nothing to think about, really; I'd already agreed to do everything that Nowak asked me. Even so, I felt I owed it to my old philosophy of non-intervention to think things over, and accustom myself to the new circumstances. I went out on to the balcony and looked across at Mount Giewont. I could see the individual trees clearly on the mountainside, the air was so clear, and the retreating snow was hard and bright. The coldness and the clarity reminded me again of what it had been like to be a boy in the Tatra highlands. I remembered how I had envied Nowak his certainty, his knowledge that there was something worth fighting for. The bomb in Cracow had shown me that nothing was as easy as that; and yet here I was, signing up to fight for the same cause, risking my own neck for an ideal. No matter which way I looked at it, it still had a tawdry ring to it, like the four lines of verse inside a Valentine card or an advertisement for a wonder-drug: it made me wonder who was manipulating whom. Perhaps that's just my fifteen years in the West talking, I thought, looking up at Mount Giewont. Perhaps I really am doing something for Poland.

CHAPTER SEVEN

'A greater understanding of the problems of the working-class and the peasants is now being demonstrated by all the organs of the State.' — Polish radio broadcast.

'I can't help what condition he's in. He's as much implicated in a serious crime as you are, and no one's getting out of being questioned.'

Magda looked angrily at the lieutenant as he stood there, his hands on his hips, his raincoat still buttoned up.

'You aren't questioning a dying man, whatever else you do. It's stupid, and it's unreasonable. Now I'll thank you to get out of my kitchen.'

The lieutenant walked slowly over to her and leaning across the kitchen table slapped her across the mouth with his leather gloves. Magda tried to move backwards to avoid the blow, and brought down the small table behind her, falling onto it and smashing the china cups. The lieutenant laughed, and called in one of the other UB men to see. Magda lay among the ruins of her crockery, her cheek an angry red where the fingers of his glove had hit it, one of her lips starting to swell.

'You swine,' she shouted from the floor, her voice high and piercing, 'you come here talking about traitors, and that's all you are yourself. My brother is worth ten of you.'

He leered down at her as she tried to get up.

'Don't give me any more trouble, old woman. Otherwise I might really start getting nasty. Let's go and see Dad now, shall we?'

Magda licked her thickening lip. 'If you take one step into his room, I swear I'll scratch your eyes out.'

The sergeant moved forward, but the lieutenant laughed, watching Magda hook her hands into claws.

'Leave the old bag alone — she's not worth messing about with.' The sergeant, relieved, moved back and his heels crunched on the smashed crockery.

'You said your father was unconscious most of the time. Did he say anything to this brother of yours?'

'He's too ill to recognize anyone.' Even in this extremity, Magda disliked telling a direct lie.

'I'll do a deal with you. If you tell me all about the town men who were here, and give me all the details, I won't go and trouble the poor old bastard. Otherwise, we put him in the car and take him down for questioning, even if he snuffs it on the way. Right?'

Magda looked down, rubbing at her cheek. Could it be so wrong to tell the police what they already half knew?

Her first duty was to her father. She looked at the lieutenant, then at the sergeant. These men were killers; they would certainly haul her father out of bed if they wanted to, and no one would ever punish them for it. They were the law here. Her thoughts turned back to her brother. If he hadn't come, the UB wouldn't be here, with their beatings and their violence and their threats.

The lieutenant watched her.

'You're just doing your duty as a citizen by telling us about them,' he said. 'Anti-social parasites, that's all they are. A good woman like you wouldn't want to shelter the likes of them.'

'Don't give me any of that talk of yours,' Magda said, but the spirit had gone out of her now. She knew what she was going to do. 'If you want the names, I suppose I shall have to give them to you, just to stop you committing a murder. I'm surprised you don't know the names already, if you come here with all these men. What did you expect to find, bringing all your guns in and damaging everything?'

The lieutenant knew that she was talking to cover her surrender, and let her go on. Then he put a piece of paper in front of her, and she wrote down on it Alex Serafinski's full name and his address in Cambridge, and what she could remember of Tadeusz and who he was.

'Did they come by car?'

Magda nodded, willing to let him make his own wrong deductions. She looked at his face with hatred, but said nothing that would provoke him. She was sitting down now, her back to the ruin of the cups and plates on the floor. That could be dealt with once these swine had gone, she thought.

The lieutenant looked carefully at the piece of paper she had handed him.

'You haven't put much about the other one.'

'I don't know anything else about him. Tadeusz, he said his name was.'

'Stupid peasant bitch,' the lieutenant said, without raising his voice, and punched her with full force on the side of the face. The blood ran out of the corner of her mouth, a surprisingly bright red.

'Pull the old bastard out of bed and put him in the car with this one,' the lieutenant said. The sergeant went down the corridor opening doors at random, until he found the old man's bedroom at the end. He sized up the heavy body lying on the mattress and went back to the door.

'I'll need plenty of help, sir,' he called out.

Old Serafinski lay with his eyes closed and his breath coming slowly and raspingly, but he was conscious. Talking to his son had cleared his mind, and shown him that he was capable of doing more than he had thought.

'Don't move, father, don't take any notice. It's only the police.' Magda was trying to force her way into the room, and the sergeant pushed her roughly out again.

'Leave her alone and get out of my house.' His voice was surprisingly strong. 'You've got no right to be here.'

The lieutenant appeared in the doorway.

'Come on, get a move on,' he shouted.

'No one raises their voice in my house,' the old man whispered, his words audible but slurred. He was sitting up now, a vast shape in his vest and blue pyjamas, the quilt lying on the floor. Nobody said anything for a moment; suddenly the old man's face turned the colour of clay, and his eyes became suffused with blood. For a second or two he swayed, then he collapsed slowly onto his side and lay there, his mouth open and a dew of sweat on his forehead.

136

'You cheap swine, you've killed him.' Magda's voice rose almost to a screech.

The sergeant stepped forward and felt the old man's wrist. 'Still alive, sir.'

'Leave the stupid old bastard. And the old girl too. We'll get on to headquarters — they'll need us for the search.' He seemed to be trying to save face.

'We'll be back for you,' he said, looking at Magda.

'Do you think I care about that?' she said.

In the season, there's as much life in Zakopane as you could find in St Moritz or Gstaad. The air is clear and bracing, the streets echo with the shouts and boasting of the young and the rich, and the bars ring with pop music and the sound of people spending money. If you come from Warsaw, you can't walk down the road without bumping into people you know, and didn't realize could ski.

But out of season, when the snow retreats and puts up a last-ditch stand in stubborn brown-grey patches as hard as leather in the hollows of the hillsides, Zakopane becomes very clean, and very quiet, and completely dead. Only the people who need to be there remain: the inhabitants themselves, and the shifting population of sufferers who move into the sanatoriums which first put the little mountain village on the map, ninety years ago. All the snow you can see at this time of year is confined to the topmost mountains which enclose the town like the sides of a bowl: Mount Gubalowka to the west, the great ridge of Mount Giewont to the south, and beyond and above that the higher peaks of Kaspowy Wierch and Kondracka, part of the High Tatra range which straddles the borders of Poland and Czechoslovakia, and acts as outrider for the Carpathians, stretching for hundreds of miles to the east. The High Tatras are some of the most beautiful mountains in the world.

Just to walk down Kuprowki Street gave me immense pleasure, and Mary seemed aware of it, judging by the sidelong glances of amusement she gave me. We were heading for the railway station, but taking the scenic route through the middle of the old town, the part built mostly of wood and inhabited once by the shepherds and those who catered for them. Nowadays, a large husk of brick and concrete and stone surrounds this wooden kernel: the bourgeois houses of the 1890s, the trimmer villas of the inter-war years, and the big glass and concrete palaces of socialism which reach up among the trees to the lower slopes of Mount Giewont.

'The boss of this *voivodship* had a massive great villa up there,' I said, pointing. I never could get myself out of the habit of delivering lectures, but Mary didn't seem to mind. 'There were amazing stories about the mosaics and the rare types of wood it was built of, all paid for by some state construction outfit he controlled. These were the days of the Sixties, when you could get away with anything if you were high up in the Party. The villa was filled with masseuses and high-class tarts, and they'd all come simpering down the ski-slopes before going back up to give his majesty another seeing to.

'And then one day it all changed, and the tarts had to leave and the wood was stripped away and stored somewhere, and the big Party boss was suddenly slopping out in gaol somewhere, doing a ten-year sentence for corruption. But that didn't stop it. The man who came in to clean everything up took over the villa in turn, and it started all over again.'

Mary laughed, and asked me who the man on the statue was. Looking at it, I finally realized the point of the joke the director of the sanatorium had been trying to make earlier that day.

'Dr Chalubinski, of course — the man who first discovered the waters of Zakopane, and built the place up.' Thinking of the director's clumsy attempt at humour made me like him more than ever.

We walked up streets and down streets, and did what we could to pass the time until midday, when our train left for Cracow. I felt full of life; it was either the air, or the aftermath of Dr Chalubinski's famous waters. I twirled my much-travelled briefcase in my hand and suggested that it was time we headed for the station.

As so often happens when you have time to kill, we ended

up walking fast in order to get there on time. I queued for tickets, my heart beating faster each time the aged woman behind the desk asked the person at the front of the queue where he or she was going. It all took a long time, and I was getting nervous.

Mary wandered around the station, waiting for me. Every now and then we would exchange exaggerated looks of impatience and agony, while the woman dealt out the wrong change and had to be shown why it was wrong, or went off altogether to talk about her chilblains to someone else behind the ticket-desk. I was only two from the front, eventually, when Mary came back from her wandering and stood very close to me.

'They're checking identity cards at the gate,' she said, in a low, urgent whisper.

'Who are?'

'The militia.'

For a moment, I couldn't think what to do. Then there was a push in my back, and I realized it was my turn. By this time I was too bemused to do anything other than ask for tickets, though it would probably have looked suspicious if we'd just walked away.

'Two singles to Cracow, please.'

It had to be repeated a couple of times, and a distinction had to be drawn between Cracow and Katowice, but eventually it was done and I had the two pieces of white card in my hand.

It wasn't that I didn't believe Mary, it was just that I wanted to make absolutely certain that militiamen were indeed doing the checking, and not simply railway workers wearing uniforms that looked similar. Unfortunately by this time the militiamen seemed to have moved further in and we had to show our tickets and walk on to the platform proper before we could even get a sight of them.

'I told you, I told you,' Mary kept saying, pulling at my jacket.

'Identity cards,' I heard a militiaman say. There was no mistaking the uniforms now.

I looked round. It seemed our only chance was to head for another platform, and then back into the booking hall and away from the station altogether; though I couldn't think how we would then get to Cracow.

139

'Oh dear,' I said, in an unnaturally loud voice, 'wrong platform. Come on.'

We broke away from the queue, leaving only a few people looking at us.

'We'd best go down this way,' I said, and added quietly to Mary, 'We'll just have to talk our way past the ticket collector.'

It would almost certainly have worked, if it hadn't been for the placing of the men's lavatory. We got to the ticket collector, and I started explaining that we'd been given the wrong tickets, and needed to go back to change them.

'Katowice, I asked for,' I said, 'and stupidly I didn't check them.' Mary laughed, and the ticket collector started to smile, and everything was fine.

'I hope she changes them for you,' he was saying, when a militiaman walked over from the lavatory. He wasn't particularly interested in us, but policemen in all countries have a habit of listening in to conversations like that. And in countries such as Poland, they have another habit as well.

'Let's see your identification cards,' he said.

Mary sensed what I was going to do and tried to forestall me.

'Here's mine,' she said, and pulled her passport out of her handbag. The policeman looked at it slowly and spelled out the name in the window at the top of the passport; then he looked at her, and from her to me.

There was nothing for it. Before he could draw a breath to call his friends I yanked Mary's passport out of his hand and punched him very hard in the stomach. My fist went in deep; it was like hitting a leaking air mattress.

'Arfh,' he said, as though he'd been thinking about it, and began to double up. I gave him another punch, this time hitting him roughly where he kept his notebook. It sent him back into the ticket-collector, who'd been watching with amazement. Gratifyingly, they both fell backwards into the ticket-collector's wooden sentry box, which in turn began to topple over under their weight, and they all went down together, with an appalling crash. People started screaming, and the other militiamen gave up checking identities and came running.

Mary and I broke away fast. We headed through the ticket hall, scattering people in front of us like dogs running through

140

a pack of sheep. Outside, there were more crowds, and a police-car parked a little way away; if I'd been more observant I would have noticed it when we arrived. I pulled Mary up short, and we made our way through the thinning crowds, walking and pushing but no longer making a display of ourselves.

In Chramcowki Street we finally slowed down, feeling that we'd probably got away with it. There were police whistles, but they weren't close. I felt curious, not having hit anyone since I was sixteen, and never having hit a policeman at all. My hand scarcely hurt. Mary was smouldering with fury.

'Why ever did you have to do something so damned stupid? You must have been mad.' She walked on ahead of me, taking short angry steps.

'What did you want me to do? Stand there while he called up the entire Zakopane police force? They were looking for us, and he read your passport.'

'How do you know they were looking for us? It could have been something altogether different. We could be on the train by now, perfectly safe, instead of being hunted through the streets like criminals.' She went on ahead of me again, turning only to say, 'I've never seen anything so stupidly irresponsible in my life.' And then, 'You obviously don't care at all about me, or my safety.'

I chose to put it down to delayed shock. She, after all, was the one who had got me into this entire mess. And anyway, we had to stick together.

'There's no point in our careering round the streets yelling at one another,' I said, in what I hoped was a calming voice. 'Why don't we head into a café somewhere, sit down and have a cup of coffee and work out what we're going to do?'

She nodded, and we turned into Krupowki Street again, where I remembered the Europejska café from my school-days.

The coffee was unappetizing, but at least it was hot, and no one wanted to see our identity cards before serving us. As we sipped it, I tried to work out a plan which might take Mary's mind off the rights and wrongs of the situation, but it was hard to know what to do. The only alternatives I could think of were to go by bus, where the problem seemed likely to be just as bad, or to hitch-hike, which would probably be worse. Or we could go back to the long-suffering sanatorium director and ask him to drive us somewhere, once it was dark. It hardly seemed the solution to our troubles.

'I suppose they *were* looking for us,' Mary said, and I was so pleased I took hold of her hand and squeezed it. 'And it was rather funny, the way they all fell down.' I squeezed her hand again, and did an impersonation of the policeman being punched in the stomach. We started laughing, the laughter of tension and anxiety.

'I'm afraid we're not out of it yet, by any means,' I said, though curiously I felt a great deal better about it now that Mary wasn't blaming me for the whole thing. 'He really was getting ready to shout out for his mates you know. I could virtually see his lips forming the words.'

We started to work out what words his lips had been forming, and that made us feel better too. We talked it over and over, and had something to eat and another couple of cups of the sour coffee.

'We can't stay here — we'll have to get out of this town as fast as possible.'

Mary nodded. 'Then we shouldn't be sitting here drinking cups of coffee.'

She was right, but I didn't want to go out in the street until we had worked out precisely what we were going to do.

'The only possibility is to head out on foot and walk down side roads and so on, as best we can, to the next place along, which is Poronin. It's only a village, but it's possible they won't have the cops out in force; there probably aren't any cops anyway. There's a small bus station, and the buses to Cracow stop there.'

We paid up, and left. It wasn't by any means our first mistake that day, but it was very nearly our last. Going out into Krupowki Street from the café we almost collided with a patrol of four soldiers, who had been roped into the business of looking for us. Probably the fact that we did almost collide with them saved us, since in the confusion they didn't get a good look at our faces. The street was crowded, and we pushed our way through the shoppers and took refuge eventually in a queue outside a clothes shop. It was a long queue, what we used to call a four-hour one when I lived in Poland, though the times have probably increased nowadays. No one would look for us in a queue, I reasoned, even if we didn't get anywhere by standing in it. My theory was tested almost immediately: the four soldiers came back along the main street and passed a few yards from us. I didn't look at them, but I could see their army boots out of the corner of my eye, and they marched straight ahead without turning.

It was a reprieve, but we were obviously going to have trouble. I took my raincoat off, although it was chilly; if they were looking for someone in a light coat they might be fooled by a dark brown corduroy jacket instead.

'I never did like hunting,' Mary said. 'When we get back, I'm going to join all the anti-hunting groups I can find.'

'Try and stop them massacring all those little birds,' I said, sounding like an Englishman. 'Have you ever seen how Frenchmen shoot down everything that moves in a forest?'

'I didn't mean France,' she said. 'I meant, when we get back to England.'

'You're kidding.'

'I'm not.'

'You mean you're going to come and live with me in England?'

'Yes.' She looked at me defiantly, as though I'd told her she couldn't. 'It's my own country, and France isn't. And you punched the policeman.'

I couldn't work it out, but I felt I didn't have to. It was just about the best reason I could think of for trying to get away from Zakopane.

'Do people who punch policemen always have that effect on you?'

'Only if the policemen are out to catch me.'

They still were. Another group of militiamen went past us slowly, looking at the people in the street but not, I noticed again, showing any interest in the queues. We weren't so near the end now, either, which gave us a little more camouflage.

Ominously, a lorryload of soldiers passed, the soldiers chatting and laughing among themselves as they sat in the back. The hunt was getting more intense.

'We've got to get out of here,' I said. 'Soon they'll be setting up checkpoints everywhere.'

'But where do we go?'

'North, I suppose, and make for Poronin. How do you feel about a five-mile walk?'

'Pretty much as I always do about five-mile walks,' she said.

'Let's start it now, then.'

We left the queue, to the amazement of people who were prepared to wait their full three hours and fifty minutes, and headed off down Krupowki Street again. The trouble was, we had done precisely what the police had expected us to do: we had gone to the centre of the city. We should have made for the emptier suburbs, the leafy promenades where the bath-chair brigade gathers, and where the police checks would have been few and far between. A police car was cruising very slowly along the street towards us. It was far too late to look in shop windows or find a convenient queue to join, though there was no shortage of them, and I could see the policemen in the car peering out at the passers-by as they went, not going at much more than a walking pace themselves.

I remembered a film, an English film, where a man avoided the police on a train by leaning over and starting to kiss his fellow passenger, who was fortunately not only a woman but highly attractive. It had worked on the British police. I looked at the car, hoping they hadn't seen us, and backed Mary up against the wall of a shop and started kissing her. She was a bit surprised at first, but she soon got the idea.

Obviously I had misjudged the Polish police for I heard the car brake sharply, and two doors slam, and I was still kissing Mary as we took off down the street, banging into enraged shoppers once again, carving our way through one queue and then another like maddened footballers, with the policemen shouting and blowing whistles behind us. I was pulling Mary along by the hand, and nearly killed us both by running blind into the road and straight under the wheels of a bus. The driver stood on his brakes, and everyone on board piled up inside and began cursing, but the driver did us the favour of starting up again just as the police got to the spot, and they had to wait while it passed before they could cross. I could still hear him yelling at me out of his window. It gave us perhaps half a minute's start. It also provided us with a different crowd of people, who hadn't seen us running along and weren't on the look-out for escapers. I walked straight towards the first available open door I could see: a big concrete building, slightly set back, with a Polish flag flying over it. Mary walked swiftly along behind me, hissing, 'It isn't a police station, is it?'

With my luck, I thought, it'll be the UB headquarters, and I took a tighter grip on my raincoat and the ever-present briefcase, ready for another débâcle. But it wasn't. An elderly lady smiled at us and handed us tickets, and before I could work out what was happening we were surrounded by a large number of stuffed animals, standing in glass cases around a tall, well-lighted exhibition hall. An enormous stuffed elk stood in the middle, looking faintly embarrassed by the outside hardware it was sporting on its forehead.

We weren't in any great hurry to get out, so we wandered around the quieter corridors, looking at several mangy stuffed bears and a whole array of chamois. The stuffing was coming out of some of them.

I like museums on the whole, but this one was distinctly melancholy. It looked as though some enthusiast with a gun had been massacring the wilder inhabitants of the Tatra mountains for years, and the people of Zakopane were less than delighted with the result. Maybe it was just that no one had spent any money on the place.

In a far corner sat a small elderly man in a dark blue uniform, who was presumably there to make sure we didn't climb the elk or steal the stuffed lynx. No one spent much money on him either. I called him 'sir', and he liked that. It wasn't always a very cheerful place to work, he agreed, but on the other hand it was interesting to meet people like ourselves. Were we planning to go climbing in the Tatras? No we weren't, I said firmly, though later I wondered if he had the gift of second sight. Didn't we want to see the Tatra vegetation garden outside? No again; we felt happier in the warmth of the museum, and were starting to think about sitting down somewhere for a few minutes. In here we felt safe; our defences were down.

Then came the noise of raised voices from the entrance hall, and I knew they'd got on to us. I felt a terrible dreariness rise up inside me, as though it would be much easier just to go out to them and say 'Here we are.' But one glance at Mary showed me that she too was at the end of her tether, and needed someone to help her along. There must have been a question in my eyes, though, because she said out loud, 'Let's keep going.' And that, and the thought of her coming to live with me in Cambridge, was enough to start me off again.

For a split second I considered trying to enlist the help of the old man; the shouting and yelling of orders was much louder now, and I knew we had to get out. But defeated and small though he seemed, he was on our side.

'They looking for you?'

'Maybe.'

'There's a back entrance to the vegetation garden; you'll find it open. I'll tell them you've gone up to ethnography.' He put his hand out, gave my forearm a little squeeze. 'You don't look bad to me,' he said.

There wasn't time to thank him, though I glanced back and saw him sitting there among the chamois, looking slightly stuffed himself, and heard the heavy steps of the policemen as they ran down the echoing corridors towards us. But we were outside in the gardens before they could catch a glimpse of us, and presumably the old man said his piece because they didn't follow out into the open air. I fancied I could hear shouted commands and acknowledgements coming through the dusty windows of the upper galleries. No one could have looked out of the windows to see us.

We found the gate at the back, a one-way affair which let us out into a quiet little street running parallel with the main shopping centre.

Zakopane isn't a particularly easy place to find your way round in, even if you knew it as a child: there's a certain sameness about the mountains surrounding it. And, since I hadn't been back there for more than fifteen years — during which time it had changed radically — then it perhaps wasn't surprising I lost my sense of direction. I speak in self-defence. Having decided that we should head for Poronin in the north, we had taken a number of side-streets and twisted and turned our way to avoid real or imaginary policemen, until I led us unerringly into the small village of Kuznice, a kilometre or so due *south* of Zakopane. I only realized it when I saw the monument to the victims of Nazism in this area, which stands by the station at the foot of the cable car to the summit of Kasprowy Wierch, nearly six thousand feet above us.

I didn't know whether to tell Mary at first, but I think she must have guessed something from the way I looked. I felt absolutely devastated by my own stupidity; we had wasted what was left of our precious energy by walking in precisely the opposite direction from the one we wanted, and we had the whole of Zakopane to cross before we could get back on our road. Time was starting to run out on us; it was three o'clock in the afternoon; and tomorrow was Wednesday: only one clear day in which to warn the entire national leadership of Solidarity that they'd be arrested if they went to Cracow on Friday.

'Is this the right place?'

'No. I'm sorry, I don't know where we went wrong, but we did. It's my fault entirely.' I felt utterly depressed.

'How on earth could you make a mistake like that?'

I let her talk; I knew that it was her way of expressing her disappointment and tiredness. She didn't even know about the Solidarity meeting; I'd thought it better to keep that to myself, in case she was arrested. It seemed quite likely that we would be, now.

'What happens over there?'

'It's the cable-car you take to the highest part of the Tatras, looking into Czechoslovakia. It's absolutely wonderful. The only problem is it's in the wrong direction. We've come south instead of north.'

She was quieter that time, and finished what she had to say more quickly. She knew perfectly well there was nothing we could do about it now, except make the best of things.

It was then that we heard the sirens. Whether someone had spotted us on the way, or they had some other means of information, didn't seem to matter. Neither of us had the slightest doubt that they were coming for us; and by the sound of the sirens, there were at least two cars heading in our direction.

There was only one thing to do, and I think Mary had the

147

same idea at precisely the same moment. The cable-car station was about a hundred yards away from us now, and we ran for it, as before: me first, pulling Mary along by the right hand and holding my raincoat and briefcase in my left. I was beginning to feel as though I'd spent my entire life doing it.

For a moment or two, the world losts its bearings and lurched alarmingly around us. Then it righted itself, and the cable-car moved smoothly forward through the air at a stately pace, leaving the trees and the few remaining chalets to drop away beneath us. It was like being in an airship: things glided past as we moved silently along.

Even the unluckiest occasionally have their moments, and this had been one of mine. There isn't much call for the cable-cars out of season, since the arthritis sufferers have better things to do with their free afternoons and the locals have all seen the view from the mountains before. Part of the time the engineers do the necessary repair work, but otherwise the cable-cars are available for use if anyone wants them, and the full staff is on duty all year round: it's part of the system of maintaining full employment in a socialist state. We had arrived at the station on a day when the cable-cars weren't being serviced, at an hour when there was someone to make it work, and at a moment when there happened to be one ready and waiting. It all seemed too good to be true.

With the police sirens dinning in our ears, we had asked as casually as possible for a couple of tickets. The man behind the counter had scarcely looked at us. 'One going right away,' he said. I never did find out whether they left on demand, or according to a timetable; in our case it didn't matter. We were up and away in our controlled flying machine while the cops were still driving round in circles trying to work out where we had vanished to. Hair's-breadth escapes were starting to become a habit with us, and I hoped fervently that the pattern would continue.

'There's the main street,' Mary called out. She was as elated as I was, and was peering out of the window at the back, spotting the places where we had had our escapades.

'And the station,' I said, joining her.

It was an uncomfortable vehicle in every way: an oval box painted yellow and green, containing two benches of wooden slats which ran down the length of the car on either side. At a pinch you could cram twenty people into it, standing and sitting. No one had cleaned the windows for a long time, but that didn't spoil the magnificent view; nothing could. I lay full-length on the hard slats, using my briefcase as a pillow, feeling the vibration of the immense cables that held us up, and laughed loudly. I suppose it was reaction to all the excitements of the day.

'Don't laugh too much,' Mary said.

I stopped and sat up.

'Look down there.'

Two little blue and white toy cars were parked in front of the cable-car station, and three ants were standing by them. A couple more ants were walking into the station itself. The chances seemed quite strong that they were wearing dark blue police uniforms. Even as we watched, suspended in air, another couple of cars drove up: black ones, this time. They might have been plain-clothes detectives, or they might have been holiday-makers hoping for a ride up the mountain, but my guess was that they were another squad of UB men, and I said so. The thought of the UB didn't frighten her as much as it did me; I suppose you don't worry a great deal about the secret police if you grow up in Highgate. But I was badly scared, especially when a minuscule van drove up and a couple of even tinier ants were let out of the back: dogs.

'Let's just enjoy the ride,' I said. 'It could be the last thing we enjoy for quite a long time.'

'We can get away into the mountains, can't we? You said the Czechoslovak border is just here somewhere — we can get across and then we'll be all right.'

There was so much wrong about her assumption that it seemed an effort to start pointing it out.

'They'll tell the men at the next cable station,' I said, beginning at the beginning.

'But you've been spending the day punching policemen in

149

the stomach — surely you're not worried about an old ticket-collector.'

'In cold blood?'

'I don't expect it will be cold by the time you get there.'

Well, maybe. But there were plenty of other problems. At the very least we would be going all night in the mountains, even if we did manage to get away at the upper station. As for her idea that we only had to cross into Czechoslovakia to be free, it was laughable. She'd read too much about people crossing the state line in America. But we all need our illusions at times.

The majestic scenery was more than enough to distract us both now. Zakopane, and its little outgrowth Kuznice, had shrunk to squares of colour in the green and brown valley. Below us were great blocks of dwarf pines, covering much of the mountainside except where there were gaps for the ski runs.

Big areas of snow, some of it white, lay in patches where the sun didn't reach it. It was a marvellous afternoon. At least, I thought, it won't be raining on us.

The cable-car to Kasprowy Wierch goes up in two stages. At roughly the halfway point, Myslenickie Turnie, you have to get out and change into another cable-car for the rest of the journey to the mountain-top, where there's an observatory and weather station. I could see it now, hundreds of feet above us: a round turret against the skyline, shaped like an English Martello tower.

We had absolutely no chance of getting that far. We might just be able to escape at Myslenickie Turnie, the halfway point, but there was no possibility that we'd be allowed into the second cable-car; they could just turn the power off if they couldn't stop us some other way. And what would the police be doing in the meantime? They wouldn't be able to follow us up by cable-car, so they'd have to take the laborious trip by road as far as they could, and hike the rest. It'd taken them quite a time. Unless — but I decided at that stage to look out at the sunshine.

The cable-car took a mild bend and started to climb more sharply. The ground was a long way below us now, maybe two or three hundred feet, and the mountain sloped away sharply, its face covered with immense granite boulders each the size of a bungalow. I remembered being here before, and I knew what was coming. We seemed to head straight for the sheer face of the mountain, then did a delicate little side-step, like a rugby player, and slipped into a narrow pass between two walls of rock that soared up beside us. The ground wasn't too far below us now, and it got closer as we went on climbing.

Suddenly, we weren't climbing any more. With a shock that threw me down the centre of the car and made me collide in a heap with Mary, we stopped dead. The bastards had switched the power off.

Looking back, I couldn't see why it had taken so long, but maybe they had to get a special dispensation, or maybe it was just that it was difficult. Either way, they had us. It would take them a long time to work their way up to Myslenickie Turnie, but when they eventually did reach it, someone would turn the power on again and we would be delivered up to them like meek little parcels. Mary and I disentangled ourselves and said nothing. It was precisely this that I'd been afraid of, earlier. We were trapped.

Both of us looked down out of the windows at the same moment, thinking the same thing, and we looked back again at each other, hopelessly. The ground below us was shelving upwards at a steep angle, but it was still a good fifty feet down with dwarf pines sprouting in profusion.

'If only they could have stopped us a bit further up, we could have done it,' Mary said.

I was very stupid. I'd known for some time now that there was something about this ride, something about the ground underneath and the forest of pines up the mountainside, but I'd forgotten what it was. Now the idea started to stir in the depths of my memory.

'Do you remember that memorial to the people who died in the war, down by the cable-car station?'

She nodded, warily. I could see she thought she was in for one of my long lectures. So she was, in a way.

'During the war, a partisan leader was picked up by the SS in Zakopane. They took him up to the mountains, maybe in this very cable-car, to shoot him. I'd forgotten all about it till now. And before he got to Myslenickie Turnie he jumped out. The

SS shot the poor sod in the forest, but at least he got out.'

'Wonderful,' Mary said. She looked out of the window at the ground, fifty feet below us, in a meaningful way.

'The thing is, he jumped out when the car was moving, and the ground was a lot closer when he did it. That's how he got away.'

'Until they shot him.'

'Be more positive,' I urged. 'We might break our necks first.' I was over-using this form of joke, I knew.

'You mean jump out of the car a bit higher up? But we're stuck here.'

I felt I had to be patient. 'When the UBEKs or the militia or whoever's in the lead get up to Myslenickie Turnie, they'll switch the power on again, so that we can fall into their laps in style. What I'm saying is that we ought to be ready so that when the power does come on we can choose our moment, not too close to them and not too far to drop, and jump. We may have a chance that way.'

'I'd rather be arrested.'

'Ah well, in that case,' I said dismissively.

'Wouldn't you?'

'Listen, Mary, I don't want to get hurt. That's my main pre-occupation in life. But at the moment I have another one as well. It's not just delivering the radio parts —' I brandished the briefcase aggressively — 'which, let's face it, you let me in for. There's another reason why I've got to get to Nowa Huta quickly, a reason I don't want to tell even you about, in case the cops worm it out of you. But I've decided I'm going to do it, and I will.'

Mary just sat there, at a slight angle because of the way the cable car was swaying, and looked at me.

'If you're unlucky,' I said, 'they'll think you know more than you do about underground Solidarity, and you could be in for a nasty time with them.' I didn't like saying it to her, but it seemed only fair. 'Tadeusz Nowak is a big figure in the underground. They'll never believe you didn't know that. And they'll want to find out all about your little group in Paris. And I mean *all* about it.'

She was looking out at the late afternoon sunshine by this stage. 'I suppose you're telling me this for my own good.' I

152

didn't say anything.

'It's just I'm getting tired of running around and I don't like heights.'

'Why not get out of them, then?'

'Very funny. I don't like breaking my legs, either.'

I couldn't make any promises about that. But I did remember that the poor old partisan had done it, and I couldn't see why we shouldn't, if we were just a little bit lucky.

'The ground slopes up quite fast,' I said, encouragingly. 'If you look, you can see.' She looked. 'It'll take us a couple of minutes, maybe, to get to that bit there, where the trees dip, and then it'll only be about twenty feet below us.'

'Twenty feet? That's like jumping from the second storey of a building.'

'But if we hang by our hands, it'll mean that our feet will only be around fourteen feet from the ground — and with your height, you'll probably only have ten feet to drop.' She grinned, briefly. 'Fourteen feet is perfectly possible.'

'On to trees?'

'We'll have to miss the trees.' Why am I bothering? I thought; much safer just to stay here and take what's coming to us. Solidarity's a goner anyway.

I think if Mary had raised any more objections, I would have given up there and then. But it was like a relay race between us, and she had the baton now.

'All right,' she said, her face brightening up. 'As long as you promise you think it'll work.'

What could I do but promise? If I were wrong, it would be one of those promises I wouldn't have to keep.

'I can see we do have one big advantage,' she said, and I looked at her warily. I didn't want any jokes now, not even my own.

'Neither the people at the ground station nor the ones up at Myslenickie Turnie can see us from here. They won't know we've jumped until the cable car comes up empty.'

'They'll be like fishermen reeling in an old boot,' I said, but what I thought was, They'll need a wheelbarrow and a shovel to scrape us up off the mountainside.

We sat there, with nothing to do. It was utterly silent, except for the wind. Hungry and tired, we lay down on the benches

153

and dozed.

It must have been about a hour later, with the sun starting to shine into the cable-car on a level with us, that the whole thing jerked into life once more, and we started moving on up the mountain. For a moment, I was completely disoriented by the suddenness of it. I may have started shouting. Mary, who always woke more swiftly than I did, was already getting herself ready.

'No second thoughts?'

'Not really,' she said, and smiled at me.

'Would you give me a kiss first?' I asked, and she did. After that I felt better. And when she discovered a bar of chocolate in her handbag and we shared it out, I felt better still.

We could see how far we had to go, though it was soon obvious that I'd misjudged the place. We passed over the fold in the mountains, where the dwarf pines dipped, a good forty feet still above the level of the ground. But it was getting closer. We'd misjudged something else as well; by now the station at Myslenickie Turnie was in sight, a squat building made out of granite blocks, partially silhouetted against the mountainside and looking extremely sinister. Beside it I could see a couple of parked cars; they must have had a terrible time getting up the stony track, and the UBEKs' tempers weren't likely to have been improved.

The cable-car was still climbing, and the ground was still shelving upwards at a sharper angle than we were. I decided it was time to open the door.

The air was sharp and exhilarating, but the cold frightened me as well; the inside of the cable car had become rather comfortable, like home. It also seemed an appalling thing to have to lower oneself out into space and hang on by the hands, especially carrying an absurd briefcase. I had contemplated dropping it but — even if I could find it again — all there would be left of the equipment would be a few slivers of broken glass and bits of wire. I was going to have to loop the handle of the case over my wrist; very awkward. I got down on my hands and knees, aware of Mary's eyes on me. If I shrank from this now, neither of us would jump, I knew. I looked back at her, as she too crouched down inside the cable-car ready to get out, and gave her a weak grin.

154

'From here to eternity,' I said.

I hadn't realized how the cable-car juddered as it went up the line; you didn't notice that kind of thing inside. With infinite care, I selected my hand-holds and clung on hard. My ears were full of the hammering of the wind, and the beating of my heart.

'Okay,' I shouted, my briefcase getting in the way no matter what movement I made. 'Now your turn.' We'd agreed we wouldn't lower ourselves until the last moment, partly not to alert the waiting police, and partly to save our strength. With a painful slowness, Mary crept towards me on her hands and knees, and then turned round in a cumbersome way a few inches from me.

'I'm scared, Alex,' she said, in a muffled voice. She could feel the extra jolting of the cable car now, just as I had. I gritted my teeth and clung on more tightly with my right hand, the one the briefcase hung from and touched her thigh encouragingly with my left, until she started to shuffle backwards. Neither of us was at our most dignified.

'How am I going to know when to stop? I can't look round.'

'I'll tell you when to stop.' It seemed to do something for me to have someone else to reassure, though I was pretty frightened myself. 'This is the easy bit,' I thought, and winced. Guided by my hand, she moved backwards, grabbing convulsively at the door-frame; from time to time the open door swung alarmingly backwards and forwards. My arms were starting to quiver with fear.

I looked down, gritting my teeth. Heights are things I've never coped with very well, and even during my childhood in the Tatra highlands I hadn't done any rock-climbing or mountaineering. But the sight was more or less reassuring: there were fewer and fewer pine trees as we got higher, and the gaps between them were certainly large enough to aim for. It looked to me as though the ground was only about twenty-five feet away now, though I knew that kind of estimate could be deceptive.

'We'll start hanging down in a moment,' I shouted, trying to sound enthusiastic about it. 'Don't forget, keep your knees bent and relax all you can. And when you land, roll over as far as possible.' I've no idea where I'd picked up all this parachuting lore: books, I suppose.

'All right,' she said, more quietly. 'But let's get it over with.'

As I'd thought, kneeling down in the doorway was the easy part. Directly I tried to ease myself out of the car altogether, the wind whipped around and buffeted me with a terrifying force. Gradually I eased my legs back, until my feet were on the very rim of the car step — and then my feet were free, and then my legs, and then I was swinging in the wind and clutching on to my hand-holds literally for dear life.

'For Christ's sake, come on,' I bellowed, the wind catching my words and ripping them out of my mouth. 'I can't hang on much longer.'

Gamely, Mary pushed herself into position on the cable-car step beside me in a way that frightened me more than ever. It took her a good deal longer, partly because she was much more cautious, and partly because there was less room. I looked down: the tops of the dwarf pines seemed appallingly close to my feet now. I yelled at her again, and this time she seemed to realize the urgency. With a little moan, she launched herself out, her jeans flapping angrily round her legs in the wind, and hung there alongside me, gasping for breath.

Somehow I found a reserve of calmness, and forced myself to relax. The quivering of my muscles lessened. I shouted to her to relax as well, but she didn't answer. I turned my head to look at her, and her face was pallid with fear. Below us, the ground seemed to be coming up fast. I peered under the body of the cable car, and saw what looked like an open stretch ahead.

'When I say the word, we'll drop. Okay?' I looked at her. 'Okay?' I yelled again. She nodded this time. There was a pause, and I thought my foot had grazed the top of a tree, though it may just have been the wind. I was unnaturally conscious of my aching arms and of the way my briefcase was digging into my wrist. My head was bent forward to its maximum, as though I were praying, and I saw the stony bare rock beneath me as the trees faded away.

'*Go!*' I screamed, and felt myself falling and tried to relax and flex my knees but had scarcely had the time to do it when I hit the ground a terrible blow, which jarred every bone in my body and left me almost winded on the hillside. I'd landed

156

on my right foot, and hadn't rolled over at all. So much for books, I thought, as I lay there, the eternal briefcase beside me. I touched it and thought I could feel the things inside it individually, but I may have been wrong.

Something else was wrong: I was alone. I scrambled up, wincing with pain, and was appalled to see Mary still hanging on to the ledge of the cable-car, her legs scissoring in the wind, too frightened to jump.

'Let go, for Christ's sake,' I screamed, and whether because she heard me, or because she couldn't hold on any longer anyway, she did let go, hurtling downwards like a letter 'X', her arms up in the air, her long hair streaming out and her legs rigid and wide apart.

'Oh my God,' I said, possibly in Polish, and went leaping off over the rocks and up the hill towards where she had fallen. I couldn't see her at first, because of the trees, but she wasn't all that far away. She was lying on the ground on her side, not moving.

'Mary!' I cried. I couldn't imagine what we'd do if something had happened to her: give ourselves up, I suppose. I knelt down beside her; she was out cold, but breathing. I felt her arms and legs gingerly. As far as I could tell, no bones were broken. There were several large rocks around, and I assumed she had hit her head on one. I sat beside her helplesssly, rubbing her hands and wrists.

Then I heard the barking and realized that the police, too, must have seen us drop. Panicking, I shook her roughly, as though to wake her from sleep. If she'd been badly injured it would probably have been the worst thing I could have done but — thank God — it seemed to do the trick. She opened her eyes.

'Where am I?' she asked, just as people do in books.

'In trouble,' I answered, feeling an immense wave of relief that she seemed to be all right. 'We've got to get away from here. Do your recuperating somewhere else.'

She looked up at me. 'You were scared too,' she said, as if she'd been conscious all the time.

'Listen,' I said, more urgently, 'those are dogs, and they're searching for us. We've got to get away from here fast.'

'I don't think I can walk.'

I pulled her to her feet, and after a little while she even managed to run. I don't know how she did it — she looked as though she felt worse than I did, and I knew only too well that I'd dropped twenty feet on to a rocky hillside. Once she fainted for a moment or two, but I forced her on as soon as she came round. I didn't know which way we were going except that it was mostly downhill. Anything to put a little more distance between us and the eager barking of those dogs.

CHAPTER EIGHT

'The anti-socialist underground still exists here and there, it is true; but it is composed exclusively of parasites and work-shirkers, egged on by the aggressive propaganda continually beamed at Poland by Western radio stations.' — Polish radio broadcast.

In spite of everything it was still cold in the room and, no matter how low they tried to keep their voices, the sound echoed alarmingly off the white tiles around the walls. They'd set up tables and chairs, and there was the desk for the ham radio too, with an ingenious system for the aerial, which went the full height of the building but was invisible from the outside. The whole complex was ideal for a secret organization: ways in and out, an elaborate system of watchers and alarms, enough places to look after anything up to twenty people for a week, or even more if necessary.

Stefan Smykowski looked round the room with a certain amount of pride. He would have preferred a window in here, but there would at least be complete security. It was a privilege for Cracow to have been chosen as the centre for the national congress of Solidarity's underground movement, and it was also a serious responsibility. He looked across at the desk where the radio man would sit.

'Tell me what it is again that we need.'

'It's called a power transistor. You can't get them here, and you can't just make them up out of spare parts.'

'And what does it do?'

The radio operator told him, but he knew that Smykowski wasn't paying much attention. They'd had the conversation before, and in this strange white environment, rather like a

159

hospital, it irritated him to have to go through it all over again.

'Damn it,' Smykowski said. He didn't care what the piece of equipment did, but he was angry at the effects of not having it. It took three men off the strength of the security staff, men who had to travel the length and breadth of Poland to pass messages which could have been sent by radio and completed in ten minutes.

'It's good that they'd decided to hold the congress here before they knew what had happened, I suppose.'

The radio operator nodded, though he was less enthusiastic. Holding the congress in Cracow simply increased the danger that they would all be caught. He'd lost two friends already in the sweeps the UB carried out for illegal radio transmitters; he wasn't keen to go and join them.

Smykowski sat down on the edge of the table.

'Three more days,' he said. 'That means that most of them will be leaving on Thursday. Not much time to send out messages by courier.' He felt that they ought to let them all know that everything was still ready and in operation. They'd have to make do with a clumsy form of telephone code instead, but that was dangerous and imprecise.

'I hate being restricted by all these mechanical things,' he said, and the radio operator nodded politely. Now that they were going to be stuck here together, they would have to get on well.

'I'm from the highlands originally, you know,' Smykowski said. 'I'm a carpenter at heart. I don't understand all your power transistors and all these other things.' This time the radio operator didn't offer to teach him.

The door opened, and the second in command of security came in.

'If Nowak left here last night, shouldn't he be back by now?'

'He should have been back last night. I checked at his flat this morning. Anna hasn't seen him.'

'He could have spent the night there. This man who came from Paris with the equipment — maybe he could have been late?'

'Maybe.' The security man shrugged; it wasn't really his concern at the moment.

'But you think he could have been picked up?'

'Not Tadeusz, no. He's too smart for that.'

'Out in the country like that, though — it was a stupid thing to have agreed to.'

'Don't worry so much, Stefan. He'll come back all right, and we'll have your radio going in no time. Give him a couple more hours, and then you'll see.'

Smykowski grumbled, and fidgeted with some papers. He didn't like irregularity.

'Is Anna around still?'

A minute or two later she came in, running a hand through her mane of curly dark brown hair.

'Did you want to see me, Stefan?'

'You're going across to Nowa Huta again, aren't you?' He handed her some papers for the strike committee at the Fourteenth Special Steel works there. There was also a transcript of foreign broadcasts.

'Just to show we still love them, eh?' He smiled and patted her shoulder. Anna brought a glow of brightness to their operations, he felt. She beamed at him now, and gathered the papers together.

'Sorry you haven't heard from Tadeusz yet. You think he's all right?'

'I'm sure he is, Stefan. He said last night before he went that he might have to spend the night there if it got too late.'

'Doesn't sound like much of a boyfriend.'

She grinned as she went out, and he watched the thick door close behind her, still smiling, before turning and winking at the radio operator.

'What about it, though?' he said to the security man. 'Do you think we ought to send out some more couriers, just to let everyone know things are all right?'

'I'm sure that if they don't hear any bad news from us they'll know it's all right.'

'But we're going to need that damned radio by Friday, that's what worries me.'

'You don't need to worry, Stefan. Those parts are in good hands. They'll be here in no time.'

'I can't believe it,' I said, conversationally. We were taking a few minutes' rest in the woodland, with the crocuses yellow and white and mauve all round us. Mary was lying down, looking exhausted. We'd just eaten the last of the chocolate. The sound of barking dogs came faintly to us, seeming further off now.

'What can't you believe?'

'I've just remembered another thing about this area. It's like being a character in my own book. I only wrote a long footnote about him, really, but even so it's weird to be following in his tracks.'

'Whose?'

'Captain Fire — Kapitan Ogien. Our parents used to frighten us by telling us stories about him after the war. He was a guerrilla chief round here and fought the Russians in 1945. If his lot caught any Russians, they did dreadful things to them — blinded them, cut their balls off, you know. Not that the Russians were any better when they caught them. Quite a lot of our parents sympathized with Captain Fire, of course: I'm sure my father did. But they didn't dare say so. The gangs used to come roaring down into places like Zakopane at night-time, shooting and yelling, and they'd kidnap all the Communist officials, the mayors and so on, and bring them back up here. We've come to the right place if we want to be outlaws.'

Mary didn't seem to be taking any notice. She knew we had to set off again soon.

Making our way through the crocuses was like walking through the carpeting department at Harrods. There were other flowers on the open ground: edelweiss, and big eight-petalled white and yellow ones whose names I didn't know, either in Polish or in English. In the late afternoon sunlight it was a glorious sight.

We stopped a couple of times to wash our feet in the freezing streams that criss-crossed the mountains, but the second time I realized it was a mistake, and that our feet were swelling too much for the relief of cold water to be worth it — we both found it difficult to put our shoes back on. However, the hunt seemed to have been shaken off and we had established fairly clearly where we were going. I'd decided that we should follow the mountains down to the plain, skirt round Zakopane to the

162

east, and head for Poronin during the night, so that we could catch the bus for Cracow early in the morning. As the crow flew, Poronin was only eight miles away. The trouble was, the crow didn't have to do it on foot.

For a time, though, the walking was relatively easy and we weren't under much pressure. We could, it's true, occasionally hear the barking of the police dogs, but it seemed to come from the west of us, higher up the mountain.

'What kind of place would you like to live in, when we get back?' I asked encouragingly.

She didn't answer for a while, grimacing with pain and effort.

'I don't know — a house, I suppose, or maybe a flat.'

'Or a cottage, a few more miles out? They're cheaper and more attractive.'

It seemed absurd to be talking about house prices in Britain when we were on the run in Poland, but it was a way of keeping our minds occupied.

'Not somewhere corny like Grantchester, but out further, in the real Cambridgeshire.' I gestured grandly with my brief-case. 'We could have a big garden, maybe even a paddock so you could keep a horse.' I had a vision of her as a little girl, perched obediently on the back of a pony in the middle of Highgate, with the traffic passing all round.

'Yes.' She sounded preoccupied. Maybe she's reconsidering, I thought, and hoped she wasn't. I was holding her hand at the time, helping her descend a small patch of bare rock, with water trickling down it. I must have pulled her a little too hard because she shouted out in pain and I saw she was on the point of tears. I hovered round her, not knowing quite what to do or say.

'Where does it hurt?'

'My side, I banged it when I fell. It hurts even more when I breathe.'

I felt her rib-cage carefully, bone by bone, but as far as I could tell she was only bruised. 'I'm sorry your side hurts,' I said, not knowing what else I could do.

'That's not the real problem.' She looked magnificent when she was angry: her face took on an added colour, and she drew herself up to her full height. Oh God, I thought, we're going to quarrel again. I could see it hurt her to grow angry at me, but it hurt me more. It reminded me dreadfully of the last phone conversation we'd had, before we broke up in Paris. Only this time we'd chosen a Police mountain-top for the setting.

It was at precisely that moment we both heard the sound of the helicopter.

We stared at each other in fear. Starting to believe we had thrown the pursuit off, we'd got careless. Instead of keeping to the woods and adding more to our journey, we'd taken the short cut across open ground. And there was a great deal of open ground, reaching for several miles in one direction and at least one mile straight ahead. The alternative was to head back up the mountain for the cover of the woods, but even that was about half a mile away.

'Perhaps if we lay flat and didn't draw attention to ourselves?'

'Out of the question,' I shouted, worked up by fear. 'We'll just have to go back, and hope we get there before the helicopter sees us.'

We turned wearily around again, and started to plough our way uphill. All the time we could hear the insistent buzzing sound of the helicopter, searching for us in the open spaces of the mountain.

'How much more daylight is there, do you think?'

I looked at my watch, and at the position of the sun, and tried to guess. 'Another couple of hours?'

'They'll find us by then.'

'Don't for Christ's sake give up now,' I shouted. 'Just try and keep going.'

But it was hard. Her breathing was heavier because we were going uphill, and it obviously hurt her. I was getting very tired too, and there was something deeply dispiriting about having to cover ground we'd already passed over. I remembered things about it — the rocks, the pattern of the flowers. And all the time the helicopter seemed to be getting closer.

There were times, in fact, when the engine note changed, and the Doppler effect led me to think it had decided to head in a different direction. But I realized eventually that it was simply patrolling the hillside, moving closer and closer to us, then veering away on a down-leg before coming back towards us again. We were only halfway to the wood, and the noise was more insistent. Soon we would see it, and the men in it would probably be able to see us.

Mary was slowing up alarmingly, her breath coming in great gasps, and occasionally she moaned as she clambered up the steep hillside. I did what I could to help her, but she didn't seem to want to be helped.

'Listen, Alex,' she said urgently, trying to catch her breath. 'I'm not going to be able to go much farther. Why don't you head off as quick as you can? Without me, you could make it to the woods, and they'll spend so much time getting hold of me they won't bother about you till it's too late.' She even managed a smile. 'Go on, please. It's best, you know.'

Perhaps it would have been. No doubt Tadeusz Nowak would have felt it was best too, and the national Solidarity committee, if they'd been asked. But somehow, with the sun shining on her, and her face twisted with the pain of so much effort, I couldn't possibly walk away from her.

'I want you to, Alex. Don't play heroes, please. I want you to get to Cracow. I know it's important.'

'We're wasting time,' I said as shortly as I could. 'Either we go on together, or we stay here together. I'm not having you do a reverse Captain Oates on me.'

She smiled again at that, and we waited there for five minutes, allowing the decision to be taken almost by default. Perhaps it was standing up and trying to walk that attracted the helicopter pilot's attention. He had been criss-crossing the valley a little way down from us, but broke off abruptly in the middle of his down-leg and headed straight across the intervening wood towards us. Both of us gave up at that point. Mary sank down on to the ground again, and I knelt beside her. I didn't even want to look at the helicopter.

It was a bright orange-red, some Russian design, I suppose, with a great perspex pod on the front that looked like a demonstration model of the brain of some huge insect. I could see the pilot and his observer quite clearly; they were wearing orange overalls that almost matched the body of their machine. The two rotors were close enough to blow the crocuses around, and whip up a storm of dust and small pebbles of granite. I even saw the pilot talking into his RT set, describing what we

165

looked like and looking round to the observer to get a confirmation of our exact position.

I could have told him our exact position: apathetic. It was all over, the will to stay free had gone. As far as I was concerned, they could do what they wanted. In the flying dust and the racketing noise of the rotors, I looked at Mary, but she was lying down in just the same position as I'd found her in after she'd jumped from the cable-car, her eyes closed as she flinched away from the helicopter's blast. There was nothing more to say, nothing more to do. I was relieved more than anything else. Nowak couldn't say I hadn't tried. I looked down at my briefcase, which I'd bought cheap in a closing-down sale in Cambridge: it had played its part well, but I wouldn't need it any more. Ahead of me, ten feet or so off the ground, the great orange insect was still hovering, and I saw the pilot turn to the observer and point. The machine bucked a little in the air, and settled down towards the ground, its rotors becoming deafening and the storm of small objects flying around quite lethal.

And then it had landed. The rotors carried on turning fast, but the lift had gone out of them. The observer opened the door and jumped to the ground, a gun of some kind in his hand. He won't be needing that, I thought dully. Beside me, Mary was still motionless, expressionless even in the face of the blast of air from the helicopter.

'Lie down, hands on the back of your neck,' the observer shouted above the din. The helicopter began to rise from the ground at an angle, heading upwards and away in the direction it had come from.

'Don't touch her,' I said, as I obeyed him, pulling my briefcase with me. 'She was hurt when we jumped out of the cable-car.'

He looked at her curiously, seeing the whiteness of her face and her closed eyes, and nodded. He didn't seem an altogether bad sort, I thought, though he was nervous. He had an intelligent face and thin long hands with blue veins on the backs. The hands were most clearly visible from my position: and the gun he was holding.

'What's going to happen now?'

'Shut up and lie there.'

'Is the helicopter coming back?'

166

'Shut up, I said.'

For a time I did, but something stirred in me, and I wanted to know.

'She can't walk any further. What are you going to take her in?'

Intelligent people aren't able to ignore questions, I've noticed. He settled back on his heels, squatting down a yard or so behind me, and said, 'There wasn't enough room in the helicopter for you. They're going to bring the militia-van here.' He had a Warsaw accent.

'Is it the militia or the UBEKs?'

'I'm not answering any more questions. Shut up.' He seemed to have lost his nervousness now.

'Do you know anything about first aid?'

'No.'

'Well, have a look at the girl anyway. She's not doing so well.'

In the exaggerated silence that had fallen since the helicopter went, I could hear his knees creak.

'Can I move?' I asked.

'No you bloody can't. Shut up.' His voice sounded as though he were stooping down. I risked a look round: he was.

'What are you, police or air force?'

'Air force. Don't ask any more questions.'

Mary moaned a little, and I saw him go down on one knee beside her. It made him look more like a human being. It was that, I think, that started me on a new train of thought. That, and the fact that I was half lying on my briefcase, and could feel the boxes inside digging into me. What remained of the Solidarity organization in Poland depended on getting those bits of equipment to Nowa Huta, and all that stood in the way was a rather decent air force man with sensitive hands. And a gun. If he had been a thug, I might not have been so keen.

'Listen, she's in a bad way,' I said.

'She'll live.'

'If she doesn't, it'll be your bloody fault. I'm a doctor; please let me see to her.' I was amazed at the fluency of my lies, though I suppose it was literally true that I was a doctor.

'Don't try anything.'

Mary was looking ill, her face white and her lips a strange

167

dark colour. Suddenly I saw what I was going to do.

'I'm going to get my case; there's something in there I need.'

He pointed his gun at me, and the barrel watched me like an eye. It seemed remarkably big. I went back to where I'd been lying and picked up the briefcase. Then I went back and squatted down beside Mary. The air force observer was about six feet away from me, but I didn't want to crowd him.

'We'll have to turn her on her back,' I said. 'I'll take the legs, you take the head. And be careful.' He started to bend down, and I held the briefcase towards him. He straightened up immediately, the gun looking at me again.

'Don't get so excited. I'll need it to treat her.' I felt the weight of it, and knew that something inside would be heavy enough: the power transistor, roughly the shape and size of a brick, wrapped up in its absurd disguise from the *chocolatier*. It would require ϵ lot of fast talking to make anyone think it was a piece of medical equipment, I could see that.

'If it'll make you relax a bit, you can see everything inside. But let's get her into the proper position first.'

He nodded, his eyes still on me warily. Lesson one, I thought: don't be a nice guy.

'For Christ's sake watch out,' I shouted at him. 'Look at her face.' He jerked his head aside to look, and the hand that held his gun moved slightly. I had no time to swing the briefcase, but I brought it down as hard as I could on the hand with the gun. He squeezed the trigger, and the bullet hammered into the ground. With Mary lying right beside him, that was a mercy.

There was fear in his face now, as well as surprise, and that gave me the necessary brutality I needed. I launched myself at him and he fell back, his legs kicking at Mary's body, his head hitting the ground. I banged his head on the ground a second time, harder than I had meant to, and he didn't get up.

'I think you must have killed him.'

I suddenly felt faint.

'He was nice, Alex.'

To my relief he grunted, and opened his mouth, though he still seemed to be unconscious.

'Don't you think you'd better do something about the gun?'

I looked down. The thigh of my trousers seemed to have been burned by the flash of the bullet, and there was another burn on my briefcase. The stench of smoke and the gases of the bullet hung around us still. I could have been killed, I thought. Then I remembered his gun, and loosened his hold on it.

'What are we going to do?' She seemed to have remarkable powers of recuperation.

The air force man lay on his back, his eyes closed and his face as white as Mary's, with a look of surprise and concentration still on it, as though he'd been trying to decide how he got there.

I looked at the gun, then stuck it in my pocket.

'We'll have to tie him up and leave him. We're going to have to get away from here very fast. They're sending a van for us.'

'I know, I heard everything.'

'So you weren't as bad as you looked?'

'I don't know about how I looked. I just thought that if I seemed to be really ill you might get the chance to do something.'

He was stirring now: in real life people don't usually stay unconscious for conveniently long periods like they do in thrillers. This time I had the gun, and the death-dealing briefcase as well. I showed them both to him, and he didn't seem to want to argue.

'I'm going to tie you up, I'm afraid.'

He looked at me. 'I wouldn't have killed you, you know,' he said, faintly. 'Even though you are a spy.'

I felt like apologizing to him, in the English manner, but there was enough of the Pole in me to think in practical terms.

'I'm going to have to take those orange overalls off you,' I said, and while Mary held the gun I pulled the jacket over his head. His skull looked mushy and wet at the back, and I sympathized with him. He winced, rolled over, and was sick.

'I'm sorry,' he said, his face a ghastly green. He was even more embarrassed when I pulled his trousers off so that he was in his underpants. He didn't seem to know what to do with his hands.

'You can't leave him like that,' Mary said, as I tied him up with his belt.

'All right,' I said, wearily, and took my raincoat off, and laid it over his puny white figure, so that he looked like the statue of the dead soldier on the Royal Artillery monument at Hyde

Park Corner in London. I tucked the orange overalls under his head, gently.

'Thank you,' he croaked, and I thought he was going to be sick again. I hung around guiltily, till I decided we'd better be going. 'I hope they come soon,' I said, without thinking. We left him lying there, a heap of old clothes on the hillside.

From our point of view they came a great deal too soon. We first heard the whine of the helicopter when we were still a good two hundred yards from the woods. Neither of us was in much of a state to run, but we did the best we could.

The pilot must have worked out what had happened the moment he saw the figure of his observer, and from there to seeing us and making his mind up where we were going was only a matter of a few seconds. No doubt he reported it all back faithfully to the UBEKs at Myslenickie Turnie. The only person who lost out in all this was the unfortunate observer. No one bothered to look after him.

We ploughed on towards the woods, occasionally turning our ankles on the rocks, and leaping from high point to high point. Something kept bumping against my thigh, and for a moment I couldn't think what it was. Then I remembered: the gun. Would it be better if I threw it away, I wondered? But I didn't want to stop even for the moment or two it would take to fish it out of my pocket.

The helicopter was near now, and swinging low down, close to the ground. I'd seen people being hunted by helicopter in films, but I had no idea what to do. In the films, they swooped down and tried to knock you over. But like so many things that happen in films, the length of time people stay unconsious for one, it bore little relation to real life. This helicopter pilot wasn't out to get martyrdom for himself by putting his precious machine at risk. Instead, he used it as a shepherd uses a dog, to herd us in the direction he wanted. He flew over us and to the side, hovering close to the ground between us and the wood. We immediately halted, uncertain what to do. We were panting and limp with fatigue by now, and Mary must have been in a bad way.

'It's no good,' she said faintly.

'We can't stop now — not after what we've done.'

170

She nodded. 'How do we get away?' Her voice was weak, and it hurt her even to talk.

'I don't know.' But I thought, perhaps, that I did. When we'd stopped, so had the helicopter, about fifty yards away from us. If he didn't want to risk his machine, I reasoned, where could we go that would make him risk it?

'We've only got one chance — that mountain scree over there.' Mary looked, and she must have felt as hopeless as I did: the scree was a good way from us, perhaps a quarter of a mile. But I knew that if we got there the helicopter would be powerless to stop us.

'Have you still got the gun?' I knew what she meant, but I wasn't prepared to consider the idea. If we — if I — shot down a helicopter and killed a pilot, they'd execute me the moment they caught us. And the chances were they would catch us. The only thing I was prepared to kill was a bird or two to eat if we got the chance. After that I'd throw the gun away.

We lurched off at an angle to our previous path; the helicopter lifted a little too, and lurched with us. It was low, but not that low. It shadowed us, moving even more slowly than we were, but trying always to keep between us and the thick wood of pine trees. It was frightening, somehow, and made me feel small and powerless, like being a child again in the arms of a powerful adult: my father came briefly to mind. Our only chance was to make the pilot think we still intended reaching the wood, and to keep him between it and us until it was time to break for the hillside. It seemed a wild gamble, but it was the only thing left to us now.

'We could always split up,' Mary said, as we stopped running for a moment. She seemed on her last legs, but I knew she had great reserves of courage and energy. She held on to her side for a moment, and I remembered the fall she'd taken.

'I'll try holding down the helicopter while you head for the hillside.' It was so simple I wondered we hadn't thought of it before.

Slowly, reluctantly, I lumbered straight for the helicopter, while Mary made her way to my left, walking now and holding her side as she went. I looked round a couple of times to make sure she was all right, and almost lost my footing as I did so. The helicopter wobbled in the air, like a living creature which couldn't think what the hell to do. But it must have decided that I was the one to stick with. It moved backwards and forwards, hanging ten or twelve feet in the air, about fifty yards from me and the same distance from the edge of the pinewood. I headed towards it, and for good measure I bent down a couple of times and picked up some good fist-sized stones, so the pilot could see me and work out what I was planning to do.

It was head on towards me now, hovering with its tail high in the air. Then it started to move, coming for me in order to show who was boss. I kept on walking. My heart was beating so hard I could almost hear it over the noise of the clattering rotor-blades. I could see the pilot by this time, grinning nastily, out to teach me not to attack air force personnel. We were only twenty yards apart, and I shied one of the rocks straight at him. It had absolutely no chance of damaging the helicopter of course, but I saw the sudden look of alarm on the pilot's face, even though the stone dropped harmlessly short.

I glanced across the open ground; Mary was nearly there now, and I only had to stay a few more moments. I was calling the pilot's bluff by making straight for his helicopter, and he had to work out some counter move. I shied another of my rocks at him, and then another, and the third hit the perspex bubble not far from his head, though it didn't have the force to crack it. He laughed at that, and did the one thing I hadn't expected. He started to put the helicopter down on the ground.

As he struggled with the door I turned and belted across after Mary, watching her as she approached the foot of the scree. Behind me, the pilot must have taken up a firing position, because as the racket of the rotor-blades died down I could hear the distinct crack of a pistol shot. But by that time I didn't care. There was another crack in the air, and something sang close to me like an angry bee, but I kept on running.

I've no idea how long it took me to fight my way across to Mary. She lay at the foot of the scree, on the boulders that had fallen down with it over the years, and her face was as white as it had been earlier.

'I don't think I can take any more of this, Alex,' she said.

'Just a bit more, my darling.'

'I thought you weren't going to do any shooting.'

'I didn't. It was all his.'

172

I looked back. The pilot had started the rotors again, and the helicopter would soon be hovering, but it wouldn't come over here: the pilot would simply watch us and report our position to the UBEKs. We wouldn't get away from them until it was dark; and there was almost an hour of daylight left. It was far and away the longest day of my life.

They were in full view even before we reached the top of the scree: perhaps a dozen men in plain clothes, and a couple of dark-coloured dogs continually barking.

The half-hour climb hadn't been easy. Fortunately, the scree was constructed of biggish boulders, rather than small stones that hang on the mountain side like a frozen waterfall. You really had to push one hard to set up any kind of landslide.

'There's no point in carrying on,' one of the plain-clothes-men shouted, and his voice echoed off the rock walls around us. 'We've got you in a corner, Serafinski.' A couple of shots rang out, but they weren't aimed at us.

Mary began to cry, as much from exhaustion as from fear.

'Don't bother about them,' I said. 'If they'd really got us they wouldn't waste their energy shouting at us. And they aren't trying to hit us.' Mary nodded, but didn't say anything. Logic was all very well, I thought — but maybe no one had explained it to the UBEKs. She looked woe-begone now, her face streaked with dirt and sweat, her hair hanging down raggedly, her sweater inside the short coat still showing its jaunty blue and white willow pattern, but it was grimy now. Her jeans were torn.

'You don't look much better,' she said, knowing what I was thinking. I grinned at her.

'I never do,' I said.

'Give yourself up, Serafinski.' The voice echoed around, and the dogs barked, not liking the competition. Somehow it irritated me. We had got so close to the top that it was a waste of time, I knew; all the same, I knelt beside a boulder the size of an armchair, and started to push at it.

'For God's sake, Alex, you'll hurt yourself.' Mary was sitting down now. She needed every moment's rest she could get. I didn't take any notice. I concentrated my attention on the little star-shaped flowers growing in between the boulders, the aptly named *saxifraga perdurans*, and put everything I had into heaving my boulder down the slope. I nearly put a little too much into it; when it began to shift, it took with it the smaller rocks which had settled underneath it and there was a gradual downward movement that had me going as well. Mary screamed, but I knew she was all right, several feet above me, though the stones must have shifted under her too. I had to grip another biggish boulder to keep my foothold, but by this time there was a small avalanche building up below us. A scree on the move is a magnificent and rather frightening sight, with boulders leaping over one another and a constant undermovement that looks like one of those walking pavements they have at airports, except that it's composed of rocks and stones. The dogs below really had something to bark about now, and the UB men shouted and pushed, trying to get out of the way of the falling stones. As I watched a single rock, not more than the size of my two fists, came leaping out of the general movement and took the foremost UBEK clean on the head as he looked up to see what was happening. He bent over backwards, and went down with the rest of the landslide. I was laughing now, though even in my own ears the laughter sounded strange. Reason was tottering on its throne after a difficult day, I decided, and turned my back on the problems of the UBEKs and their dogs.

The movement beneath our feet came to an end, and I decided it was safe to climb the last eight or ten feet to the top. Mary needed to be pulled. I would have carried her, if her side hadn't hurt her so much. We would have to hole up for the night soon.

It's always the same with mountains: you reach one height, only to find more beyond it. There were more beyond now, and although the gloom was growing I could see there wasn't any real cover anywhere for some way round.

'The cops won't take as long as we did to climb that scree,' I said. 'We must find somewhere we can shelter pretty quickly.'

Mary looked around listlessly, and asked, 'What's wrong with those old ruins over there?'

Maybe her eyesight was better than mine, but it was some moments before I could see any ruins. They were about a hundred and fifty yards away, four or five shapes that appeared to be out-crops of rock, but which — when you peered more closely — turned out to be crudely constructed huts. From the way the weeds and grass were growing over them it seemed that none of them had roofs. I thought about it. In a way, they were the natural place for the UBEKs to search, once they had scrambled to the top of the scree. But it would be twilight before they stood where we were now, and I doubted if any of them would spot the ruins then. The dogs, of course, might follow us, but we would have to take that risk. I looked down again. Only about five UBEK men were climbing the scree, together with the two dogs. The rest seemed to be looking after their colleague who had been hit by the flying rock, or else telling the others what to do. As for the helicopter, that had taken the injured observer away and hadn't come back. The odds were lengthening in our favour.

One of the UBEK men down in the valley saw that I'd reached the top, and shouted something to the others. I gave them a rude Polish sign and moved away. We were in a hurry now.

Mary made it to the ruins, but only just. If I'd hoped there might be some alternative, I knew now that there wasn't; I was pretty exhausted myself. The huts looked better from a distance than they did close up. They certainly offered no shelter from the weather, and they seemed to have been burned, which would have explained the missing roofs. As we lay there, Mary all but unconscious, my mind worked overtime as it always does when I'm most in need of sleep. Who could have established a settlement here in the mountains, and when? This could never have been a village: it was too small for that. A camp, then? I looked around me some more. The walls were overgrown with moss and lichen, but in one or two places you could see that they had once been painted. Whitewashed, I guessed, but the fire would have dealt with that. Down by the floor, though, the fire hadn't caught. I rubbed away at the lichen: there were flakes not of white but of red. I gave it up and settled my back against the wall. It was rather more important to know if the UBEKs were coming, and I set myself to listen for them. All the same, I couldn't help thinking about it. White and red paint.

175

When the answer came to me, it was so sudden that I jerked upright out of an uneasy doze as my semi-conscious mind presented the solution. Captain Fire: his men must have set up camp here, and painted this wall in Poland's national colours. It felt extraordinary to be there when I'd written about it, as though one of us must be a figment of the other's imagination. The Russians, or maybe the Polish Communists, had tracked him down here, taken him and his men prisoner, and burned their camp. Captain Fire had been executed in Zakopane, and nothing had ever been said officially about him again in Poland; no one was allowed to get the idea that there had been any resistance to the establishment of People's Poland. And now here we were, the historian inhabiting the ruins of his own history. Somehow the precedent didn't seem a particularly encouraging one.

A dog barked. Another echoed the first. They seemed unpleasantly close. I understood what had happened, though. The dogs, nimbler on their feet than the heavy, reluctant UB men, had reached the top of the scree quickly, and were racing across the valley looking for us. The men would be along later, to take us once the dogs had pinned us down. I looked across at Mary, who was slumped against the wall asleep: no point in waking her. There was no point in peering out to locate the dogs, either. They'd be here in their own good time. I searched around for something to protect myself with, but there was only the rubble from the walls. I gathered together a few convenient rocks, as quietly as I could, but we would have to get to much closer quarters than I wanted if I had to use them. There was only one other thing, and I shifted my position slightly to grasp it and see what it felt like.

It felt remarkably good, as my hand curved round its butt. Though I'd always hated guns, and in the Polish army had been famous for never cleaning my rifle properly — and never being able to put it back together again once I'd taken it apart — there's no doubt that if you're being hunted down by a couple of dogs trained by the Polish secret police to attack and bring you down on sight, a gun is a heart-warming thing to have in your hand. I had it in my hand now, and I squinted down the barrel, aiming at the corner of the building.

The barking was much closer to us. The dogs had found the

huts all right, and were trying to work out where we were. It was very nearly dark now, but that wouldn't protect us. I prayed Mary would stay asleep until something happened.

I fancied I could hear the dogs, leaping from rock to rock, or sniffing round the edges of the camp. They must have got our scent, but they were taking their time following it. Maybe the huts had a smell of their own, from the unwashed partisans who had once lived here, and maybe the smell was like one of those whistles that are too high for the human ear to hear: too faint for the human nose to notice. I knew I must be getting really nervous if I was making jokes to myself.

A stone clinked. I shot bolt upright, my hand trembling slightly as I held the heavy gun away from me. I wouldn't have much chance to get the shot in, I knew that. There was another sound too, as though the dog was snuffling somewhere. I wanted to stand up and run out and blaze away, shouting and screaming; it was as much as I could do to sit there, with my back against the Polish flag, waiting for one of the dogs to put its muzzle round the ruined door-frame.

Another clink, this time on the far side of the building. Thank God there were no windows; the only way the animal could get in was through the doorway. They must have known we were there: that was why they were hunting in silence.

I could hear the blood throbbing in my ears, and my heart beat with a kind of sombre regularity which I could feel in every part of my body. Suddenly I wasn't cold any longer.

I moved my hand slightly to relieve the ache in the arm and a dog appeared silently in the doorway and stood there. It was a mongrel, but you could tell from the silhouette that it had Dobermann blood. It was a good deal taller than I had expected, with a fine massive head. In the gathering darkness, it didn't see me. Instead, it backed away a little from the gloom of the place, sniffing eagerly at the ground a short distance away.

What alerted the dog to our presence, I don't know. It might have been an involuntary move by Mary, who was still asleep, or the slipping of a pebble. It made the dog leap with fright, keyed up as it was with nerves, and then it was in the hut and on me, before I had had a chance to think. Somewhere outside, the other dog started barking and running round to search for it.

Until the dog actually touched me, I was too paralyzed with fear to shoot. But I felt its teeth sink into the cloth of my sleeve, and sheer panic took over. The sleeve was the right one: no one had told the dog that some people are left-handed. Shouting out, my hand trembling and my arm agonizingly painful from the creature's jaws, I rammed the barrel of the gun against its dreadful head, as it tore and worried my arm. Then I jerked wildly at the trigger.

In the confined space of the hut the noise was cataclysmic. The dog's head seemed to dissolve before my eyes, though its teeth stayed locked in my arm. I shook its remains off, quivering with the horror of what I had done, and the fear of what it had done to me. It's happened before, I thought, but for the moment I couldn't remember where. Two other things happened: Mary screamed out in fear, sounding hysterical, her voice cracking and bubbling, and there was a loud growl as the other dog came leaping through the doorway to avenge its dead mate. I was sickened by the noise and blood, and too afraid of hitting Mary to fire at random across the hut. The second dog was slower in its reactions than the first, and was unsighted by the darker shadows of the hut. But it quickly saw the body of the first one, and came for me. Curiously, I felt I had all the time in the world, this time, and I knew immediately what I was going to do. In the split second before the dog leapt at me, I shot at its foreleg. It must have been a good shot, because the dog was knocked to the ground near the other one. I hadn't wanted to kill it, and I was glad it wasn't necessary. The dog was brave enough, though: as I went across to see how Mary was, it tried to lunge at me and bite me, but I kicked it down. Hurting the dogs was almost worse than attacking the air force observer; but that was because he'd known what he was doing, and he wanted to take me prisoner. These dogs were trained to do what they did; it wasn't a question of choice. And besides, they were such magnificent animals, bold and powerful and healthy. Destroying them was like smashing some beautifully designed machine. I shuddered, and my arm ached so much I nearly cried out. The other dog whined and whimpered, and getting up on its three good legs it limped out of the cabin. I let it go, sick of destruction.

Mary couldn't speak for some time, and I got the impression

that she didn't want to, even when she could. The sudden explosion of violence and noise had disoriented her, and when she saw the dog's blood on my torn sleeve she shrank away as if I were some murderer. She didn't even ask me if I had been hurt.

'I'm afraid it wrecks our chances,' I whispered, trying to show her that she should keep quiet as well. 'They must have heard the shots. It's just a question of when they find us.' I looked up at the sky: it was almost dark, but the UBEKs would still have about fifteen minutes during which it would be light enough to see.

'Why did you have to shoot?'

There was no answer to that, if she couldn't understand. I did what I could to make her comfortable, then sat down to nurse my damaged arm. It throbbed badly, but when I pulled the sleeve back I found that the creature's powerful teeth hadn't broken the skin, though even in the gathering darkness I could see the line of bruising like a big double 'U' on the upper and lower sides of my forearm. Maybe they're trained not to draw blood, I thought, and felt guilty, but I realized that was pure sentiment. Imagine the UB training its dogs not to draw blood: it was like telling the Inland Revenue not to charge people money. There was nothing to be done about the sleeve of my jacket: that was badly ripped, showing the lining underneath. It was already too dark to see the blood, but at least I knew now that it was the dog's and not mine.

It was difficult to concentrate on what we were going to do now. So much depended on whether the UBEKs decided to continue with the search, now that the dogs were gone, or whether they would call it a day and start searching again in the morning. I decided it was worth risking a look out of the doorway to see if they were around.

They were, but down by the edge of the scree still, silhouetted against the western sky, with its slight tinge of colour. I would have been completely invisible to them. There seemed only one possibility now: that they would wait until morning. But would they camp out where they were, or head back to their base? I wouldn't find that out, I thought, unless I fell over them in the darkness. Either way, it seemed a good idea not to make a noise. I crawled back and reported what I had seen to Mary.

'I can't move from here.'

'We'll have to move fairly soon, if we're going to get away.'

'All right, but not for a bit. I must get some sleep.'

I remembered Tadeusz Nowak listing lack of sleep among the hardships of life on the run. I could see him sitting in Magda's kitchen, his mouth ringed with the *barszcz*'s red, telling us how you were always cold and hungry — and needed more sleep. That seemed so long ago, I could hardly believe only twenty-four hours had passed — I felt as though I'd been a fugitive for months. Tadeusz had been right in what he'd said about the cold and hunger and fatigue. There was little I could do about the first two discomforts, and before I too could sleep I dug a hole in the rubble and buried the gun. I didn't want to see it again, ever. I had done more than enough killing and wounding already in my life.

We had timed it reasonably well: at seven-thirty, Poronin was just starting to come to life, and there were enough people in the streets for us not to be as obvious as we might have been an hour before. Mount Gubalowka towered over us again, though the day was so overcast, compared with the previous one, that there could have been other mountains which were invisible now. I remembered Poronin from my schooldays. We used to come to the Lenin museum on the village outskirts on little day trips. Lenin held some meetings with other exiles there in 1914; at that time he was proposing a free and independent Poland, and there was a statue of him outside; though of course by the time the statue was erected, Lenin's successors had made sure that Poland was as much part of their empire as it ever had been. But when I used to go there, I hadn't yet graduated to blowing up statues.

We sat in a little park in the middle of the village, with neatly kept privet hedges all round us, and small copper beeches to shelter under if it rained. An old woman trailed a big cart around as she swept up the last leaves of the autumn, bunching them together with a board and dumping them in the cart; when, that is, she wasn't stealing glimpses at us.

180

I suppose we looked pretty dreadful. People can take a ragged man with a dirty face, but a ragged young woman with a dirty face is something else. We didn't even look like gipsies. I tried to think if there was some way we could clean up before we went to the bus station, but I couldn't think of one. The old woman carried on scraping the leaves into piles, and looking at us round her headscarf.

'What do you think?' I asked Mary. She had sunk into a doze, exhausted by our long walk through the mountains, and scarcely opened her eyes to look at me. I felt alone, and uncertain. It was such a chance to take.

'Excuse me,' I said. She wasn't as old as she had seemed: maybe fifty. She looked at me in some surprise, and then looked round to see if there was any help handy. There didn't seem to be.

'Yes?' She sounded frankly hostile; people like us weren't wanted in Poronin.

'My wife and I have had an accident, and we've had to walk all the way from Murzasichle.' It was almost true; that was the nearest village to the east, a tiny place which I hoped the street-cleaner wouldn't know. 'We've got to get to Novy Targ to get our car repaired, but — as you can see — we need to clean up a bit first. Is there anywhere we could do that? We're on holiday from Warsaw, you see, and my wife's expecting, and you know how it is—' I was running out of inventions, but the word 'expecting' had done it. She no longer suspected us, she felt sorry for us and probably despised us for being from Warsaw and going around by car.

'You can go to my house, with pleasure,' she said, with the old-fashioned courtesy I remembered so well from my own childhood. 'My mother's in the house, and if you tell her Agnieszka told you to go there, she'll let you wash and tidy up. Poor little thing,' she said, looking across at Mary's five feet eleven. 'You should have been more careful.' She glanced at my sleeve, with the blood on it. 'What sort of accident was it?'

I couldn't think of any more lies for the time being.

'Dreadful, dreadful,' I said, and I spoke from the heart.

An hour later, having been refused any way of thanking the old grandmother for the hot water, the use of a small precious cake of gritty soap, and the careful job of mending she had done on my jacket, we were standing at the bus station in the centre of Poronin. I was too tired now to care about security, and led Mary to it without any precautions. But Poronin was a small place, with no police station. And if there had been reports on the radio of a new Captain Fire in the mountains, attacking helicopters and picking off UBEK dogs, no one there seemed to know anything about it.

There was a big crowd waiting for the bus. Long-distance buses, especially in the early morning, are something in Poland that nobody forms queues for; there aren't enough of them for people to be that patient. I had explained it all to Mary quite carefully, but neither of us was quite prepared for the shoving match that broke out when the Cracow bus finally appeared. There was no possibility that we would all get on — not even half of us, and perhaps not a quarter. The bus was already nearly full, and only a few seats and the gangway were empty.

The pushing began directly the bus came in sight, as people who were on the outer edges of the crowd began to realize how small their chances of getting on were. We were about in the middle of the crowd by this time, having quietly wormed our way through it during the preceding fifteen minutes. But halfway through was nowhere near enough. The pneumatic doors of the bus hissed open, and a few passengers confused the issue by getting off. That blocked two entire files of waiting people, and gave Mary and me a better chance. Losing any sense of decency, I rammed my way forward, pulling Mary after me. No one seemed to think I was acting unfairly; most of them were trying to do precisely the same thing to the people in front of them. Shouting and screaming echoed round us, and a savage fight suddenly erupted between a couple of older men. Somehow I got my foot on the bottom step of the bus, and fought my way between two women who were trying the same thing. One of them beat me to it, and slipped aboard as though she had got the last place on a *Titanic* lifeboat, but the other stood no chance. Sticking my left arm straight out in front of me, and hoisting Mary up and through the crowd with my left, I climbed on. I was so delighted that I hardly noticed when the bus conductor grabbed hold of my arm at the point where the UBEK dog had chewed it the previous evening. Only one other person got on after us, the stout woman I had forced aside.

As the doors hissed shut, and the bus jerked away from the stop towards the open road, she bore us no ill will at all. We bumped against each other jovially as we stood, holding the rail of the luggage-rack, and smiled our apologies to each other. The bus smelled of sweat and onions, and it got hotter and hotter as we drove on. I loved it, and felt we had got out of everything remarkably well. I hoisted my long-suffering brief-case on to the rack, and wondered for the hundredth time whether the crystals and the power transistor had survived. I winked at Mary, and gave the stout lady I was pressed up against a big grin. We were going to make it now.

'Do you think they'll be watching the buses from Zakopane?' It was marvellous to be sitting together. I held Mary's hand, and felt her fingers curl anxiously round mine.

'Almost for certain. That's why I think we ought to get off before we get to Cracow city centre.'

'And you don't think they'll be watched before?'

'Nothing we can do about it if they are.'

My anxieties had been succeeded by a warm sense of fatalism. If we were going to get through we would; if not, we would simply endure it as best we could. I looked at Mary's anxious face.

'Don't worry, love.'

She pulled her hand away from mine.

'The trouble with you, Alex, is that you don't take charge of things enough — you just accept what happens.' Having left a trail of wounded men and animals behind me I felt this accusation was unfair. I put it down to her tiredness.

I debated whether I should tell her now what lay ahead of us at Nowa Huta, and the effort to stop the national gathering of Solidarity leaders. I decided not to, looking at the strain on her long, tired face. The dark shadows under the eyes had become pouchy and swollen. She sat with her head against the window and went off to sleep, while I thought of the time we had last sat together in this way, in the plane from Paris.

There were ugly long buildings in concrete beside the road now, with tall television aerials like telegraph poles on the roof. And there were the endless lines of people queueing: for meat, for clothes, for bread, for vegetables. Factory chimneys belched out smoke overhead, and only the boxes of flowers on every balcony of every apartment block showed the human influence — but then, of course, it was the people who grew the flowers, and the state that grew the queues. I remembered what people in Cracow used to say, in the year or so before I left: Things are getting better now. We can go in for growth, like Western countries. You watch, within ten or twelve years we'll be the France of the socialist bloc, and Cracow will be its Lyon, or its Strasbourg.

Perhaps a touch of *Schadenfreude* afflicted the returning exile, but the outskirts of Cracow didn't look at all like Lyon or Strasbourg to me; they looked worse, if anything, than they had looked fifteen years previously.

I felt gloomy, and woke up Mary in a mood of depression. At a suburban stop, in the middle of the concrete wilderness, we left the warmth of the Zakopane bus and settled down at the stop to wait for a local one. The wind blew down the barren street, and the air smelt of brown coal. Mary was sorry for her irritability now, and kissed me hard and lovingly to show it. That was one good thing, at any rate.

They built Nowa Huta after the war, as one of the biggest steel-making complexes in the world. The idea was to syphon off some of the peasant over-population in southern Poland, but the effect looks like the planners' revenge on the countryside. The government used to be proud of it, and photographs of Nowa Huta featured in all the official books about Poland, showing the vast chimneys — like the barrels of guns — spouting grey fumes into the air until someone told them that pollution wasn't a good thing any more. So as their contribution to cleaning up the atmosphere they stopped putting photographs of Nowa Huta in the books.

I had always hated the place, especially after coming from the clean air of the Tatras. But it's good to feel a sense of mission, and as I walked through the straight streets and passed the grimy blocks of flats I congratulated myself on all the barriers I'd surmounted to get there with my information and my bits of equipment. I had left Mary at a bath-house in Cracow; she'd be safe, and able to rest till our rendezvous in the city at three o'clock. There were immense problems ahead of us, but at least we had arrived in Cracow on time.

I knew nothing about factories, never having been inside one in my life; and it never occurred to me that getting in might be difficult. It was only when I got closer, and saw the crowds moving around the street in front of the gates that I realized things weren't going to be as easy as I'd assumed.

A placard hung on the gates reading *Strajk Protestacyjny*, and the gate itself was almost hidden in bunches of flowers and red and white flags of Poland. Behind the gates were dozens of men, perhaps more, and behind them, almost blocking out the view of the factory buildings, an immense barricade of iron and wood and old scrap had been piled up for the full width of the gate and beyond.

The gate itself was chained and barred, and in front of it, leaving a healthy gap, stood a line of about thirty ZOMO riot police, wearing their blue-grey tunics and carrying scarred plastic shields. The visors on their helmets were turned up. They didn't seem to know whether they were there to stop the strikers getting out, or the crowds of women and children gathered in the street from getting in. There was a tremendous din, as hundreds of people talked and shouted and chanted, and cassette machines played competing kinds of music, mainly Polish national and rock.

No one seemed to be in charge, on either side of the gate, and no one seemed to know what to do. I couldn't see any way of getting near it.

But as always in Poland there were ways. As I stood looking at the gates, a thin, wasted-looked woman stopped beside me. She was about forty-five, and she was still in her housecoat, although it was nine-thirty in the morning. She had crossed her arms over her chest as working-class city women do everywhere. Perhaps it was my briefcase she noticed first, or perhaps my air of general innocence.

'You look lost,' she said. It's unusual in my part of Poland for women to speak to men in the street, and for a moment I wasn't sure how to answer. She saw my uncertainty.

'My husband's in there,' she said, jerking her thumb over her shoulder.

'I'd like to get in there myself.'

'It's not hard, if you really want to. Those ZOMO are just rubbish. There's a place round the back that they haven't covered. If I show you who to go to, you can ask them how to find it. There's a group that gets things in to the men, you see.' She looked at me more carefully, as if she were afraid she'd made a mistake. 'They won't let you in if you're not genuine.'

'Oh, I'm genuine. I've got a letter to prove it.' I had, too; I'd persuaded poor Nowak to write a note to the chairman of the strike committee, vouching for me.

In the street silence fell, and only the clashing music went on playing. I turned round to see what had happened. A taxi had driven to within about twenty-five yards of the factory gates, and had stopped. It was difficult to see what was going on in the taxi, but there seemed to be a lot of people inside.

Suddenly a shout went up — a shout of anger. 'They're from DTV!' DTV was Polish National Television, much hated by everyone as the mouthpiece of the military government. Indeed, behind the taxi, on a wall that faced the factory gates, someone had painted the slogan *DTV KLAMIE*: Polish TV Lies. But no one hustled them or interfered with them; it was as though they were figures from their own medium, entertainers who had suddenly appeared in our midst. You could see now the big lens of their camera as they filmed the scene at the factory gates.

The line of ZOMO troopers watched the taxi from a distance but took no action to interfere with it. Maybe the ZOMO thought they were from DTV as well. Then someone shouted an order, and three ZOMO troopers ran forward. The taxi driver started to move off, but the leading ZOMO man went down on one knee and aimed his rifle at him. The taxi driver stood on the brakes. The other two men wrenched at the handles of the doors, and pulled out the people inside.

There was a little groan from the onlookers who had given the game away by shouting out. As the cameraman was hauled out of the taxi, trying to protect his expensive equipment, everyone could see the bold letters on the side of it:

186

'Swedish TV'. The three ZOMO men had been joined by others now, and they were laying into the television crew and their driver with the butts of their rifles, grunting as they did so. It was painful to watch, and the women standing nearby started shouting out at the ZOMO, but they took no notice of anyone else, clubbing and kicking away at the soft bodies in front of them.

Somehow the reporter, unencumbered with equipment, managed to break away from the group and headed for the crowd. The women shouted encouragement at him, and started to move forward to hide him in their ranks, but he veered away, perhaps too dazed to understand what was happening, and made for the gates of the factory. His momentum took him through the thin line of ZOMO men there, and their slow reactions helped him. He hung for a second or two on the bars, while people yelled conflicting things at him in a language he couldn't understand. The men on the other side of the gate tried to help him up to the top, but he was only a few feet up when a screamed order sent two ZOMO men across to him. One of them struck him a terrible blow on the leg, enough to break the bone, and he fell back on to the cobbles, his leg folded untidily beneath him. His forehead carried a long gash, and he lay there panting, not making a sound, like an animal waiting to be finished off. The other ZOMO man kicked him almost casually on the point of the chin, so that his body arched up and fell back again. He was still silent. They pulled him away, while the others dealt with his colleagues, closer to the taxi. A wail of sympathy and anger went up from the crowd, but with the ZOMO around in force no one felt able to go and help. I was sickened by the whole thing, and turned away. A ZOMO van drove over from a side street to take the three Swedes to hospital or to prison. Beside me, the woman in the housecoat was watching with tears running down her cheeks, but as I turned she took hold of my arm.

'I'll show you how to get in,' she said.

Having seen what happened to someone who tried that, I wasn't as enthusiastic as I had been, but there was no point in waiting there any more. I had always known that the ZOMO were thugs, many of them recruited from Poland's gaols, and I had seen a little of their handiwork on British television. But the shock of seeing it in reality at close range was something altogether different. As I followed her I could still hear the sound of the baton on the reporter's leg, and see the way he dropped to the ground.

The smell of defeatism was almost as strong as the cigarette smoke inside the manager's office, where the strike committee was in almost continual session. There were full ashtrays everywhere, and once they'd filled the ashtrays they had taken to filling the dirty cups that littered the table. The windows were firmly shut, to avoid any kind of electronic eaves-dropping, and the thin yellow curtains that the manager had selected were pulled across, making a permanent twilight. All along the walls, the manager shook hands in photographs with Party dignitaries and deserving workers; little presentation boxes and statuettes stood on a sideboard near the door, where the manager no doubt kept his drinks when he was there.

He hadn't been there for several days now, and the room showed it. As for the strike committee, everything had been made worse by the decision to meet in this room, cut off from the strikers and the atmosphere downstairs. In a way, I thought, when I got a chance to look about me and think, the strike committee was affected by the same problems the manager would have had. The only good thing about holding their meetings up here was that every time someone became restless, which was about every other minute, they could walk over to the window, lift the curtain, and look out. You could see the main gate from there, as well as the only physical achievement the strike committee could so far point to: the barricade blocking the way into the factory. It looked as large as a small-sized house from this angle, but I had an advantage the strikers didn't have, if you could call it an advantage: I'd seen on television what ZOMO armoured personnel carriers could do against such barricades and I could guess that this one wouldn't be enough to keep them out.

'I've read the letter of introduction from Tadeusz Nowak,' the strike committee chairman began, clearing his throat and looking past my head at a picture of the factory manager

188

shaking hands with a man three inches taller and a great deal better off. 'And I can only apologize if we seemed in any way doubtful when you first arrived. I hope you'll understand that in this kind of atmosphere . . .' His words trailed away apologetically, and I nodded. I did understand; I'd been surprised that they'd let me in so quickly. They hadn't even made me open my chocolate boxes, and although that constituted a lapse of security, I was grateful for it.

'Is there any possibility that Tadeusz might be able to come here and join us?' An elderly man, thick-set and not very well shaven, leant across. 'He had such an effect on everyone, he could make the workforce do anything he wanted, just about.' He looked round him at the others who were sitting there. 'Without him, frankly, we're in trouble. And because he's not here, there've been rumours that he didn't want to stay and take the consequences. It's bad for everyone.'

I told them what I thought the chances of his being able to get there in time for the strike were. It didn't take me long. The elderly man nodded, as though he hadn't expected any good news anyway, and rubbed his chin resignedly.

'When do you expect something to happen here?' I put the question as tactfully as I could.

'We don't have any way of telling. Now they've cut our phones off. . . .' The chairman's voice trailed away again. No wonder they miss Tadeusz, I thought.

We sat there for a little. I tried not to look at them too closely, and they tried not to look at me. I got the impression that every one of them would be happy if he could only change places with me, and get away; even though they didn't know a quarter of the problems I had to face. It just shows, I thought: decency and courage aren't enough. You need something else as well.

I was still working out what that something might be, when the chairman cleared his throat again.

'Is there anything else before we . . . send you on?'

In that atmosphere, I couldn't think of anything, I looked around for inspiration, and saw the photograph of General Jaruzelski on the wall. He was the only person who hadn't shaken hands with the manager, it seemed: if the strikers had taken his photograph down, it might have done them some good. But it gave me the necessary inspiration to make a little speech.

'I just thought I ought to say how much I admire you for what you're doing here, and to remind you that it isn't just the people of Nowa Huta, or even just the people of Poland, who are watching you, but the people of the whole world.'

I was embarrassed then, never liking to listen to inspirational speeches myself. I didn't even think it was likely to be true; knowing as I did the way of the West, and the general lack of awareness of what was going on in Poland. But for an instant it felt as though it ought to be true, and I certainly did admire them for their courage. The atmosphere seemed to lift a little, and one or two of them exhanged glances and sat up straighter.

The chairman of the committee thanked me at some length, and then pressed a button on the intercom on the manager's desk.

'Would you ask Anna to step in?' he said, for all the world like a deferential old manager himself. He caught my look, and said, 'We make use of these things, you know,' as though he thought I was going to present him with the bill.

The door opened, and a girl came in. She was about twenty-five, with a quick, lively face framed in lush dark hair curled like a Restoration wig. I liked her immediately.

'Anna is our go-between,' he said, not making it clear exactly who it was she went between, though I could guess. He smiled at her, and so did most of the others on the committee. You could tell that things improved when she came into the room.

'Would you be kind enough to take Dr . . . ,'

'Serafinski,' I said.

'Serafinski — to see our friends?'

She gave me a quick grin and nodded. I said my goodbyes and left them to it.

'Someone said you'd been with Tadeusz,' she said. I couldn't think how the news had travelled so fast, but there was no reason why I shouldn't nod.

'Can you tell me how he is? Is he all right?'

I told her, and she grimaced. Nevertheless, as we walked across the factory yard, she had a smile for almost everyone.

'He and I, we're friends. We live together,' she added, looking at me cautiously.

'I liked him the moment I met him,' I told her truthfully. 'I was only sorry we couldn't come back here together. He's just the kind of person I get on with.'

'Me too,' she said, and gave my arm a squeeze.

'Don't you find it hard to get in and out of the factory all the time? You must be about the only woman here.'

'There are the cleaning women,' she said, evidently not fishing for compliments. 'I know all the boys in here. They're great.'

We talked a good deal as we made our way out of the factory by the side gate, and headed off down the road, well away from the ZOMO and the scene of confrontation at the main entrance. She was an enjoyable companion, lively and enthusiastic. She had visited England, she said, and had even spent an afternoon in Cambridge. But she liked the US better. She glanced at me as though she thought she might have hurt my feelings, but I've never been one of those people who think there's one best place, or one best country, in the world.

'How are we going to get there?'

'By bus. Best not to talk too much when we're on it. They're everywhere round here.' Her face took on a sour look, which went oddly with her cheerful expression. 'One day these bastards will be thrown out, though.'

'And replaced by other bastards?'

'Perhaps not quite such bastardly bastards.' She laughed, and it made me feel less tired and less strained immediately to hear her.

'Isn't all this a bit of a risk for a girl like you to take?'

'Believe me,' she said seriously, grabbing hold of my arm again in a way I found very pleasant. 'It's the most dangerous job in the world.' It was only when she started laughing that I realized she was making fun of me.

'I'm a university teacher,' I said, apologetically, 'I have a licence to be pompous.'

'Will Tadeusz be safe down there?'

'He told you where he was going?'

'Everything can't be a secret, you know. What a curious life you must lead with your wife in England, never telling her where you go when you leave home.'

'I'm not married, so I don't have to. My girlfriend isn't the kind to ask me anyway. And she lives in Paris.' We were on the bus now, and were both doing what she'd said not to do as we headed for the centre of Cracow. I looked at my watch: it was one o'clock. 'Is it much further?' She shook her head but didn't say anything. 'I've got to meet my girlfriend by three at the latest.'

'In Paris?'

'No, in Cracow.'

'Oh, you'll be there, don't worry.'

I wondered whether I should tell her what Nowak had said about there being a traitor in the organization, but I decided not to. Security was security, and there was no point in telling things unnecessarily to people who didn't have to know.

We dodged around until two o'clock, while I grew increasingly nervous. Every time I suggested to her that we ought to hurry, she laughed and told me not to worry, and that everything would be fine.

'When do you leave Cracow?' she asked.

'That depends on what help your people can give me. I've done one or two other things that may cause me trouble.' I felt rather proud of myself, now that the shock had worn off. I didn't tell her about the observer, and I glossed over the worst bits about the dogs. She was sympathetic, all the same.

'I think it's marvellous, all the things you've done for us. I can't believe we won't do something just as good to get you out of the country. Solidarity still has a lot of pull, you know, in spite of everything.'

'But can you get us on a plane to England?'

'Does it have to be a plane?'

We both laughed, and I decided not to labour the point. It was two-fifteen, and I was starting to get really worried.

But just as I was about to remonstrate with her yet again, she said, 'We're going to walk down this street and then turn off to the left. I want you to wait at the end of the side street while I go on. After a minute or so I'll come back and find you.'

We were in the centre of Cracow now, in an area I knew fairly well. The shops were crowded, with queues outside a good many of them. Everyone carried plastic bags or string ones, but few contained much.

The side street was quiet, and when she went on round the corner, leaving me to wait, I stood in the doorway of an old building and looked carefully around me. No one had followed us down here, and no one had stopped in the main street to watch what I was doing. Anna's methods were time-consuming, but at least they were effective. She was gone for a good ten minutes. You and your bad time-keeping, I remembered Mary saying to me once. It's just a sign that you take me for granted. I hoped she wouldn't have grounds to say it again. I blamed myself very much for not having realized how long all the cloak-and-dagger business might take.

Anna's small energetic figure appeared round the corner again, her curly hair swinging and her breasts moving pleasantly as she ran. I returned her smile with interest as we met halfway.

'Sorry to keep you, but we have to do this kind of thing. You do understand, don't you?' She grabbed hold of my arm again, and I did understand; or at least I said I did.

'I've told them all about you, and they're waiting to see you.'

I felt nervous as we walked on, and swung my briefcase to give myself a little more courage. I had been looking to this meeting as the most important thing in my life, and now that it was about to take place I realized it was nothing more than the end of a chapter. After this would begin the far more difficult business of smuggling ourselves out of Poland. I supposed it would happen; everything else had gone right for Mary and me in the end, and it seemed reasonable to hope that things would continue to do so. But I had no idea how, and the only people who could help were themselves prisoners of an elaborate system of security.

Anna nudged me enthusiastically. We were in a narrow street which ran parallel with the main shopping street. You could see a good way in either direction, and there were very few people about. If it was here, I thought, the place had been well chosen. But it wasn't there. Instead, we turned down a small alleyway, just large enough for a delivery truck to get through, and found ourselves in a yard with workshops and store-rooms on two sides of it. On the side facing us was the back of a meat store, though only the blood and the discarded cheese-cloth from the joints of meat proclaimed it; that, and the sign *Mieso* over the door.

Anna looked round carefully, but there was no one watching.

'The butcher's,' she said, and headed for it. I hung back a little, more out of tiredness than anything else. 'Come on,' she said, and put her arm cheerfully round my waist. 'Journey's end.'

CHAPTER NINE

*'Anti-socialism, hostility to Marxist-Leninist ideology,
is rooted most strongly in older people, and particularly
the peasants. And therefore, in the natural order of
things, it is dying out . . . '* — Polish radio broadcast.

It was doubtful whether the old man could see anything at all
now, though his eyes were still fixed, perhaps by accident or
perhaps by force of habit, on the picture of the Sacred Heart on
the opposite wall.

We all think death is such a momentous thing, Dr Galka
reflected, because our lives are so important to us. And yet it is
the most commonplace thing there is. You can slip into death a
thousand ways, and scarcely notice it. This at least is a quiet
death. Galka thought of some of the harder ones he had seen.

Serafinski's head was a little higher than his body, propped
up by the pillows. His eyes were red and his face an ugly grey
colour. So this is how his life ends, Galka thought, as though
he were watching the last reel of a film. We played dominoes
together a week ago, and neither of us foresaw this then. The
old man's hands were purple, the veins full.

The priest had finished giving him the last rites, and Galka,
who had been forced to leave the room, was still angry at the
intrusion. Death is a cult for them, he thought irritably. The
old man's understanding has gone, he neither sees nor knows.
How then can he be numbered among the righteous by
anointing him? Galka cleared his throat with annoyance, and
the priest, who disapproved just as strongly of him, paused for
an instant in his prayers and glared at him.

But Galka was wrong. Even after the last massive infarction
there was a centre of consciousness left in the old man's mind,

195

as though he were standing alone in a fog. Some details were still perfectly clear to him, though nothing else was observable. He remembered his son's visit, for instance, and felt the discomfort in his neck from the angle of the pillows. But the fog was spreading, and soon even his son slipped away from him.

Magda held his hand and wept, and for a moment he was conscious of a last habitual twinge of irritability. Then that passed as well, and he was aware only of an immense tiredness which radiated up from his feet in the darkness now surrounding him. There was no question of pain; he was slipping slowly into a dark vacuum. To his surprise, he found he could control the speed of it a little. If he wanted to, he could distinguish between Magda and Galka and the priest. But mostly he didn't want to; he was too tired, it wasn't worth it, he wanted to rest.

Galka noticed a flicker in the eyes, and looked significantly at Magda, but she was too busy weeping. He ignored the priest, who was still praying. The priest and he disliked each other, he felt, not necessarily on confessional grounds, but because they each competed for the homage of the villagers. Magda buried her face in her handkerchief, too overcome to watch her father's moment of death.

And so the old man's life trickled away, going faster in the last seconds, just at the last grains of sand race quickly out of the hour-glass, while the three people by his bedside were each absorbed in their own concerns; the priest with the precise details of his ritual, the doctor with his free-thinking hostility, the daughter with her grief. So the precise moment at which Karol Serafinski ceased to exist went unmarked.

It was the priest who noticed first, and he crossed himself slowly. Galka, looking away from him to the body on the bed, felt for the pulse and touched the old withered neck, and nodded. Magda, for the first time, looked up and saw what had happened. Galka, genuinely moved, put his arm round her and guided her tired, dissatisfied head on to his shoulder.

I shall be like this soon, he thought, looking at the greying face on the pillow, already losing its likeness to the man he had known. Then, in a moment of superstition of his own, he put his free hand on the heavy grey hand of his friend. It was still warm.

196

Galka believed that, after physical death, consciousness lingered for an instant or two, and the dead could see the actions of the living. If you're still there, Karol, he thought, I want you to know how fond I am of you. He was too embarrassed to say it aloud.

For a few minutes more the four of them stayed there: the priest quietly repeating the prayers for the dead, the daughter weeping on the doctor's shoulder, the doctor still touching the hand that would soon be cold and stiff. And the old man himself, grey and mysterious.

It was an extraordinary place for an underground organization to hide out in, but perhaps it was well chosen for all that. The butcher's counter was no doubt almost empty, with a few scraggy cuts of meat and no sausage, but that only made it easier to accommodate the Solidarity people in the storerooms. There was a good deal of suitability, in all sorts of ways, in having their headquarters in a butcher's cold store.

'I hope you'll forgive the strange surroundings, Dr Serafinski,' the small man at the head of the rough deal table said as he stood up to shake my hand. He was stout and balding, with the thick hands of a craftsman, and a fussy manner.

I looked around the high, windowless room, entirely clad from floor to ceiling in white ceramic tiles. It was like holding a council meeting in the corporation public lavatory. I thought I could smell the sickening reek of old blood and fat, but I may have been too imaginative. I'd had enough of that kind of thing over the previous couple of days.

'We've got a great deal to thank you for. Anna here has explained everything about the way you got here, and the care you took of our colleague Tadeusz Nowak. How was he when you left him?'

'He seemed to want to get back to you pretty quickly. He was worried about not being at the Nowa Huta strike.'

I noticed one or two of them exchange glances, and I thought of the air of hopelessness in the factory manager's office. No one had introduced me to the other people round the table, but it didn't matter. The less I knew about them the better for all of us.

Someone brought in coffee, and I caught sight of the ham radio set-up in the corner. I wondered how I was going to break the bad news to them that they were being betrayed; things seemed too formal at the moment to be able to do anything like that. I scratched my head reflectively, and drank the coffee. It tasted of old butcher's meat as well; everything would here. There was a Solidarity poster taped to the wall commemorating the Katyn Massacre of Polish officers by the Russians. In a place like this, I thought, every day is a Katyn Massacre for cows and pigs.

'Do you have the—' Smykowski's voice dropped for a moment, and the radio operator piped up, from his desk in the corner, 'It's a power transistor.'

'It's in here,' I said, hoisting up my briefcase and putting it on my lap. If the damned thing is smashed, they'll serve me up as cuts in the shop, I thought, and felt I had some careful priming to do.

'I don't know if Anna told you, but we had a bit of trouble getting here.' It all sounded so unlikely now — being hunted by helicopters and policemen and savage dogs. In my tired state, I might almost have been hallucinating. 'I had to hit someone with it,' I said. 'And I jumped out of a cable-car.'

The radio operator's face registered horror. Maybe power transistors were more easily damaged than I'd thought.

I hadn't prepared them for the appearance of the things, either. *Hautval Chocolatier*, read the magenta letters on the pink paper. The bright green ribbons were still curled, which said something about the skill of the girl who'd done it. Some dents, however, marred the packages. As for my briefcase, it seemed everything that had happened to us had left its mark in one way or another; especially the burn-mark from the bullet.

'I think you'd better open these,' I said, trying to force a laugh as I handed them to the radio operator. 'I told the customs they were a special present for my sister.' One or two people smiled, and that was all. They knew better than I did how much depended on the state the equipment was in.

Until they knew, no one liked to congratulate me too much. I sympathized. What they didn't realize was that something even more important to their organization than the radio parts still waited in my briefcase. I pulled out Nowak's letter to Smykowski.

For a moment I thought I should open it myself, and find out the traitor's name. But better not, I thought for the second time since walking in there. I shivered a little; they hadn't finally managed to drive the cold out, any more than the smell.

'Well done, anyway, Dr Serafinski, for bringing these things all this way.' Anna was irrepressible, and I was grateful to her. 'And for enduring so many hardships.'

'It sounds as though you're planning to give me a medal!'

She looked round at the others, who were all watching the radio operator's face, trying to gauge what his reactions were.

'I just thought someone should thank you.'

'Yes, of course, thank you very much indeed. Very good of you.' Smykowski's voice had, I thought irrelevantly, a touch of the highlander's brogue about it.

'Mr Smykowski, I've also got a message for you.'

'Ah, yes, thank you very much.' He wasn't paying any attention at all. 'Perhaps you could put it with my other papers.' By this time he was over by the radio operator's desk.

'It's extremely urgent,' I said, but he took no notice.

'What do you think?' he was asking.

'Much too soon to say yet,' the radio operator said shortly, without looking up from the fiddling he was doing with his screwdriver.

Smykowski walked around the cold store for a bit, his big hands behind his back, and his short figure looking slightly absurd. What better man to have as an underground leader, I thought, than one who looks so ordinary?

Nobody said anything. I wondered if any of them was the traitor. Three of the four people who had been sitting at the table when I came in were standing now, trying not to get too near the radio operator and irritate him, but wanting to be close enough to see for themselves if the equipment worked. The fourth was still sitting down.

'I expect you'd rather tiptoe away before they find out what's happened.' Anna was looking at me in an amused way, and I smiled back at her.

'I'd rather tiptoe away because I've got an appointment to

keep,' I said. It was two forty-five; Mary would be waiting for me in fifteen minutes. Even without Anna's security procedures it would take me half-an-hour to get to the rendezvous. I blamed myself again for having been so optimistic about the time it would all take; if Mary were kept waiting for a long time, it would make her conspicious, and for us that meant danger.

'Why don't you just go off now and come back later with her, after you've done everything that you need to? They'll be finished by that time, and you'll have their undivided attention again.'

I thought about it. 'The trouble is,' I said, 'I've also got this urgent message from Tadeusz to hand over to Mr Smykowski. I must give it to him before I go.'

'Tell me, and I'll give it to him.'

'It's not only a verbal message, he sent a written one as well.'

'Tadeusz wrote Stefan a note? I don't believe it. I've never had a note from him in my life. I used to say he couldn't write. Well, anyway, why not hand it over to me, and I'll give it to Stefan when you go?'

I was very tempted. Mary was going to be angry, as well as worried, about my lateness. To give Anna the letter would be the obvious way out. Maybe that was why I didn't do it.

'I'm sorry to sound stuffy,' I said. 'But I promised Tadeusz very definitely that I would hand it to Mr Smykowski in person, and that I'd give him the verbal message, too. He was very insistent about it.'

'Well, I don't care,' she said, obviously irritated. 'I just thought I'd save you a bit of time, that's all.'

I smiled at her again, but it didn't help.

'Why should he write a letter?' she asked, after a while.

'No good asking me. He didn't explain.'

She looked away again, annoyed. She was still looking away, and I was still trying to work out what I should do, when I sensed a change in the atmosphere by the radio operator's desk. I walked over there, my shoes clicking on the white tiles. All the whiteness gave a strange feeling of distance to the room, or maybe I was just expecting to see the moisture rising from everything as it would when the cold store was really cold. Above the heads of the little group gathered round the radio were the hooks they hung the joints from. I felt like Cassandra, as I walked across towards them.

The radio operator made an important noise, and pulled his sleeves back. This was the moment. He checked that the car battery on the floor was correctly hooked up, he adjusted the tuning, and then pressed the switch to 'on'. A meter indicator came on, but that didn't seem to satisfy him, though everyone else began to straighten up and smile at each other. Seeing his concentration, they bent down again. He consulted a typed list of wavelengths beside him, twitched the mike key a couple of times, and said matter-of-factly, 'Who do you want me to contact first?'

It was a magnificent moment. People were standing up and shouting suddenly, and hugging each other. I got Anna, and did more hugging than shouting, but she was still annoyed with me and didn't respond. Then everyone came over and shook my hand, and patted me on the back, and told me how brave I'd been, and how much I deserved the praise and gratitude of the entire Polish nation.

'Of course, we should have thanked you before, but we just wanted to see that everything was working properly,' Smykowski said, beaming.

'Of course. I'm very glad. There are just a couple of things . . .'

'But first, my dear friend, we must send our messages. Time is getting very short.'

'Who do you want first, Stefan? Warsaw?'

'Yes, make it Warsaw. Say: "All now ready for inspection!" They'll know what that means. Then get on to Gdansk, and Wroclaw, and . . .'

'I don't think you'll want to say that, when you've heard what I've got to tell you,' I said.

Everyone went quiet. I had wanted to tell Smykowski on his own but he was too worked up about the radio set now, and I was worried that the right moment would pass.

'Tadeusz Nowak told me that he's worked out that your cell here was being systematically betrayed. And he asked me to give you this letter' — I fumbled undramatically in my pockets while I tried to find it — 'so that he could explain to you what had happened.'

No one moved. Perhaps they all had the dreadful feeling that they were equally under suspicion, and that they wouldn't be able to disprove the charge if it were made against them. I was the only one entirely in the clear.

In the white room, our breath still clouding a little in the surrounding cold, Smykowski reached out to take the letter. It looked very dog-eared.

'Do you still want me to go back to the factory, Stefan?' Anna's voice sounded hard in those strange acoustics. Smykowski didn't say anything at all. Perhaps he was a slow reader — or perhaps Nowak's handwriting was hard to decipher. In the general atmosphere of suspicion, nobody liked to move or breathe too loudly, in case it should be taken as a sign of guilt. Even I found it difficult to know what to do with my hands and feet, so I stood there, like the others.

All Smykowski could do was stand there with the letter in his hand and say, 'But we've always trusted each other here.'

'Does Nowak give any names?' one of the others asked, the anxiety too much for him.

'Yes.' Smykowski looked down at the letter again, as though he might have misread it. He turned round slowly.

'What are you going to do about it?' Anna asked, even before the small, untidy figure had stopped to look at her.

'I don't know,' Smykowski said. He went back to his seat at the table and read the letter again, first to himself and then out loud.

It was very short.

'You've shopped two of my closest mates, you bitch,' the radio operator shouted, and he lunged at her. He didn't get through the group.

I had no idea what I should do now. I wasn't interested in getting mixed up in their private house-cleaning session, I wanted to get away. I also didn't want Anna to be smashed up by anyone.

I looked at her. She didn't seem particularly upset by what had happened, though I couldn't tell from her expression. You never can. She seemed almost to be smiling.

'We'll have to lock her up somewhere,' somebody said. They didn't see her as a person any more, I thought.

'The congress must go ahead still.' That was Smykowski.

'Look,' I said, 'I'm sorry if this is none of my business, but you've got to assume that the police know everything about you now, and that they're just waiting for you to get every-body gathered together here before turning you all over. It'll be the biggest thing they've done since martial law. And the moment Anna disappears, they'll know you've worked out what's happened, and they'll move in and get you anyway.'

There was a good deal of nodding at all that.

'The one thing you've go to do is to tell all the other regions that the congress is off. And you'd better do it quickly, in case they've got this place bugged.'

That made them move. I wondered, as I saw them working out who to tell, and what to say, whether Tadeusz Nowak, with his fast mind and his gentle manners, wasn't the real boss here, but hadn't chosen to exert his authority. No wonder they missed him. As for Anna, they left her standing there, though the radio operator was watching her pretty closely. But when she made her move, I was still the nearest person to her.

She must have worked it out fairly carefully in advance. First she threw a nearby chair into my path, so that I fell into it and landed on the floor. Then she charged the door of the cold store, which was two feet thick and resembled those doors they lock bank vaults with; but because it was so cumbersome, the Solidarity people usually left the door pushed to, rather than closed.

Her impetus took her straight through and out into the passageway beyond. There was a security man there, but she was past him in an instant and he stood staring at her as I picked myself up and got out of the way of the chair. The radio operator was moving fast behind me, crowding me in the doorway.

I suppose I should just have left him to it, and concentrated instead on getting Smykowski to work out how they were going to help me out of the country. But even at that moment it seemed there were more important things to do; it was the attitude, of course, which had got me into all this in the first place. I pushed him against the door, not too hard, and said, 'You've got all those messages to send. I'll do the chasing.' The shock sobered him up, and he nodded. I was getting into the habit of being aggressive with people.

Out in the corridor, the security man was still wondering why Anna had gone running past him. I gave him something else to worry about, almost colliding with him as I went through the doorway. Even the split-second glance showed me there wasn't much point in asking him which way she'd gone, and I headed out into the courtyard.

I am not a particularly fit man, and had been leading the sort of life in the previous few days that only very fit men should lead. My legs and arms ached, I was tired, and I was hungry. Beyond that, though, I wanted to go home, and my only chance of doing so was if I found Anna before she found the police. So I started to run again, slower now that I had a moment to think about it, but trying to keep within my capabilities; I didn't want to fade out a hundred yards down the road. And at least I was doing the chasing this time; it made a change. I burst out into the quiet side street, but there was no sign of her. I looked round fast, trying to remember from my earlier impression of the place whether she would have gone to the left or right. I knew there must be look-outs around, but I couldn't see anyone in the street. As I hesitated, furious with myself for being so slow, a movement caught my eye. An elderly man was sitting in the window of a flat in a building across the road, and pointing down the street to my right. I winked my thanks to him, and headed off as fast as I could. She must have had a start of about half a minute on me now, but if I got to the street corner fast, I might see which way she would go on the main street which lay beyond.

I thundered along, my legs a mass of darting pain, my feet leaden, my head starting to ache, but with a curious feeling inside me which I recognized later as exhilaration. There is a slightly indecent pleasure in hunting somebody; especially if you feel you have a good chance of catching them.

I got to the street corner, and saw her briefly at the end of it, glancing round to see if she were being chased, the magnificent mane of dark curling hair shaking over her face as she turned her head again and darted down the main street to her right. It was her second big mistake of the day.

At this point a certain amount of geography is needed. By turning right out of the cold store, right at the corner of the short side-street that led to the main shopping street and right in the main shopping street itself, Anna was covering three sides of a rectangle. It took me only a matter of a few seconds to run the length of the short side-street, and turn into the main street after her. But then things changed radically. Cracow was stiff with men in uniform; militia-men, soldiers who were patrolling the streets and soldiers who were off-duty but on the look-out for trouble. And in the atmosphere of Poland at the time, running constituted trouble.

Why Anna herself wasn't running any more, I couldn't be certain. She had only to go up to the first person she saw in uniform to be safe from me. But she didn't. I watched her walk quickly past a group of three paratroopers who were sauntering idly along the street, and looked at each other as she went. As for me, I had to walk as fast as possible without seeming to, and that meant keeping on the inside lane, hugging the shop fronts where the crowd was thinnest.

She had a good twenty-yard start on me at first, but I'd had more experience of cutting my way through crowds than she had, and I soon began to catch up. Once I had to force my way through a long and patient line of shoppers, who didn't like it, and once I cannoned into an elderly man who was selling gold-fish at a makeshift table, just as he was ladling one out of a big glass jar into somebody's jamjar. The ladle shot up into the air, and the fish slipped out of it and landed wriggling on the pave-ment. I managed to avoid treading on it and was off, still apologizing, before the man had stopped cursing me and begun picking up the shocked and winded goldfish.

Anna was walking fast along the outside of the pavement, only a few yards ahead of me. I don't think she knew I was there. It was then that I saw a militia-man standing at a fixed sentry post, and knew that something would have to be done.

Whether I had kept a map of the area in my head, or whether it was pure luck, I don't know; on my past record I doubt if it could have been luck. I realized at that precise moment that the shop outside which the policeman was standing was a butcher's; and that almost certainly it must have been part of the complex where the Solidarity leaders were.

I risked running a few paces, and took hold of her arm just before she drew level with the bored militia-man. It was as sweet a piece of diversion as I have ever seen. My speed took her straight through the open door of the shop, and we ran full tilt into an old woman who was just turning away from the counter with a parcel in her hands.

Nobody said anything for a little, and then the old woman let us both have it. Nobody had any manners any more, didn't we have eyes in our heads, look how she'd almost dropped her entire ration for a week.

'Disgusting,' someone else said.

Anna seemed on the point of saying something.

'I caught her in bed with another man,' I announced loudly, shifting my grip on her arm.

'Disgusting,' the woman said again, though which of us she meant wasn't clear.

'We've got three children,' I added. That didn't go down particularly well either, but I felt I had to gain time until I could decide how to get through the shop into the part at the back.

'Let me go, you bastard,' Anna shouted, so loudly I was worried that the militia-man outside might hear.

A man in a stained white coat came out of a back room and walked quickly towards us.

'What's all this, Anna?' he asked, looking angrily at me. I suppose he could see I wasn't a militia-man myself, nor from the UB. The other shoppers were gathering round now: it was a good deal more interesting than looking at bare shelves and empty refrigerators.

'I've got an urgent message—' she started.

'Let's go into the office and talk it over,' I said, to drown out her voice. A man behind the counter, also dressed in a stained white coat, was coming forward with one of those pointed things they sharpen knives on.

'For God's sake, there's no time.' Anna seemed to be working out the advantages of screaming and bringing in the militia-man.

'You heard her.' The sharpening implement looked increasingly unpleasant.

'Said she was, you know, in bed with someone,' a woman was saying behind me.

'Let her go.' The sharpener was within swinging reach of my head now.

'Smykowski wants to see her.' It was my last card, and it worked. The sharpener wavered and dropped, and the man who was wielding it looked around the semi-circle of faces to see if the name had registered with any of them. It hadn't.

'Come into the office,' he said, and I didn't take my hand off Anna's arm. She was silent now, and didn't struggle, though I was digging my fingers in pretty hard. Just before we went into the office she drew in a deep breath, as though she were going to scream, but I twisted her arm savagely and told her I'd break it if she made a noise. A week earlier it would have been an empty threat, but now I might have done it. She seemed to think so, anyway.

'Don't start preaching to me,' she said, directly we were sitting down in the office. The man with the sharpener listened without saying anything, wiping his hands absently on his apron as though he'd got something unpleasant on them. I hadn't said anything anyway.

'What do you know about the kind of pressures they can put on people? You live a long way away from all this. What can they do to you, or your family?' It set me thinking.

They could do a great deal to my father, and to Magda, and I had scarcely spared a single thought about either of them from the moment I had escaped from the house. I hadn't even looked back at the house as I'd left it.

'They blackmailed me, that was all. I didn't want to do it. They blackmailed me.' She looked at me with a curious intensity, and I saw that she wanted me to believe her.

What could I do? I nodded, and shrugged my shoulders. I liked the girl.

'You could have told them — let them know the police were on to you.'

She rounded savagely on the butcher. 'Don't you dare even say a word to me.' He looked down at his apron, embarrassed.

'Maybe you'd better let Smykowski know, and we'll follow you.'

He went out.

'Listen,' Anna said, urgently. 'I'll do a deal with you. Stefan will be so angry with me they could do anything. They could even kill me. If you let me get away, I swear I won't go to the police or tell them anything.'

207

I didn't have the energy to make that kind of decision. All I could think of was that I was going to be late for Mary. I only had to wait a little before the decision would be taken out of my hands.

'Did you really tell them all about everything? Even Tadeusz?'

'He'd have been safer doing six months in prison than running around being shot at by those swine.'

'The swine you were working for.'

'Oh, for God's sake.' The fight seemed to have gone out of her for the last time. When Smykowski and the others came into the room, she didn't even look at them and the dark hair hung round her face like a screen.

I didn't ask what they were going to do with her and I didn't need to. They were far too uncertain to do anything decisive, I could see that. For a moment or two I had one of those strange insights into the future and the nature of things that you get when you are close to exhaustion; I knew that they would argue among themselves until the point came where they either had to escape or be arrested. I made hasty arrangements about how they would look after me and Mary that night — an address, a name, and a telephone number for use in an emergency — but I wasn't altogether confident that they would come to anything.

They were still shouting at Anna when I left, and she was still looking down at her hands, examining the stubby chewed fingernails I had never really noticed before. She wasn't saying anything, and they weren't doing anything to make her talk. If they had stopped shouting occasionally she might have said something. They were nervous and angry, and she had been weak and cowardly, but not everyone can be strong at the right moment.

As for me, I had helped them warn off the national leadership from coming to Cracow, which was something. But I still had to find Mary, and it was after three-thirty.

CHAPTER TEN

'The Politburo enjoins Party organizations as well as the organs of the State to support efforts to smash social sabotage, as well as all kinds of diseases, perversions and irregularities which are still present in many sectors of socio-economic life . . . There will be resistance, but it cannot long survive . . .' — Polish radio broadcast.

The late afternoon sun threw the shadows of the ZOMO troops across the cobbles, like a line of cyrillic letters on a Russian poster. Everything was quiet; the crowd of onlookers outside the factory were bunched together in front of the ZOMO line, curious and hostile but not moving. Behind the factory gates, and the signs and the flags, the strikers stood or walked around in twos and threes, waiting for the inevitable attack. Up in the manager's office the chairman of the strike committee looked out at the barricade and wondered how Tadeusz Nowak would have handled the whole thing.

Someone banged urgently on the office door, and the chairman went over to open it himself.

'Tadeusz is back!' was all the messenger said, before he rushed downstairs again. The chairman and the entire strike committee streamed down after him, and for the first time in two days the chairman felt that maybe something would go well after all.

Nowak was sitting down in one of the machine-rooms, his face very pale and his arm in a sling. It hadn't been a good idea to come, he realized, but he was incapable of staying in the sanatorium at a time when the strike he had helped to call was under threat. He grinned at them as they came into the room, but didn't get up.

'I'll got for a walk round when I'm feeling a bit stronger,' he said, and laughed self-deprecatingly.

The news had spread everywhere in the factory within half an hour, and was being repeated by the crowd of onlookers outside ten minutes after that. Everyone felt that things were looking up now.

At exactly four-thirty, a whistle blew. People jerked their heads up to see where the noise had come from, but within seconds the sounds of the factory on strike were drowned by a confused sound of grinding metal and the squeal of inadequately oiled tracks. The ZOMO armoured personnel carriers were moving.

Men crossed themselves, and swallowed hard. The riot squads were going into action. The half-tracked vehicles screamed over the cobbles, lumbering towards the main gates two at a time, then stopped about ten yards away. One carried on.

It took the locked and barred gates at a speed of not more than five miles an hour, shredding the strike notice and the Polish flags and the bunches of flowers under its tracks, and leaving them black and unrecognizable on the ground in its wake. For a second or two the gates held, pushed inwards to their fullest extent. Then, with a shriek of metal, the armoured vehicle struggled for its purchase on the cobbles, and the chains and the bolts gave. The gates burst open; the way to the barricade lay clear.

It had taken the strikers twelve hours to build the barricade. They had used all the bulky metal they could find from frames of scaffolding to the cars of the factory manager and his deputy. It was a powerful barrier, and an impressive one, twelve feet high and twenty or thirty feet long, with baulks of wood behind it to give it strength and support. Most of the strikers believed it would keep the ZOMO vehicles out, and they were drawn up behind it in defiant lines, brandishing anything they could find to use as a weapon.

Other armoured personnel carriers moved forward now to make their way through the gates and support the lead vehicle. It had crossed the few yards to the barricade, and the driver inside revved up the engine to near-maximum. No one did or said anything, either inside the factory or outside it. This was the moment that would show whether the workers or the authorities were to have control.

The carrier's tracks came into contact with a piece of scaf-folding sticking out from the bottom of the barricade, like a sharpened stake pointing at a cavalry charge. The tracks seemed almost to suck the metal under, pulling it down and crushing it, and using it and the other objects it brought with it to climb up higher on to the barricade, which shifted and moved under the ten tons of the great machine. This was at a steep angle, climbing and crushing its way through. It barely touched the bumper of the manager's attractive green *Chaika* which had been perched on the nearer side of the barricade on a pile of rusty steel girders. As it, too, was sucked under the tracks half of the car disappeared, the windscreen popping out whole, and then shattering in the air into thousands of small fragments.

The armoured personnel carrier made its way down, at a less steep angle than before, and, moments later, having left a clear path to its successors, it headed into the open yard of the factory. The men who had been drawn up behind the bar-ricade let out a groan of dismay, and broke in front of it as the doors opened and a dozen ZOMO troops in full riot gear threw themselves out of the back and began laying into the strikers. But the troops were heavily outnumbered for the time being, and the constant rain of cobblestones and the occasional fiery arc of a petrol bomb kept the ZOMO at bay for a little longer.

Vehicle after vehicle crossed the barricade. Soon there were nine armoured personnel carriers in the factory yard, and the ZOMO troops from outside streamed in through the gates. One was cut off and surrounded by a group of demonstrators; he was beaten to death as he lay there, his helmet rolling off to leave his head unprotected against their kicks. But elsewhere the ZOMO were able to lay into the strikers as they pleased. Since they controlled the entrance, few people were able to escape; the sight of their comrades being beaten savagely with riot sticks and the ZOMO's less authorized weapons damped down the determination of many of the men. Small groups resisted for a while but the ZOMO isolated them and fought them to a standstill.

A snatch-squad of eight ZOMO troops found the machine-room where Tadeusz Nowak and most of the strike committee were waiting. The sight of Nowak's sling seemed to excite one ZOMO man and he gave Nowak a savage slash across the arm with his baton. Nowak breathed in hard, but didn't say anything, even when the ZOMO man pushed him against the wall and kicked his legs apart viciously in order to search him. Then he was hustled down the corridor and thrown into a lorry which had been brought in through the open gates. Nowak caught his arm a jarring blow on someone's knee as he was pushed into the lorry, but still he didn't say anything, though his face was white with pain.

It was another couple of hours before the convoy of lorries and armoured personnel carriers and their attendant jeeps left the factory. No one remained inside, and a ZOMO patrol stayed at the gates to make sure the place wouldn't be reoccupied. On its way to the main prison, between Nowa Huta and Cracow, the convoy had to pass down a narrow residential road with high blocks of flats on either side. As the third vehicle passed the middle of the street a sudden volley of bricks and cobble-stones met it, and the lorry behind cannoned into it as it braked sharply, its windscreen smashed. From the houses came a further hail of missiles, and a crowd gathered and started to pelt the jeeps. For the most part the ZOMO kept the convoy under control, but it was dark now, and the street lights had been deliberately broken to help the ambush. The prisoners in two of the lorries managed to overpower their ZOMO guards, and jumped out before anyone else could stop them. Within seconds, they had vanished down side streets or inside houses. The last group was composed of three men, who went more slowly than the others. A woman who was watching carefully from her doorway called to them urgently, and they headed towards her front door. The battle was still going on behind them, and no one noticed their going. Two of the men slipped in immediately. The last took a little longer, and he turned round briefly on the doorstep to see if they were being followed. They weren't. The lurid light of a petrol bomb shone briefly on the sling supporting his injured arm. Tadeusz Nowak was a free man again.

212

Adam Mickiewicz was on his plinth in the main Market Square, with the pigeons hanging round him in clouds and the four graces or virtues or continents or whatever sitting round the base collecting their share of the pigeons' attention too. It wasn't the original statue, of course — the Germans destroyed that. It had a gritty post-war look to it, as though they hadn't got it out of the mould quite cleanly. But he was still in the same attitude as he always had been, hitching cloak up round his middle, holding a book of his poems in his right hand, and looking down his nose at passers-by. 'Born in slavery and chained by my swaddling bands,' I quoted to myself; it was a quotation from Mickiewicz I had put on the title page of my book about Poland, and I thanked him for it as I went past. I felt it described my situation admirably, and I thought sadly about my father, wondering if he were still alive. But the trials I had gone through somehow lessened my guilt about him. He would, I felt sure, have understood and appreciated the reasons for my escape from the house. He had never liked policemen, and secret policemen least of all. I was proud of him for that; and not only for that.

But there was no time to pause. I was walking across the square as fast as I could without attracting attention to myself. I was a good two and a half hours late for Mary, and the light was starting to fade.

I stopped beside the Church of the Virgin Mary, set at a strange angle at the corner of the Market Square. When I felt sure I couldn't be seen from the square, I dodged into a corner by one of the buttresses of the church, and waited. A dozen or so people went past, but they all looked perfectly harmless to me. I looked back: no one was tailing me. For the moment, I was clean.

I had become obsessive about this business of being followed. After all I'd gone through I was determined that no carelessness on my part was going to get me arrested. I headed round the square, going parallel to it in a series of short cuts and turnings, so as to get round to the south-west corner. It took me a long time, and it gave me a tour not just of Cracow, but of Polish Catholicism too; I went from the Dominican church to the Franciscan one, with the cathedral on Wawel Hill looking down at me. My swaddling bands hadn't altogether chained me there, I thought, trying to remember the last time I had been inside a Catholic church as a worshipper.

In my panic I scarcely noticed the slanting buttresses of the seventeenth-century buildings which had always been my great delight in Cracow. Sweat was running down my chest and back, all adding to the pungency of a shirt I hadn't taken off for two days. The streets were quieter now, as more sensible citizens were thinking about having something to eat in the comfort of their own homes, and my footsteps echoed between the high walls.

I turned into the Straszewskiego at an oblique angle, and headed for the park adjoining the street. There I was completely on my own: no one could follow me unnoticed. In the gathering dusk I could see the handsome baroque dome of St Anne's church now, with its regulation cupola on top, and worked round towards it, covering a wide semi-circle between the ornamental trees. I had come cycling in this park when I was a student, and I'd once brought a girl here, in circumstances which turned out to be deeply embarrassing. I spotted the bench involved, and avoided it superstitiously.

Scarcely anyone was ascending the great white marble steps of St Anne's, though there was a constant trickle of people leaving. Mary wasn't among them. As I went up the steps towards the door I prayed — genuinely, I think — that I would find Mary inside. My heart was thudding with nervousness.

Someone was playing the organ: an explosion of sound that must have been written at roughly the time the church was built. The smell of incense hit my senses, and brought a great crowd of memories to me, so many I couldn't possibly distinguish between them. It was getting dark inside the church, though the last rays of the sun still shone through the magnificent west window, high above me. There was certainly enough light for me to see Mary, but none of the bent backs, the kneeling figures, belonged to her. I looked around again with a dull certainty. She wasn't here. She wasn't in the aisles, she wasn't in the side chapels, she wasn't in the magnificent transept. She had either left or been taken away.

I sank down on a seat, the disappointment as strong as the anxiety and the tiredness. Aimlessly I looked around at the splendour of colour and form that surrounded me. The dying

214

sun shone on golden sceptres and golden crosses and golden books held by the sculptured figures that crowded the walls. Bishops ten feet high smashed the feet of their processional crosses into the throats of fallen believers in no uncertain manner. Christ was crucified in agony twenty, thirty, fifty times over. The pulpit was an amazing floating weight of marble the colour of a piece of liver on a butcher's slab, and golden angels in mid-flight held a golden canopy over it to make sure everyone could hear the sermon. I craned my neck upwards, hoping for inspiration, and saw that the *trompe l'oeil* ceilings were thrown open to the heavens, and God Himself was having a look down to make sure the congregation was listening.

The music stopped, and the organist climbed down into the body of the church. An old woman passed me, her bracelets clinking as she crossed herself. Someone started moving meaningfully around with a bunch of keys. I had about as much idea what I ought to do as the couple of gilded cherubs brandishing their unplayable golden ram's horns had.

'I thought you weren't coming.'

I spun round, and my chair squawked loudly on the black and white pavement. The ancient party who was going round with the keys locking everything up clucked her annoyance at the sound.

'Mary — for God's sake. I was so worried.'

'Maybe you can imagine how I felt, then, waiting here for three hours.' Her voice was cold and expressionless; I'd heard it sound like that on a couple of dreadful occasions before.

I couldn't decide whether or not to start explaining. There was so much of it — the factory, the underground meeting, the uncovering of Anna and the search for her.

'Have you got somewhere to stay tonight?'

'I think so — the underground people were all in upheaval, but I think they'll be . . .'

'Because I've had to find somewhere for myself. I'm not sure whether they can take you or not. I didn't mention you. I decided something had happened to you, and that it was an emergency. So about half an hour ago I rang someone.'

'Rang someone?' It seemed so outlandish, so impossible, that it was almost funny. I tried to see if God the Father was still there, but it was too dark. The brightest thing in the church now was the altar-lamp, glowing like a ruby.

'I had to look after myself. I thought you probably wouldn't be coming back.'

I started to apologize for it all, but she wasn't interested. What I really wanted to know was who she'd telephoned.

'Phoning can be a tricky business here, Mary. Who did you get on to? How did you know about them?'

'Oh, there's nothing for you to worry about. It was someone I had on the highest recommendation.'

'Yes, but who from?'

'From Jan Dolanski, before I left Paris.'

'Jan Dolanski told you to ring someone?'

'Only if I was in real trouble. It was a special friend, some-one who would be able to help out. He gave me the number.'

'But why didn't you tell me?'

'Why should I have? You'd only have said you'd be there on time, like you always do and like you never are.'

We were starting to raise our voices now, and I think we were talking English. Both of us realized at the same moment, and started hushing each other. The old lady with the keys had come to have a look at us, and no doubt to help us on our way.

'So what did this Polish Samaritan say?'

'He said to wait here in the church, and he'd come for me. I spoke to him only a few minutes ago.'

'Was he at his home or his office?'

'At his office — but why are you keeping on like this, Alex? If you hadn't been so late I wouldn't have had to bother him in the first place.'

'But of course you'll ring again, and tell him there's no need to trouble him, because I'm here now.'

'I don't think there's any of course about it.' It was getting difficult to see her now, but I could make out her excellent profile — the strong jaw, the straight nose, the softer outline of the hair. She was sitting beside me.

'You won't come with me?'

'It depends on the kind of arrangement Jan's friend feels he can make.'

Jan's friend, I thought. The keys clinked suggestively again, further off this time. We'd probably have to wait outside for

216

Jan's friend to turn up.

'How long did he say he'd be?'

'He had to get a few things together, but fifteen minutes, he said. I expect he'll keep to it.'

Maybe he won't have to fight his way through ZOMO riot troops and set traps for traitors, I thought.

I stuck my feet straight out ahead of me. 'I only got involved in this because you wanted me to bring all that stuff, Mary. And you only came because I did. Don't you think that means we ought to stay together?' I made an effort to take her hand, but she pulled it away.

'It all depends,' she said.

'In other words,' I said, feeling the constraints falling away, 'you're saying you'll pick and choose between the offers you get?'

That made her really angry. 'I'm not going to hang around here listening to cheap insults.' She stood up; it was almost too dark to see her at all now. In the failing light she looked imposingly attractive.

'Mary, I'm sorry. Please forgive me. Of course you're free to do whatever you want. But if you want to come with me I should be very happy.'

I thought later — when I had no shortage of time to do so — that she was going to answer me favourably, but I can't really say now. Before she had a chance to reply, something happened.

A man came out from behind a pillar and said, 'Police: nobody move.' He had a gun in his hand; other shapes behind him seemed to be more policemen. Several of them appeared to be wearing hats, from which I deduced they were from the UB.

I did move. I was so keyed up by the events of the day that I couldn't have done anything else.

I threw myself at the pulpit, and took shelter behind it for a moment. A shot hit the marble, and went screaming its way across the church to break some glass.

I dodged backwards, keeping the pulpit between me and the flash of flame that had erupted from the policeman's gun, hoping to find a side chapel somewhere.

Mary's voice suddenly screamed out, as loud as any gun.

'Alex, Alex, they're taking me away. Alex, I'm sorry, I'm sorry.' Someone put a hand over her mouth, and I heard her struggling.

'I love you, Mary.' My voice filled the church like an organ voluntary: the louder the better, I thought, they'll never be able to hear exactly where the sound comes from. 'I love you. I love you.' I couldn't shout any more, and I heard the door slam in the sudden silence. Mary had been taken out of the church.

'Come on, Serafinski,' said a drawling voice. 'You can't possibly get out now, you know. Give up and you won't be hurt.'

Earlier, I'd probably have done it. But now I was on my own, and didn't stand a chance of getting away anyhow; so I carried on trying. At the back of the church, near the door, a fedora-hatted thug was starting to light church candles with his cigarette-lighter. I could hear it click unsuccessfully several times. But if I thought St Anne was handing me a miracle, I was wrong. One of his friends had a box of matches, and they did the trick.

I was moving backwards all the time, and in the eery silence I found a sudden absence of marble and statuary which seemed to be an opening. I backed cautiously into it, waving a hand behind me to check for obstructions. What I found eventually was an altar rail; I was in a side chapel. From the body of the church, bright lights were advancing: the men of the UB, still in their hats, were processing down the aisle with candles. Their leader, out in front, addressed me.

'Listen, Serafinski, we know all about you and where you've come from. Throw out your gun and you'll be all right.'

That's why they're so nervous of tackling me, I thought: they don't know that I got rid of the gun after shooting the dogs.

'I'll take a couple of you with me, at least,' I shouted, hoping the echo would do the trick again.

A shot rang out, and smashed something beautiful a good way away from me.

If I climb on to the altar, I thought, I might be able to break the glass and get out of the window. I looked up. A light some-where far off outside glimmered through the stained glass very faintly: I caught sight of a bishop, or perhaps a saint, looking down at me. I couldn't do it. Some things were worth more than my liberty.

With a noise I could feel in my heart, I hit something; a pile of somethings. It was a long time since churches and I had had much to do with one another, but as I bent down, knees creaking horribly, to work out precisely what they were, the word 'missal' came to mind. I had stumbled on a pile of prayer books neatly heaped up in the corner of the side chapel.

Beyond me, in the darkness, men in fedoras were stalking me through the church, lighted candle in hand, guns in their other hands. Missals. Missiles.

I picked one up, patting the floor and the heap until I had it safely in my grasp. Like a blind man, I didn't even bother to turn my head to look. I held it between thumb and finger of my left hand, and skimmed it out high in the air into the nave of the church, up towards the high altar. It may have gone as high as twenty or thirty feet. Best of all, it came down on the pavement of the church flat on its cover. The bang was sensational.

Within half a second, three things had happened. The candles had been blown out, I had thrown myself on the floor, and gunfire cracked out everywhere. Bullets sang and shattered things and played off the walls like squash balls. Someone yelled out in what I hoped was pain.

I had scattered the pile of missals in my fall, but there was one that dug into me as I lay there, and once the first storm of gunfire had died down, and the fedoras were advancing on the eastern end of the church, I picked it up again, and flicked it out as though I were playing ducks and drakes with flat stones across a pond. This time I aimed at the back of the church — the west end.

That took them completely by surprise. There was a lot of noise of chairs falling over, and more gunfire, though not so much as last time, but no yelling. I wondered if they were getting suspicious.

I should have a game plan, I thought; some idea of how I would actually get out of the church, rather than merely to scare my persecutors. If I could only work my way down to the west end of the church, I thought — and then rejected the idea. They would certainly have the entrance staked out. The only other way of escape would be through the vestry and into the priest's house.

I tried hard to work out the plan of a Catholic church in my mind, but in a place of this size, the priest could have any number of ways to get to his house. I would have to depend on luck.

I took a couple of missals with me and inched my way out of the chapel into the nave. My eyes were getting better accustomed to the dark now, and I could make out vague shapes. Once I touched something with my back, and almost shouted out: the prophet Isaiah had prodded me involuntarily with a marble finger. I went down on my hands and knees after that, feeling my way along. There were too many other marble fingers and marble staffs and marble crosses around.

Every now and then I could hear noises around me: men who were also feeling their way along came into contact with one another, or with items of church furniture and they seemed to be getting closer to me. I found refuge in a group of statuary: a tomb, perhaps. Time to clear a little space for myself, I thought.

Even as I skimmed the next missal away from me, I knew it was flying wrong. It went up in the air reasonably high, but it must have come down on the edge of its leaves: a dud. I heard the noise it made in landing, and so did the UBEKs: a kind of limp sound, with something of a rustle to it.

'You're wasting our time, Serafinski. Give yourself up and we won't hurt you.' The voice made me jump, and I think I must have jerked upright. As I did so, my outstretched arm came into contact with a surface less cold and comfortless than marble: something made of wood. I knew then what it was, and what I was going to do.

Inside, the confessional smelled of guilt and intimacy and disclosure: smells that took me back a long way. Father, I have sinned. Well, I had, of course, but I didn't want to stress that side of it too much, at a time like this.

Remember, Father, I was the one who decided not to go through the stained glass windows. They did all the shooting and lighting candles and wearing hats. The missals were just self-defence, Father. On balance, Father, on balance.

'Give yourself up, Serafinski. You're wasting **our** time.'

The voices were closer now. They must have decided I didn't have a gun. I'd fired all my missals.

I didn't answer. I was keeping my head down in the approved position.

Father, I have sinned. I have committed sins of the flesh, Father. I have neglected my family, Father. I have neglected my father, Father.

> *Not today, O Lord*
> *O not today, think not upon the fault*
> *My father made in compassing the crown.*

'Serafinski, you're trapped. You might as well save yourself and us any further trouble. Come out and give yourself up.'

Father, I have sinned.

'Serafinski, you can't escape.'

Father.

'I'm over here,' I said.

AFTERMATH

'The Grave's a fine and private place,
But none I think do there embrace.'
— Andrew Marvell: 'To his Coy Mistress'

A spattering of rain fell across them and some people turned aside to let their shoulders or their backs take it, hunching down their heads in the cold. Dr Galka scarcely felt it. He'd fortified himself against the weather with a couple of glasses of good-quality vodka before leaving home, and he looked straight ahead of him, the rain wetting his face and making it shine. The vodka had had little effect on his emotions, he found; he had hoped he wouldn't feel much about the burial service, but to his shame the tears still ran down his cheeks. He hoped they might be taken for raindrops, if anyone noticed.

He had lost patients before, plenty of them; he was no miracle-worker. But this wasn't just a patient. Magda was standing near the crumbling edge of the grave, where the soil lay black on the grass. She wasn't crying, but her nose was red and every now and then she scraped her hair back with a red hand. The swelling on her face had gone down a little, Galka noticed. She would be free to marry now: maybe some farmer, a little older than herself, who wanted land and wasn't interested in beauty.

He looked at the details of Magda's mother — born 1908, died 1972. He had only the vaguest recollection now of what she looked like, though he could remember her from when he first came to the village: in her early thirties, gentle and quiet, not exactly beautiful because village women round here didn't go in much for beauty, but delicate and shy. All gone now.

The heavy coffin had taken the strength of four men to lower into the open grave. Friendship and memories went with

222

it, Galka thought, and the love of others, and no doubt their resentments and anger as well. Galka looked at the gathering round the grave. Most of them here out of duty, he thought, and watched the umbrellas go up, and the black gloves clutch politely at white handkerchiefs. The priest's braying voice cut through the stiff breeze, emotionless and formal.

The UBEKs were hovering around the graves at the back of the graveyard, keeping crude watch in case of trouble, as though there would be any at the funeral of an obscure old farmer in a remote highland village: three men in raincoats, one short and stocky, the other two large and menacing. They were talking loudly. Galka wondered if one of them had knocked Magda about. Someone ought to complain about it, but he knew nobody would. Fragments from the burial service were blown to him, like the rain, but he didn't take much notice of that kind of thing. His lack of interest in Christianity was the only thing he had in common with the three UBEK thugs.

Bored and miserable, Galka looked away from the huddle around the graveside. The clouds hung low and ragged over the mountaintops, but the fields and meadows beyond the simple whitewashed wall were stunningly beautiful, and the sweep of the valley as fine a sight, Galka thought, as you could find anywhere in the world. The village lay below them, the walls of the houses white or faced with wood, the roofs as steep as arrowheads. The knell from the church tower came to them occasionally, when the wind veered. Out in the lane a cart went slowly by, and the old man who drove it stood up as he held the reins and faced the graveyard respectfully, waiting until the horse had ambled the full length of the whitewashed wall before slowly sitting down again. Further on, down between the field, Galka could see a small boy sitting on the back of a horse and pulling a mudsleigh. Nothing much changed here; they still lit the pagan harvest fires, the *dozynki*, in this area, and relics of ancestor worship had lingered on until the middle of the nineteenth century.

Easy to get sentimental about the land, he thought, especially if you don't spring from it yourself. He remembered his own home, in the industrial area of Elblag, and how he had been persuaded to come here for his own health, all those years ago. And now he was outliving all the friends he'd made.

The crowd round the grave was starting to break up, and Magda moved across to stand and endure the handshakes and condolences of the whole funeral party. Galka looked at the heap of black earth that would soon cover the coffin of a difficult and tyrannical old man, and then he looked away at the incomparable beauty of the valley. It's all happened so often before in this place, he thought, and yet none of us can quite imagine it will happen in our turn.

The rain had moved off the village and beyond it, the shafts clearly visible from the hillside where he stood. Soon it will be spring, he thought. The realization gave him the necessary strength to walk over to the lounging group of UBEK men, who stood keeping an eye on the disappearing crowd.

'Your behaviour is disgusting,' he said, 'and if you louts are under any kind of discipline I shall make sure your commanding officer knows about it.'

In their surprise, none of them said anything to him, and he strutted off towards the line of sympathizers. A little offering to the shade of my friend Serafinski, the doctor thought; and then, So what if there's trouble? I'm too old to care.

It was only when they fished out my briefcase from behind the counter and handed it to me that I decided I really was going home — that it wasn't just another attempt to break me down. God knows where they'd found it; the last time I remembered seeing it was in the cold store along with the underground leadership. But I knew why they were giving it back to me: no one is more concerned with private property than a policeman working for a Communist state.

After that, there was some driving around, and an airfield. The Pope had once spoken there, someone said to me confidentially, as though he thought I would feel an extra sense of uplift when we took off. I didn't. I was white from a year in gaol, and my clothes, the ones that had gone with me to my family house and across the mountains and back to Cracow, hung loosely on me. But Poland is a place where a lot of people go short of food, so it doesn't show so much when prisoners come out of gaol thin.

It had been a long time. Mary had been let out after exactly ten days, because the French government had made a fuss with the Polish authorities on the grounds that she worked for a French organization. I was in for a year because the British government didn't get round to doing much about me for a long time; after all I wasn't born in Britain. Eventually, though, someone had persuaded Warsaw that it would look better if there weren't too many foreigners in its prisons. We cost the Polish state money. Not much, especially in my case, but a bit.

I hadn't been treated too badly. They hadn't gone over me with rubber truncheons, or wired me up to electrodes. They just questioned me a lot, and I gave them a good deal of back-chat and refused to answer questions until I'd seen the British consul. And since there was no British consul in Cracow, I didn't answer many questions. They didn't seem to care. Other people could tell them everything that I knew, and I didn't know a great deal. Some of the time they wanted to know about George Grandison, and the college's links with MI 6, and it was harder to prove to them I didn't know anything about that. I did, however, give them a close account of Patrick Binney and his activities, in the hope that someone might visit Cambridge and shoot him in the leg with a trick umbrella. Maybe they twigged eventually that Patrick Binney had absolutely nothing to do with British Intelligence. In any sense of the term.

They told me they had arrested everyone in the Cracow and Nowa Huta underground movements, though I doubted it. They actually confronted me once with Stefan Smykowski, and neither of us said a word. I heard they hadn't caught Tadeusz Nowak.

Beneath us, the fields were shrinking, and Cracow was no more than a brown smudge on the horizon, covered over by the fumes from Nowa Huta. I would never see it again, nor the highlands, nor my father. They gave me old copies of the *Morning Star* to read, and didn't believe it when I told them there were newspapers in England that had nudes in. I found it difficult to believe myself, after a year in solitary. Everyone in the plane was quite pleasant, and they fed me a meal that must have come from a LOT airliner, judging by the taste. There were only five of us aboard the military aircraft.

'I tell you what,' I said, cheering up as we headed through the clouds and found the sunshine, 'you can all defect, and I promise we won't say a word about what's happened to me.'

That upset the atmosphere for a bit, but I noticed that a lieutenant in uniform grew distinctly thoughtful. I sang a few Solidarity songs too, just to help the time pass. They couldn't stop me now, I decided. I showed them the marks on my brief-case and told them which ones were connected with the UB. They quite liked that; secret policemen are never popular, and rightly so. They didn't approve of the way the UBEKs had shot up the inside of St Anne's either.

'Here's to the Thought Police,' I said, and raised my glass of mineral water.

'We'll be in Berlin in fifteen minutes,' the pilot announced.

The hand-over wasn't at all dramatic: no bridges, no early morning mist, no double-crosses. I went throught the Fried-richsstrasse checkpoint and only had to show my dog-eared passport once. The lady with the bosom back at the hotel in the Tatras would have been outraged.

As for the British Army, they couldn't have been less interested.

I held a brief press conference, and answered questions from journalists who knew nothing about who I was or where I'd been.

'All this happened in Poland, did it?' a reporter asked. Another wanted to know what I would do when I got back to Oxford. One of the Western freedoms I was starting to be re-educated in was the freedom to be pig-ignorant. Long may it last, I thought, as I repeated it all again for some television reporter, and watched him asking cutaway questions for the camera that he'd never actually asked me. After that I was free to go. I spent the night in a British Army base, and signed a form that said I would repay the Foreign and Commonwealth Office the cost of my air fare back to the Britain. By that stage I would have agreed to foot the bill for the British Army of the Rhine.

I spotted Grandison the moment I emerged from the customs hall at Heathrow. He looked very big in a raincoat that was the general size and colour of an army tent. He threw away his noisome cigar when he saw me, his face more on fire than ever.

'You can't say I didn't warn you,' he boomed, though I could, of course. Several Pakistanis turned to watch him, and a television cameraman came leaping over towards me. Grandison suddenly became rather shy and left me to walk towards the exit on my own. The cameraman didn't take any notice of him.

'I've got us a car, dear boy.'

He had, too; a vast, old-fashioned Daimler that reeked of his cigars and felt as though we were driving down the M4 in a tithebarn. The driver was blocked off from us by what seemed to be several thicknesses of plate glass.

'They wanted to know a lot about you, Grandison.'

He rather liked that. I told what I had said about Patrick Binney, and he liked that even more.

'We aren't going all the way to Cambridge in this hearse, are we?'

'Lunch first, my dear chap. There are a couple of characters I'd like you to have words with.' My heart sank.

By the time we reached the West End it was pouring with rain, and people were finding it hard to know whether to get their umbrellas blown inside out, or keep them down and be soaked. Cars stopped unwillingly for pedestrians on zebra crossings, and pedestrians systematically underestimated the braking length of cars. Taxis had disappeared from the streets.

Ahead of us, as we crossed Trafalgar Square, a sleek black official Rover with twin aerials carved its way through the traffic in a way that shocked our driver to the core. He was still shaking his head when we pulled up behind the offending car in Pall Mall, outside a large Italianate warehouse of a building. A tall man in a wrinkled grey suit got out of the Rover and hurried up the steps holding a magazine over his head. I knew who he was: I remembered him, his suit and his magazine, from a sleazy café near Westminster. I knew what the building was, too. Barry had designed it to look like a Roman palace, before he discovered the Middle Ages and went on to bigger things, like the Houses of Parliament.

'Are you a member of the Reform Club, Grandison, or is it your spy friend over there?' Got you, I thought.

'He's the Garrick, as far as I remember; the Reform's one of mine.' You had to admire him: he always trumped the aces.

The sallow man in the grey suit was waiting for us inside. He made a movement with his head and his left hand which was meant to show that we'd met before.

'You know Gregory Stallard of MI 6, of course.' I nodded. Then Grandison turned to a superb figure in double-breasted blue stripe, and said to me, 'But you won't know Henri-Luc de Bernay, of the Direction Générale de la Securité Extérieure.' His pronunciation matched the Frenchman's suit for splendour. We shook hands, and Grandison left us to shuffle and ignore each other, before coming back holding drinks over his head to protect them from the crowd. There is always a crowd at the pre-lunch drinks bar at the Reform.

'Hello, George,' the chairman of a big nationalized corporation which lost millions of pounds a day called out, and then said, 'Another one all round?' to his group. Grandison inclined his head to him graciously, and didn't spill a drop. He liked being recognized by the famous, and I saw now why he had brought us here.

Lunch was spoiled for me by various things, not the least of which was the piercing gaze of Mr Gladstone, who hung over our table and looked at me as though I'd been going out with one of his fallen women. It would have been bad enough, anyway. De Bernay was superior and Stallard was sinister. I told them everything I knew and a bit more, and they gave me the general impression that they knew it all already. Maybe they were only scoring off one another. After a time I became angry.

'I can see why we've got MI 6 here, Grandison, but why the French connection?'

There was a pause; I had been guilty of bad manners. Grandison hung over us like the Matterhorn and said, 'If only you'd wait a little, Serafin, you might find out.'

I went back to the roast beef. It reminded me of something they used to give us in gaol.

It was over coffee, on the grand balcony overlooking Barry's atrium, that I found out what the superb M. de Bernay was doing there.

'This Dolanski,' Grandison said, lighting up his cigar

theatrically and bringing each new detail of the discussion in with the fast skill of a croupier raking in the chips, 'tell us about him, de Bernay.'

De Bernay told us, in beautiful English. Dolanski was a double agent who informed on French Solidarity to Polish intelligence, and on Polish intelligence to the DST, the French security service. Difficult to decide whom he gave the greater information to. Useful, greedy, and without scruples. Not very important, de Bernay concluded, with a look at me.

Stallard jerked the edge of his coffee-cup in my direction. 'If you're thinking of popping over to Paris for any reason, Dr Serafin, you won't disturb our Mr Dolanski, will you? I shouldn't like to think he was being disturbed.'

'Wait a minute,' I said. My mind wasn't working very fast. Everything seemed to go very silent, and they all looked at me. 'You mean you knew about Dolanski, all along?'

Nobody nodded or said yes. On the other hand, nobody said no either. Grandison looked about him for some MP or captain of industry to greet, but there wasn't anyone up here just now.

'If you knew about him, you must have known that he would warn the Poles that Mary and I were coming. With all the stuff.' Grandison was looking warily at me now, as though I were an unexploded firework and he were trying to work out whether to risk having a closer look at me. 'And you didn't tell me.'

'Sorry about that,' Stallard said. 'This thing was bigger than both of you.'

'Thanks,' I said, but at least he had the honesty to be cynical.

Grandison looked at the other two, and said, 'Dolanski was more important than de Bernay was implying. The Poles suspected him. We had to give him something worth while.'

'Like me,' I said. Grandison spread his hands as if to say, 'Don't be so vulgar.' But he was embarrassed now.

'Regard it as a sabbatical,' Stallard said. 'You must have learned a lot.'

There were any number of retorts to that, but I couldn't think of a single one. I was completely out of jokes. I wanted no more than to get away, to go to a bookshop or walk down a busy street and try to remember what being a real person was like. I thought I had done something for my country, and all I had really done was to play a bit-part in someone else's spy movie.

I stood up, and didn't shake hands with anyone. I told Grandison that I'd see him back in Cambridge. I didn't say when.

Downstairs, the porter handed me my briefcase as though it had gone bad some days before. He especially disliked the mark the helicopter man had made on it with his gun.

Grandison was waiting for me by the steps that led down to the front door.

'I wanted you to know,' he said, and I believed him; up to a point. I looked at him for a moment. The smell of his cigars hung about him, and his face was as mottled as ever. We were going to have to live alongside one another for years to come, I reflected; it was my turn to offer him a face-saving exit.

'The Thought Police,' I said dismissively, for the second time in two days.

'Oh, I'm not sure that thinking plays much of a part with them.'

I almost smiled.

'Dear boy,' he said, as though he were trying to tack it on to his previous words. He still looked embarassed.

What the hell, I thought, and stuck my hand out. His felt as old and heavy as another hand I'd touched, a long way away from the Reform Club.

It was overcast in Paris, but at least it wasn't raining. I took the Métro to Cardinal Lemoine and walked. The restaurants looked good to a hungry man, and I liked the way they were spreading the cloths and getting ready for dinner, though it was only six o'clock.

The narrow lift twitched and groaned, and I thought of the past and learned a new rude word in French from some scratches on the door. Music floated out from Mary's flat, together with a smell of cooking that reminded me of home; home in Poland, that is. I rang the doorbell.

'Alex,' she said, as though the thought of me hadn't entered her head for years. 'Why ever didn't you call to say you were coming? I read all about you in the papers.' She filled the doorway, and didn't move out of it.

I knew what the smell was, now that it had an unimpeded path to me. 'Kolduny?' I asked. She nodded, and went on standing there.

'I can't stay for long.' That proved to be the password, and she stood aside. Her flat looked even better now; plants everywhere, and books starting to pile up on the floor. A contralto was singing songs from the Auvergne on the record-player.

'I'm sorry, Alex, I've got someone coming for dinner.'

'I'm sorry to have dropped in like this.'

She went and took care of the kolduny for a moment, and I looked at the picture of Jan Dolanski in its silver frame on the window-sill, next to a jug of red carnations. Then she was back.

'Did they treat you badly in gaol?' I asked.

She shook her head and smiled.

'I wondered if you'd ever written, or anything.' My voice trailed away.

'I knew it would never get to you.' She was a woman who lived her life by principles: mere human feelings played less of a part. The principle of security seemed to have claimed her now: hence the silver frame with the silver-haired Dolanski in it, looking satisfied with life, as well he might.

'If only you hadn't come on a Saturday,' she said, to remind me that my time was short. I felt panic-stricken: there were so many things to say, and I wasn't going to get through any of them.

'I've been hearing about your friend Dolanski,' I said.

'He's explained everything to me. There's nothing more to be said.'

'How's his collection?'

'I wish you wouldn't say that kind of thing, Alex.'

After that we talked about the Institute, and how nice her flat was looking, and the problems she was having with the French government, and some more about the Institute. She had just signed another three-year contract with them. We didn't talk about her work with Solidarity, and we didn't talk about me.

The moment arrived to ask her to come back to me, but I didn't, and we talked about something else instead.

At the end, I said, 'Oh well,' and started to move. She was on her feet at once.

'I hope you enjoy the *kolduny*,' I said.

'Thank you. If you come to Paris again, please let me know beforehand. We could go out somewhere for dinner, maybe.'

I nodded. Goodbye, Mary, I said, but I waited till I was in the lift, and I didn't say it out loud.

It was growing dark as I walked across the Pont de la Tournelle, and the lights in the expensive shops and tea-rooms which are starting to overrun the Ile St Louis were shining out into the street. I walked down the Rue Saint-Louis-en-l'Ile and managed to keep myself from thinking about anything until I got to the point where you can almost see Notre Dame. I wasn't going anywhere in particular.

On the bridge that joins the Ile St Louis to the Ile de la Cité a small crowd had gathered in a circle. It had obviously been a larger crowd, but people were moving away as the light faded and the cold increased.

A barrel-organ, magnificent in light green and gold paint, was standing there; it had small figures on the front of it that rang bells and clashed cymbals and generally joined in the fun at selected moments. But it wasn't playing now. A man with a dark head of hair was kneeling down beside a hurdy-gurdy and turning a handle to feed the slotted paper through its works. As it played its nasal tune, he sang the words, and his head shook with the intensity of it, and the veins on his forehead stood out. The words were all about love.

I had thought I was doing something for Poland, and I had ended up doing something to help Stallard and his friends. I had thought I was doing something to bind Mary closer to me, and I had ended up helping Dolanski to take her away from me. I had thought I was doing something for love, and I had ended up helping treachery. It was quite funny, really, if you could only see it in the right way. I knew I would, eventually.

The last fold of paper went through the hurdy-gurdy, and those of us who were left clapped dutifully and dropped money in the up-ended top hat.

'V'là, messieurs-dames,' the man said, and bowed low in order to make fun of us. He and his brother started putting everything away in boxes, and the little crowd broke up.

I headed towards Notre Dame. Once I heard a girl shouting something, and I turned round quickly, my heart beating fast, but it wasn't for me. I felt cold, and walked on a little quicker.